Game of
LOVE

The Remingtons, Book One

Love in Bloom Series

Melissa Foster

ISBN-13: 978-0-9910468-5-0
ISBN-10: 0991046854

Cover Design: Natasha Brown

WORLD LITERARY PRESS
PRINTED IN THE UNITED STATES OF AMERICA

A Note to Readers

When I met Jack Remington and his family in *Bursting with Love* (The Bradens, Book Five), I wasn't really sure what to expect from them, but I knew that each family member resonated with me for different reasons. I was excited to write about Dex Remington, a twenty-six-year-old PC game developer, and delve into a world vastly different from the rest of the Love in Bloom characters. Dex and his love interest, Ellie Parker, took me on an exciting, passionate, and unexpected journey. I hope you fall in love with them and the rest of the Remingtons just as I have.

Game of Love is the tenth book in the Love in Bloom series and the first book of The Remingtons. While it may be read as a stand-alone novel, for even more enjoyment, you may want to read the rest of the Love in Bloom novels.

Melissa Foster

For all of us to remember that our circumstances do not define us. Our choices do.

PRAISE FOR MELISSA FOSTER

"Contemporary romance at its hottest. Each Braden sibling left me craving the next. Sensual, sexy, and satisfying, the Braden series is a captivating blend of the dance between lust, love, and life."
—*Bestselling author Keri Nola, LMHC*
(on The Bradens)

"[LOVERS AT HEART] Foster's tale of stubborn yet persistent love takes us on a heartbreaking and soul-searing journey."
—*Reader's Favorite*

"Smart, uplifting, and beautifully layered.
I couldn't put it down!"
—*National bestselling author Jane Porter*
(on SISTERS IN LOVE)

"Steamy love scenes, emotionally charged drama, and a family-driven story make this the perfect story for any romance reader."
—*Midwest Book Review (on SISTERS IN BLOOM)*

"HAVE NO SHAME is a powerful testimony to love and the progressive, logical evolution of social consciousness, with an outcome that readers will find engrossing, unexpected, and ultimately eye-opening."
—*Midwest Book Review*

Chapter One

DEX REMINGTON WALKED into NightCaps bar beside his older brother Sage, an artist who also lived in New York City, and Regina Smith, his employee and right arm. Women turned in their direction as they came through the door, their hungry eyes raking over Dex's and Sage's wide shoulders and muscular physiques. At six foot four, Sage had two inches on Dex, and with their striking features, dark hair, and federal-blue eyes, heads spun everywhere they went. But after Dex had worked thirty of the last forty-eight hours, women were the furthest thing from his mind. His four-star-general father had ingrained hard work and dedication into his head since he was old enough to walk, and no matter how much he rued his father's harsh parenting, following his lead had paid off. At twenty-six, Dex was one of the country's leading PC game designers and the founder of Thrive Entertainment, a multimillion-dollar gaming corporation. His father had taught him another valuable lesson—how to become numb—making it easy for him to disconnect from the women other men might find too alluring to ignore.

Dex was a stellar student. He'd been numb for a very long time.

"Thanks for squeezing in a quick beer with me," he said to Sage. They had about twenty minutes to catch up before his scheduled meeting with Regina and Mitch Anziano, another of his Thrive employees. They were going to discuss the game they were rolling out in three weeks, *World of Thieves II*.

"You're kidding, right? I should be saying that to you." Sage threw his arm around Dex's shoulder. They had an ongoing rivalry about who was the busiest, and with Sage's travel and gallery schedule and Dex working all night and getting up midday, it was tough to pick a winner.

"Thrive!" Mitch hollered from the bar in his usual greeting. Mitch used *Thrive!* to greet Dex in bars the way others used, *Hey.* He lifted his glass, and a smile spread across his unshaven cheeks. At just over five foot eight with three-days' beard growth trailing down his neck like fur and a gut that he was all too proud of, he was what the world probably thought all game designers looked like. And worth his weight in gold. Mitch could outprogram anyone, and he was more loyal than a golden retriever.

Regina lifted her chin and elbowed Dex. "He's early." She slinked through the crowded bar, pulling Dex along behind her. Her Levi's hung low, cinched across her protruding hip bones by a studded black leather belt. Her red hoodie slipped off one shoulder, exposing the colorful tattoos that ran across her shoulder and down her arms.

Mitch and Regina had been Dex's first employees when he'd opened his company. Regina handled the administrative aspects of the company, kept the production schedule, monitored the program testing, and basically made sure nothing slipped through the cracks, while Mitch, like Dex, conceptually and technically designed games with the help of the rest of Thrive's fifty employees—developers, testers, and a host of programmers and marketing specialists.

Regina climbed onto the barstool beside Mitch and lifted his beer to her lips.

"Order ours yet?" she asked with a glint in her heavily lined dark eyes. She ran her hand through her stick-straight, jet-black hair.

Dex climbed onto the stool beside her as the bartender slid beers in front of him and Regina. "Thanks, Jon. Got a brew for my brother?"

"Whatever's on tap," Sage said. "Hey, Mitch. Good to see you."

Mitch lifted his beer with a nod of acknowledgment.

Dex took a swig of the cold ale, closed his eyes, and sighed, savoring the taste.

"Easy, big boy. We need you sober if you wanna win a GOTY." Mitch took a sip of Regina's beer. "Fair's fair."

Regina rolled her eyes and reached a willowy arm behind him, then mussed his mop of curly dark hair. "We're gonna win Game of the Year no matter what. Reviewers love us. Right, Dex?"

Thrive had already produced three games, one of

which, *World of Thieves*, had made Dex a major player in the gaming world—and earned him millions of dollars. His biggest competitor, KI Industries, had changed the release date for their new game. KI would announce the new date publicly at midnight, and since their game was supposed to be just as hot of a game as they expected *World of Thieves II* to be, if they released close to the release for *World of Thieves II*, there would be a clear winner and a clear loser. Dex had worked too hard to be the loser.

"That's the hope," Dex said. He took another swig of his beer and checked his watch. Eight forty-five and his body thought it was noon. He'd spent so many years working all night and sleeping late that his body clock was completely thrown off. He was ready for a big meal and the start of his workday. He stroked the stubble along his chin. "I worked on it till four this morning. I think I deserve a cold one."

Sage leaned in to him. "You're not nervous about the release, are you?"

Of his five siblings—including Dex's twin sister, Siena, Sage knew him best. He was the quintessential artist, with a heart that outweighed the millions of dollars his sculptures had earned him. He'd supported Dex through the years when Dex needed to bend an ear, and when he wasn't physically nearby, Sage was never farther than a text or a phone call away.

"Nah. If it all fails, I'll come live with you." Dex had earned enough money off of the games he'd produced that he'd never have to worry about finances again, but he wasn't in the gaming business for the money. He'd been a gamer at heart since he was able to string coherent thoughts together, or at least it felt that way. "What's happening with the break you said you wanted to take? Are you going to Jack's cabin?" Their eldest brother Jack owned a cabin in the Colorado Mountains. Jack was an ex–Special Forces officer and a survival-training guide, and he and his fiancée Savannah spent most weekends at the cabin. Living and working in the concrete jungle didn't offer the type of escape Sage's brain had always needed.

"I've got another show or two on the horizon; then I'll take time off. But I think I want to do something useful with my time off. Find a way to, I don't know, help others instead of sitting around on my ass." He sipped his beer and tugged at the neck of his Baja hippie jacket. "How 'bout you? Any plans for vacay after the release?"

"Shit. You're kidding, right? My downtime is spent playing at my work. I love it. I'd go crazy sitting in some cabin with no connectivity to the real world."

"The right woman might change your mind." Sage took a swig of his beer.

"Dex date?" Regina tipped her glass to her lips. "Do you even know your brother? He might hook up once in a while, but this man protects his heart like it carries all of the industry secrets."

"Can we not go there tonight?" Dex snapped. He had a way of remembering certain moments of his life with impeccable clarity, some of which left scars so deep he could practically taste them every damn day of his life. He nurtured the hurt and relished in the joy of the scars, as his artistic and peace-seeking mother had taught him. But Dex was powerless against his deepest scar, and numbing his heart was the only way he could survive the memory of the woman he loved walking away from him four years earlier without so much as a goodbye.

"Whoa, bro. Just a suggestion," Sage said. "You can't replace what you never had."

Dex shot him a look.

Regina spun on her chair and then swung her arm over Dex's shoulder. "Incoming," she whispered.

Dex looked over his shoulder and met the stare of two hot blondes. His shoulders tensed and he sighed.

"It's not gonna kill you to make a play for one of them, Dex. Work off some of that stress." Sage glanced back at the women.

"No, thanks. They're all the same." Ever since the major magazines had carried the story about Dex's success, he'd been hounded by ditzy women who thought all he wanted to talk about was PC games.

Regina leaned in closer and whispered, "Not them. Fan boys, two o'clock."

Thank God.

"Hey, aren't you Dex Rem?" one of the boys asked.

Dex wondered if they were in college or if they had abandoned their family's dreams for them in lieu of a life of gaming. It was the crux of his concern about his career. He was getting rich while feeding society's desire to be couch potatoes.

"Remington, yeah, that's me," he said, wearing a smile like a costume, becoming the relaxed gamer his fans craved.

"Dude, *World of Thieves* is the most incredible game ever! Listen, you ever need any beta testers, we're your guys." The kid nodded as his stringy bangs bounced into his eyes. His friend's jaw hung open, struck dumb by meeting Dex, another of Dex's pet peeves. He was just a guy who worked hard at what he loved, and he believed anyone could accomplish the same level of success if they only put forth the effort. Damn, he hated how much that belief mirrored his father's teachings.

"Yeah?" Dex lifted his chin. "What college did you graduate from?"

The two guys exchanged a look, then a laugh. The one with the long bangs said, "Dude, it don't take a college degree to test games."

Dex's biceps flexed. There it was. The misconception that irked Dex more than the laziness of the kids who were just a few years younger than him. As a Cornell graduate, Dex believed in the value of education and the value of being a productive member of society. He needed to figure out the release date, not talk bullshit with kids who were probably too young to even be in a bar.

"Guys, give him a break, 'kay?" Regina said.

"Sure, yeah. Great to meet you," the longer-haired kid said.

Dex watched them turn away and sucked back his beer. His eyes caught on a woman at a booth in the corner of the bar. He studied the petite, brown-haired woman who was fiddling with her napkin while her leg bounced a mile a minute beneath the table. *Jesus.* Memories from four years earlier came rushing back to him with freight-train impact, hitting his heart dead center.

"I know how you are about college, but, Dex, they're kids. You gotta give them a little line to feed off of," Regina said.

Dex tried to push past the memories. He glanced up at the woman again, and his stomach twisted. He turned away, trying to focus on what Regina had said. *College. The kids. Give them a line to feed off of.* Regina was right. He should accept the hero worship with gratitude, but lately he'd been feeling like the very games that had made him successful were sucking kids into an antisocial, couch-potato lifestyle.

"Really, Dex. Imagine if you'd met your hero at that age." Sage ran his hand through his hair and shook his head.

"I'm no hero." Dex's eyes were trained on the woman across the bar. *Ellie Parker.* His mouth went dry.

"Dex?" Sage followed his gaze. "Holy shit."

There was a time when Ellie had been everything to him. She'd lived in a foster home around the corner from him when they were growing up, and she'd moved away just before graduating high school. Dex's mind catapulted back thirteen years, to his bedroom at his parents' house. "In the End" by Linkin Park was playing on the radio. Siena had a handful of girlfriends over, and she'd gotten the notion that playing Truth or Dare was a good idea. At thirteen, Dex had gone along with whatever his popular and beautiful sister had wanted him to. She was the orchestrator of their social lives. He hadn't exactly been a cool teenager, with his nose constantly in a book or his hands on electronics. That had changed when testosterone filled his veins

8

two years later, but at thirteen, even the idea of being close to a girl made him feel as though he might pass out. He'd retreated to his bedroom, and that had been the first night Ellie had appeared at his window.

"Hey, Dex." Regina followed his gaze to Ellie's table; her eyes moved over her fidgeting fingers and her bouncing leg. "Nervous Nelly?" she teased.

Dex rose to his feet. His stomach clenched.

"Dude, we're supposed to have a meeting. There's still more to talk about," Mitch said.

Sage's voice was serious. "Bro, you sure you wanna go there?"

With Sage's warning, Dex's pulse sped up. His mind jumped back again to the last time he'd seen her, four years earlier, when Ellie had called him out of the blue. She'd needed him. He'd thought the pieces of his life had finally fallen back into place. Ellie had come to New York, scared of what, he had no idea, and she'd stayed with him for two days and nights. Dex had fallen right back into the all-consuming, adoring, frustrating vortex that was Ellie Parker. "Yeah, I know. I gotta..." *See if that's really her.*

"Dex?" Regina grabbed his arm.

He placed his hand gently over her spindly fingers and unfurled them from his wrist. He read the confusion in her narrowed eyes. Regina didn't know about Ellie Parker. *No one knows about Ellie Parker. Except Sage. Sage knows.* He glanced over his shoulder at Sage, unable to wrap his mind around the right words.

"Holy hell," Sage said. "I've gotta take off in a sec anyway. Go, man. Text me when you can."

Dex nodded.

"What am I missing here?" Regina asked, looking between Sage and Dex.

Regina was protective of Dex in the same way that Siena always had been. They both worried he'd be taken advantage of. In the three years Dex had known Regina, he could count on one hand the number of times he'd approached a woman in front of her, rather than the other way around. It would take Dex two hands to count the number of times he'd been taken advantage of in the past few years, and Regina's eyes mirrored that reality. Regina didn't know it, but of all the women in the world, Ellie was probably the one he needed protection from the most.

He put his hand on her shoulder, feeling her sharp bones against his palm. There had been a time when Dex had wondered if Regina was a heavy drug user. Her lanky body reminded him of strung-out users, but Regina was skinny because she survived on beer, Twizzlers, and chocolate, with the occasional veggie burger thrown in for good measure.

"Yeah. I think I see an old friend. I'll catch up with you guys later." Dex lifted his gaze to Mitch. "Midnight?"

"Whatever, dude. Don't let me cock block you." Mitch laughed.

"She's an old...not a...never mind." *My onetime best friend?* As he crossed the floor, all the love he felt for her came rushing back. He stopped in the middle of the crowded floor and took a deep breath. *It's really you.* In the next breath, his body remembered the heartbreak of the last time he'd seen her. The time he'd never forget. When he'd woken up four years ago and found her gone—no note, no explanation, and no contact since. Just like she'd done once before when they were kids. The sharp, painful memory pierced his swollen heart. He'd tried so hard to forget her, he'd even moved out of the apartment to distance himself from the memories. He should turn away, return to his friends. Ellie would only hurt him again. He was rooted to the floor, his heart tugging him forward, his mind holding him back.

A couple rose from the booth where Ellie sat, drawing his attention. He hadn't even noticed them before. God, she looked beautiful. Her face had thinned. Her cheekbones were more pronounced, but her eyes hadn't changed one bit. When they were younger, she'd fooled almost everyone with a brave face—but never Dex. Dex had seen right through to her heart. Like right now. She stared down at something in her hands with her eyebrows pinched together and her full lips set in a way that brought back memories, hovering somewhere between worried and trying to convince herself everything would be okay.

Her leg bounced nervously, and he stifled the urge to tell her that no matter what was wrong, it would all be okay. Dex ignored the warnings going off in his mind and followed his heart as he crossed the floor toward Ellie.

Chapter Two

NO WAY. NO fucking way did Dina just leave me alone on my first night in the city. Ellie stared at the table. *You know how to get to my apartment, right? Just give us an hour; that's all I ask,* Dina had said before handing her an extra key. Great. Dina and a guy she'd known for less than an hour might or might not be having sex while she slept on the couch. *I just need to get through the interviews; that's it. I can do this.* Her mind weaved through the tangled afternoon of rushing to Union Station, missing her train and having to wait for the next one. Spending three hours on the train practicing for her interviews before pulling into Penn Station, exhausted and late. She was contemplating ordering a drink—or five—when very definitely male fingers touched her table. Why did they look familiar?

"Ellie?"

Ellie sucked in a breath at the sound of his voice. *Dex. Oh, God. Dex.* Her gaze followed those familiar fingertips to the large hands that had kept her safe when she'd climbed into his window late at night. Her heart remembered, thundering in her chest as her eyes traveled up his sinewy, muscled arms, and she took in all six-foot-something of him, ending at his seductive, midnight-blue eyes. Jesus, they still slayed her.

"Dexy?" His name came out as one long breath. She needed to stand, to hug him, to say hello, but her body wouldn't obey. She was frozen in the booth like a wallflower. Ellie was no wallflower, damn it. She closed her eyes for a beat and centered her mind. *It's Dex. Just Dex.* The truth was, Dex had never been *just Dex.* But she knew better than to get too attached to anyone. Even Dex. *Especially Dex.* Self-preservation was a skill Ellie had honed at a young age.

Ellie didn't have time or energy to dwell on the unkindness of her upbringing. She soaked up the good memories, and knowing she was always on the brink of chaos, she swept the bad memories under the carpet with mummified silence and pushed on. No matter how shitty the day appeared—and she'd seen her share of shittiness in her twenty-five years—nothing compared to moving from one foster family to the next, all the while praying her mother would finally find sobriety and do the right thing by her. But her mother had drunk herself to death when Ellie was eight, ending her internal longing for the mother she'd never have. Admitting to the awfulness of her upbringing would be like falling right back into that needy little girl, and she was never going back there.

Dex ran his hand through his dark hair. He still wore it long on top and a little shorter in the back. And damn if he didn't have that sexy facial hair thing going on. The hair on his chin was lighter than the hair on top of his head—closer to the color of Ellie's. Not quite black, not quite dark chocolate. His thick eyebrows and dark lashes still shadowed his eyes, giving him that serious brooding look that had always made her heart skip a beat. *God, you're here. And you're hot. No. I can't go there. Shit.*

"I can't believe you're here," he said, sliding into the seat across from her. "It's been—"

"Too long." Ellie cleared her throat to strengthen her voice. She didn't want to rehash the details of when she'd come to see him four years earlier. She'd fought the painful memories day in and day out, tried to forget the weekend ever happened—*Oh, how I tried to forget.* But she could no sooner forget a *day* with Dex, much less the best weekend of her life. She hadn't even been brave enough to return the few messages he'd left, trying to figure out why she'd gone away. The thought of hearing the pain in his voice was too much. She'd had to leave. She'd had to separate herself from him. Dex was better off without her hanging around his neck like a needy, fucked-up noose.

She dropped her eyes to the table, barely able to breathe past the guilt of what she'd done. He was right there with her again. He was always there for her—and she was always soaking him in, taking the comfort he had to give. *And breaking his beautiful heart.* She kept her eyes trained on the table to keep from...what? Begging for forgiveness? Crawling into his arms and telling him how much she loved him? How he'd scared the living shit out of her four years earlier when he'd professed his love for her? *Fuck.* There was nothing she could say to fix what she'd done, and she was in no position to make up excuses or promise a damned thing, which was why she hadn't had the courage to call him when she'd decided to return to New York. She'd worried that he wouldn't want to see her again after the way she'd left the last time. The way she'd always left, without so much as a goodbye.

"Four years," he reminded her.

She cringed. It was silly of her to think he'd let her off the hook for leaving without saying goodbye. For not answering his desperate attempts to reach her. For not explaining why she'd left. As she looked at him now, she didn't see any such demand in his eyes. Then again, Dex had never demanded a thing of her.

He reached across the table and touched her fingertips.

Ellie stared at his hand, desperately wanting to answer the pull in her heart and take his hand in hers. Dex's hand had been her lifeline on too many nights to count, but now she didn't reach for his fingers. She couldn't. It would be too easy to crawl into the safety of him and allow herself to soak up the comfort he'd surely provide—and too easy to forget that she came with even more baggage now, tangled all around her like a wicked web. She was a different woman than Dex had known before. A stronger woman. Even if it hurt like hell to be strong sometimes. Even if looking at Dex, knowing how badly she'd hurt him, sliced her heart wide open.

Dex made no move to pull his hand away. "What are you doing in New York?"

Running away. "Applying for teaching jobs." Ellie

wanted to pour her heart out to Dex and let him erase the hurt of the last few weeks and help her to start fresh. She needed to forget, but Ellie sucked at forgetting. That was part of what made her strong. Remembering every shitty thing that had ever happened to her allowed her to never fall into the same circumstances twice. Of course, running away helped, too.

"So you did it."

Dex's lips curved into a smile that said so much more than he was happy for her. He'd believed in her when no one else had. God, she missed that. *God, I've missed you.* He leaned back. His rumpled black T-shirt clung snuggly to his chest. Tattoos snaked down his left arm. New tattoos that she hadn't seen before. Ellie felt a stirring down low in parts of her that had been quiet for a very long time, which confused the hell out of her because she and Dex hadn't progressed to being *those* kinds of friends in the past. Although, had she stayed...No. She wouldn't think about that. His eyes never wavered from hers, and as Dex's long fingers trailed away from hers, she longed for them to return.

"Yeah. I made it, Dex." She met his gaze and shook her head, feeling her own lips wanting to smile and hesitating. The tension in her shoulders eased. "Some days I can barely believe it, but I have the paper to prove it. I've got a master's in minority and urban education from the University of Maryland. They gave me a scholarship, which was really helpful." Pride swelled in her chest alongside the familiar comfort of being with Dex that she was trying *not* to allow herself to enjoy. He had a way of doing that to her. Sneaking comfort in through the cracks in her armor.

"I never had any doubt," he said.

"I heard about Thrive. I guess all those years of tinkering paid off." She remembered many nights when she'd crawl through his window to find him wearing nothing but boxers and sitting beside a stack of technical books and magazines. She'd maneuver around memory boards and computer paraphernalia, articles and notebooks. God, there were always notebooks scattered about his bedroom floor. He'd lift his arm, and she'd crawl in bed beside him and settle into the safety of him. His arm would drop to her shoulder and he'd pull her close while he read, and she calmed her nerves or slept. Or sometimes, she just breathed in the security of him.

Dex nodded. "Yeah. It's a nice gig."

Nice gig. That was so like him, downplaying his success. She'd seen his picture on the front of *Gamer* magazine several times over the past few years. One of her fifth-grade students had written a report about him right before she'd left Maryland. It had been a well-written report, noting not only his multimillion-dollar business but also his double degree in computer science and mathematics from Cornell. At the time, she'd thought about contacting him, but given the way her life had been unraveling with each breath, she hadn't wanted to cast her chaos onto him again. Not after they'd shared that weekend together and she'd realized just what Dex had meant to her—which scared the shit out of her at the same time.

Not after she'd run.

She always ran.

And now here he sat, making time for her once again while she ran away from the shit storm caused by dating a man she hadn't known was married—a man who had hurt her both emotionally and physically. God, she couldn't let Dex know. Right after he killed the asshole, he'd probably look at her differently, even though she hadn't known he was married. She couldn't be seen as a victim again. It was too damn hard. Goddamn Bruce Kellerman. She was done with men. She pushed the thought of Bruce aside. She had bigger problems to deal with, like trying to get a job and find an apartment, not to mention making it through the night worrying about some strange guy in the next room.

"Hey, do you have time for a drink?"

No. I need to find Dina's place, and I...hell. The familiar comfort of being with Dex was too good to ignore. "Yeah, sounds good."

Dex flagged down a waitress and ordered a beer, then lifted his eyebrows to Ellie. "Rum and Coke?"

She rolled her eyes. "God, am I still that high schoolish?" She wished she could order something more adult, like a cosmo, a manhattan, or a martini, but the truth was, her high school taste for rum and Coke had stayed with her like white on rice. "Yeah, bring it on." She might as well relax and enjoy the evening. Her first interview wasn't until ten the following morning, so even if she stayed out a little late catching up with Dex, she'd have time to sleep in.

Chapter Three

DEX COULD HARDLY believe Ellie was there in front of him, and damn, she looked more beautiful than ever. He'd thought she'd disappeared forever when they were teenagers and she'd been sent away to a new foster home. He'd been devastated about her leaving, but when he'd gone to her house the day she was supposed to leave and found she'd left without saying goodbye, he'd been completely inconsolable. She'd stolen his heart as a teenager, but until she'd shown up four years ago, he hadn't realized how much he'd still loved her. In one brief weekend she'd filled his heart so full he thought he'd died and gone to heaven, and just as quickly as she'd reignited his love, she'd shattered his heart and left him a broken man. Ellie wasn't safe. She was Kryptonite. She'd only bring him more pain. But he'd never been able to walk away from her, and as he drank her in, intoxicated from just being near her again, he was powerless to turn away.

Two drinks later, the tension around her eyes

eased, and he saw hints of the softer side of her, the side she'd hidden from the world but that he'd known so well. He wondered if anyone else had gotten into those places in her heart over the years.

"Why New York?" His stomach did a little tumble of hope. *Did you come back to see me?*

Ellie shrugged, fiddling with the rim of her glass. "Roots, I guess. I spent more years in New York than anywhere else, with the exception of college, of course."

"How was Maryland?" Dex knew he was walking on eggshells. At their closest, Ellie hadn't talked about the harsh realities of her life. When the foster family she'd lived with treated her badly, she'd gone mute. She'd cuddled beside Dex without a word. It didn't take long for him to recognize the faraway look in Ellie's eyes for what it was. She'd been running back then, too, only she'd been running emotionally, not physically. Back then he'd wanted to understand what had driven her into that muted, unhappy state—what he'd come to know as her *silent place*. He'd gone to her house late one night and peered through the windows. Listening through the thin walls of the rambler, he'd heard yelling, and at the time, Dex had wished his older brothers, Sage, Kurt, Rush, and Jack, had been there to knock the shit out of her foster father, but Jack had joined the military, Rush was off training for the Olympics, and Kurt and Sage had been away at college. Only Dex and Siena were still living at home, and when he'd finally found the courage to ask Ellie about it, she'd shut him out. That had been the first and only time he'd brought it up. Sitting with Ellie now, he wondered if she'd shut him out or let him in.

Ellie dropped her baby blues to the table and fiddled with the edge of her glass. He recognized the straightening in the curve of her lips, the hooded expression in her eyes, and he knew she wasn't going to let him in now, either.

"It was okay. Not bad like it was with my foster family in our old neighborhood, but not exactly good, either."

She finished her drink and fisted her hands in the side of her hair, up high on the crown of her head. When she let go, her hair had a tousled look, parted in the center and falling in thick waves down her shoulders. *Bedroom hair.*

Coming out of the bedroom with tousled hair and that sweet, sexy look in her eye would require Ellie to let someone into her world. Damn, he wanted to be in that world. Dex looked away, trying to dissuade his mind from thinking of Ellie in that way.

Christ. Stop it. It's Ellie.

Dex needed a runner in his life like he needed to miss his release date. She couldn't be counted on. He knew that. She'd had no qualms about tearing his heart out. He'd been there, done that with her, and it had hurt like hell. But then again, it was Ellie, and for Ellie, he had no idea what he would or wouldn't risk. Just being with her stifled his ability to think straight.

An hour later, Ellie's eyelids were at half-mast. She'd had three drinks, in contrast to the one that used to send her stumbling as a teenager. She hung her purse across her shoulder and sighed. "I'd better get going." She swayed on her feet and grabbed the table as she slid from the booth.

Dex reflexively put an arm out to steady her and rose to his feet. When had their height difference gotten so vast? Ellie was so strong and stubborn that he'd envisioned her taller, not nearly as petite and feminine as she was. He had the urge to wrap her in his arms and hold her until that guarded look fell away.

"Where are you staying?" he asked.

She looked up at him and put her hand on his chest. Dex tried to ignore the way his heartbeat sped up and his chest tightened from her touch. Jesus, she'd touched his chest too many times to count when they were younger, but he didn't remember it inciting a rise in his pants. Or maybe it had but he'd been really great at ignoring it. *Fuck.* That weekend she'd come back had changed everything—and nothing at all. It didn't matter. This was Ellie, and he wasn't going there with her. He suppressed his desire to let Ellie in again.

"Thrive!" Mitch yelled from across the bar.

Ellie turned quickly in Mitch's direction and clung to Dex's chest to steady herself. "Hey, I think he's calling you."

"Yeah, that's Mitch. Every time I come into the bar, he does that. It's kind of his way of greeting me. He and Reg work for me. We were just about to have a meeting before I saw you." He put his hand on hers and pulled it from his chest—missing it instantly and chiding himself for feeling that way. "Come on. I'll introduce you."

"Hold on." She leaned over the booth and tugged her suitcase from beneath the table.

How the hell did I miss that? He realized that she

hadn't answered him about where she was staying. "Wait. Is this your first night here?"

She looked at the suitcase, then back at Dex, as if she were trying to figure out the answer. "It is," she finally said.

"Are you here for a week?"

"No. This is all my stuff. I'm moving here."

Holy shit. Your entire world fits into one suitcase? He remembered when Ellie had left her foster family when they were kids. She'd told him that people had a lot of wasted stuff and that she preferred to keep only what she needed. He realized now that she'd probably said that to protect herself, so he wouldn't think less of her. *Damn it. I could never think less of you.* Everything about Ellie was so much more valuable than material belongings could ever be. Nothing and no one in his life had ever replaced her, and he didn't know if anyone or anything ever could. He reached for the suitcase, and she struggled to get it out of his hands.

"I can do it, Dex."

Same old Ellie.

"I know you *can.* I was just trying to help."

"Thanks, but I've got it." She flipped her hair over her shoulder with one practiced snap of her chin and tugged the heavy bag behind her.

He could hear the unsaid words in his head. *I don't need your help. I can do it myself.* That's what she'd said when they'd first met. She'd been in fifth grade, he in sixth. Because Ellie was a year younger than him, he'd immediately put her into the *ignore* column of his brain. Ellie had been living with a family a few blocks from Dex's house, and when she'd stepped off of the bus, she'd dropped her binder. He'd stopped to help her pick up the contents and she'd snapped at him. *I don't need your help. I can do it myself.* Having grown up with a four-star-general father, Dex knew when to step back and shut up. But standing back and watching her run after the papers that had been carried in the wind went against everything his hippyish, peace-to-all-creatures mother had ever taught him. He'd picked up the papers that had fallen at his feet, and Ellie had glared at him with those beautiful—though at that moment dart-throwing—eyes and hadn't said thank you when he tucked them into her binder. In fact, she hadn't said anything at all, and neither had he. But like two peas in a pod, from that day forward, they'd walked home side by side in amicable silence. When they'd reach the corner of Marlboro and Carlisle Streets, where Dex turned right and Ellie turned left, Dex would lift his hand in a waist-high wave and Ellie would lift her chin and walk away.

During those afternoon walks home, Dex had been drawn to Ellie's strength as much as her quiet vulnerability. Dex was a quick study, and he'd learned what made Ellie comfortable and what set her off. Like a baby hawk, he'd imprinted onto Ellie with silent adoration. When Ellie climbed into her silent place and shut him out, he was there for her. That was all she needed—and maybe even all she wanted.

Chapter Four

ELLIE STRUGGLED TO maneuver the bulky, heavy suitcase through the crowded bar, stopping to wait for people to move out of her way every few steps as she followed Dex toward the bar. There was no way in hell she'd be able to find Dina's apartment with the way New York was suddenly spinning around her. She made a mental note that rum and Coke was now officially off her list of valid options for alcohol. She hadn't eaten since early that morning, she was tired, and she was pretty sure that she was about to meet Dex's girlfriend—and quite possibly the skinniest woman she'd ever seen.

Dex stopped short and turned around. Ellie smacked right into his chest, which felt really good and smelled even better. *Note to self: Dex smells way too good after rum and Coke. No more rum and Coke.*

"I'm sorry." Dex laughed. "Are you okay?"

No. I'm horribly embarrassed and I suck at the moment, but you smell really good, so I'm just gonna leave my nose pressed between your pecs for another breath or two. She looked up into his smiling eyes. *Jesus, what am I doing? It's Dex. Ugh. Moron move number seventeen for the night.*

"Sorry." She pushed away from him and wobbled, sober enough to note that his jeans hung dangerously sexy across his hips.

He put his hand on her shoulder. "You sure you don't want me to take that bag?"

She narrowed her eyes in the way she knew he'd understand.

He sighed. "You are one stubborn woman."

"Thank you," she said with as much snarkiness as she could muster.

Dex shook his head and waved a hand, leading a path to a barstool.

"Thank you," she said as she climbed up on the stool. The stool began to spin, and with one hand holding her suitcase, she reached for the bar to stop the motion—and missed, sending her suitcase keeling to the side while the stool continued its obnoxious whirl.

Dex grabbed her knee and steadied her.

"I've got it." Ellie felt herself falling right back into the girl she had been so many years ago: tough, resilient, in control...and cold. *Shit.* She was acting cold and she didn't like it one bit, but the alternative was not good. Acting on her feelings for too-sexy Dexy was dangerous.

"Regina, Mitch, this is Ellie Parker."

Ellie heard Dex introduce her, but his hand was searing a hole in her jeans right through to her bone. She forced her gaze from his hand to his friends' curious eyes.

"Hi." Ellie noticed that Regina was also staring at Dex's hand. *Oh great. Now I've pissed off his girlfriend. Why the hell didn't he tell me he had a girlfriend instead of sitting at my booth for so long? Now the skinny girl would give me the evil eye forever.* She pushed Dex's hand off her leg with a quick brush of her elbow. *Better. Sort of.*

"Mitch." The scruffy guy with a head of curly hair held out his hand.

Ellie shook his warm, doughy hand.

"Ellie. Ellie. Ellie." Mitch looked at Dex. "Ellie?"

She could see him trying to place her. It was glaringly obvious that Dex had never mentioned her, which stung, though she knew it shouldn't. She'd kicked him to the curb when she'd left. Why would he ever want to talk about her—or for that matter, why was he being so nice to her now? *Because it's who he is. I should get the hell out of here before I do something stupid and hurt him again.*

"Parker," Dex said. "We went to school together."

"School. College?" Regina crossed her arms and dragged her scrutinizing gaze from Ellie's head to her toes.

"No, high school." Dex took a step closer to Ellie. A step she recognized as protective, as he'd done when they were younger. His body angled a little bit in front of her, his shoulders back, his leg touching hers.

I don't need protecting anymore. She felt heat radiating from him. *Oh God. Maybe it's all in my head. I'm drunk and Regina can tell. She thinks I'm here to scam on her boyfriend.* Panic clenched her gut, and Ellie slipped into protection mode. She sat up straighter and locked eyes with waify Regina.

"We lived around the corner from each other." Ellie hoped she didn't sound as swoony as she felt.

"Ah, cool," Mitch said. "So you know all the Remingtons?" He waved the bartender over. "Another round, please?"

The Remingtons had their issues, like all families, but she'd never felt safer than when she was in Dex's room at night, and being in Dex's arms was not something she should be thinking about when she was three sheets to the wind.

Ellie waved her hand at the bartender. "No, no, no. None for me, thanks." She slid off the chair to her feet and waited for the room to stop spinning again. "I really should get going." She looked toward the back of the bar, then the front. Damn, she couldn't remember Dina's address, and she was feeling very light-headed. She dug out her phone and texted Dina.

What's your addy again?

"So soon?" Mitch asked. "Stick around. We'll grab a bite to eat and you can tell us about what Dex was like as a teenager. Give us something to tease him about."

Regina tapped her upper lip with her index finger. Ellie noticed a tattoo crawled across her shoulder. She squinted to get a better look.

"Viper," Regina said.

Ellie started. "Sorry. I was…er…sorry."

"It's okay." Regina's stare didn't relay anything even close to *okay*.

"Um, do you know where the ladies' room is?" She needed to splash water on her face and get her head on straight before trying to hunt down Dina. She worried that Dina was too busy with the guy she took home to even look at the damn text.

"Sure. I'll show you where it is." Dex laced his fingers with hers.

Regina's stare rendered Ellie mute as Dex led her through the bar and down a set of stairs. The stairs were steep, and she was glad for the stability of Dex's hand.

"Your girlfriend hates me," Ellie said.

"Girlfriend?" Dex stopped on the stair below her, and Ellie nearly toppled over him.

"You have to stop doing that." Her hands were on his chest again. He stood two steps below her, leaving them eye to eye, as they'd been in grade school when they'd first met. She remembered how sweet Dex had been. The other kids never spoke to her, and when she'd dropped her binder, they'd trudged right through the mess. But Dex had stopped to help. She'd wondered what he'd expect in return. She'd learned through the foster system that help was never free. But he hadn't asked for anything, and day after day, Dex had waited for her when they got off the bus, and he'd silently walked with her toward her house. *You've always been there for me.*

"Sorry." He cocked the right side of his lips into a sexy, lopsided grin. A grin that still felt familiar even after all the years they'd been apart. "Regina's not my girlfriend. She's my employee, and a good friend."

Ellie arched a brow. "Coulda fooled me. Whatever she is, she hates me already." She swayed on the stairs, and Dex put a hand on her waist to steady her. He was always steadying her. *Especially tonight.*

"She doesn't hate you. She's just protective of me, that's all." He took her hand again. "Come on." With one hand on her lower back, he guided her down the rest of the stairs to the ladies' room. "She'll grow to love you—like you—just as much as I do. Promise."

"Stop holding my hand. Your protector doesn't like it." Protector? Like Dex needed protecting. Who was she kidding? Hadn't she proved that he needed to be protected from her when she'd left without saying goodbye? Twice. Ellie looked over her shoulder at Dex as she opened the door to the ladies' room, stirring memories of when she'd left four years earlier. Sneaking out while he was still asleep. She swallowed the guilt that tried to strangle her as the door swung closed behind her.

She went to the bathroom, washed her hands, then splashed cold water on her face and stared at herself in the mirror. Her eyes were glassy, her cheeks rosy. *Damn it.* She never drank. Why did she have to drink tonight of all nights? Fucking Bruce, that's why. Asshole. She'd had a great job in Maryland and she'd loved her roommates. Sure, they were a little messy and a little loud when she was grading papers, but she'd liked them, and they'd liked her. Then he fucked up her life. She could no sooner have stayed in Maryland than she could have pretended they'd never dated. Her gaze shifted to the door. And then there was Dex. The other reason she drank tonight. He was so unexpected, and everything about him was comforting and safe. She didn't need safe. *Safe is never really safe.*

CHRIST. WHAT AM I doing? He hadn't thought of Ellie in...a day. Maybe. *Shit.* Who was he kidding? Ellie lingered in the back of his mind like a wave. Memories of her came and went, some more powerful than others, but always making an appearance. He wondered what had become of her and where she was living. But mostly, he wondered whose window she was crawling into at night. She was just as tough as she'd always been, but something dark lingered in her eyes, and Dex wasn't going to sleep well until he found out what it was. She came out of the ladies' room and he rose from the bottom step, where he'd been sitting.

"Where did you say you were staying tonight?" he pushed.

Ellie's smile faded. She dug in her purse for her phone. "Um. A friend's."

Shit. Everyone knew *friend* was code for boyfriend, or hookup. Tough Ellie wasn't the hookup type. Or at least she didn't used to be. "Well, don't you think you should call him?"

She typed a text and lifted her eyes to his. "Her. Dina. I know her from college. Or at least I thought I knew her. She left earlier with some guy, but I can't remember her address. I can call information."

"Ellie, your friend bolted the first night you arrived?" Dex leaned against the wall.

Ellie shrugged. "It's okay. She said she'd be at her apartment."

"What kind of friend does that?" He crossed his arms, and when Ellie tried to walk past him, he touched her arm. He felt her muscles tense beneath his touch. "Hey. You sure you're okay?"

She opened her mouth to speak, but nothing came out. She clenched her jaw shut. "Mm-hmm."

"Ellie, it's me. I know that look, remember?" He stepped closer. Ellie didn't like to be held in public, but in private she'd nearly crawled beneath his skin. The stairwell counted as private, and hell, he needed to hold her. Dex wrapped his arms around her and held her until she stopped her halfhearted struggling. He held her until the rigidity in her back and arms eased; then he rested his cheek on the top of her head and rubbed her back until her heartbeat calmed. Finally satisfied that her demons were at least a little further at bay, he drew back. Her beautiful blue eyes were open wide—staring past him. She pushed away.

"Anyway, it was good to see you, too." She stormed up the stairs and past Regina.

"Ellie!"

"Meeting, remember?" Regina said as he flew past.

"Right. Gimme an hour?" He took the steps two at a time and caught up with Ellie outside of the bar. She was dragging her suitcase down the sidewalk, her boots clomping purposefully away.

"Ellie, wait. Did your friend text back?"

"No." She picked up her pace.

"El. Where are you going? It's after midnight." She was so freaking stubborn that it was beginning to piss him off. He grabbed her arm. "Talk to me."

She spun around and faced him. "What do you want, Dex? I'm in your life for a few hours and I already made an enemy. I'm chaos. Walking, living, breathing chaos. You don't need me in your life, and I don't need saving."

"Saving?" His muscles were on fire. People moved past them on the sidewalk, arcing out around the angry girl with the suitcase and the guy who must have looked like he was ready to punch a wall. He took a deep breath and closed the gap between them, then lowered his voice. "You are not chaos, and I'm not saving you. You've never needed saving, Ellie."

Her chest rose and fell with each angry breath. "Right."

"Right." He grabbed the suitcase and whipped it out of her hand. "But there's no way in hell I'll let you walk the streets after midnight with no clue as to where you're going. And I don't care if you fight with me about it, because I'm a friend, and that's what friends do."

"Right." She didn't move.

"Right?" Was she really agreeing with him?

"Right, and that's why Regina is watching you."

Dex whipped his head around. Regina and Mitch stood outside the bar watching the scene unfold. *Damn it. What the fuck are they doing?* Couldn't he have an hour to himself? The truth was, in game development and especially this close to the release date, no, he couldn't have an hour to himself. Every Thrive employee counted on the release to be a success. He felt Ellie's fingers prying his from the suitcase.

"Ellie." Her name was almost a whisper.

She looked up at him with an expression that said, *Don't.* She shifted her gaze to the dark alley beside the bar.

"All it takes is one wrong person to drag you into a dark alley like that. Don't make me worry. Please? I'll walk you to your friend's house."

She stood with her hand atop his for what seemed like an hour but in reality was only seconds; then she gave a barely there nod of her head, though her eyes clearly said, *Whatever. Let's just get out of here.*

Dex looked back at Regina and Mitch. "One hour," he hollered.

Mitch pointed at him, then steepled his hands in the gesture that they'd come to know to convey, *Your place.*

He nodded, agreeing to meet them at his place in an hour; then he swung an arm over Ellie's shoulder and finally breathed again, ignoring the rigidity that had once again claimed her body.

"Let's find your friend's apartment."

Chapter Five

BY THE TIME they called information, tracked down Dina's address, and reached her apartment, the sharp edge of Ellie's buzz had softened. She never would have been able to decipher the directions if it weren't for Dex. She was glad for his company, too, even if she had no idea how to handle her racing heart when he was around. She hadn't remembered how alone a big city could make a person feel.

The foyer of Dina's apartment was barely large enough for Ellie and her suitcase. To her right was a cozy living room with just enough room to walk in front of the couch and put her feet up on the coffee table. To her left was the smallest—and maybe the messiest—kitchen she'd ever seen, and just beyond, a full bathroom. The door to the bedroom was off the living room and it was closed, with no light snaking out from under the crack and no signs of life behind it.

"Do you think she's here?" Dex asked.

Ellie shrugged. Now facing the reality that she

didn't really know Dina at all, the nerves in her neck tightened. She reached up and rubbed the ache. What had she been thinking when she called Dina? They'd hung out with the same group of friends, having shared the same floor in the dorms. She'd seemed nice enough, and they'd often talked in the middle of the night, when Ellie couldn't sleep and would hunker down on the couch in the recreation room. She knew then that Dina came out of her room those nights as a hint for the guys she'd picked up for one-night stands to take off, but she'd never carried that thought through to her decision about calling her for a place to stay. She'd been so damn desperate to leave Maryland that, in lieu of Dex, Dina had seemed to be her only option.

"I don't know. It's awfully quiet. Maybe they went to his apartment after all." Ellie set her suitcase on the coffee table, then flopped on the couch. "I'm sorry, Dex. I didn't mean to make a scene in front of your friends. It's been a long day, and I'm just a little frustrated."

Dex smiled and shrugged. "No worries. You kinda took me by surprise, El. I still can't believe you're here. I wasn't sure I'd ever see you again."

"That makes two of us, and I have an interview tomorrow at ten." She covered her face. "Please apologize to your friends. I never drink, so you can blame it on that." She peeked out from between her fingers and saw Dex arch his brow. She sighed and threw her head back against the cushions. "Okay, fine. It's me. It's always me. I still haven't learned how to gracefully extricate myself from uncomfortable situations. Whatever."

"They're cool, Ellie. They won't care. Listen, give

me your number, and I want to give you mine, and my address, so you have it."

"Okay, but you don't have to worry about me. I'm fine." *Liar, liar pants on fire.*

He handed her his phone. "It's not you I'm worried about. Put your info in here."

She handed him her phone. "You too." She watched him inputting his information. His kindness was being smothered by the elephant in the room—and making her feel like she was going to suffocate. She had to get it out in the open. "Dex, don't you hate me for the way I left...after that weekend...?" It hurt so much to say it out loud. To acknowledge what she'd done, how she'd cast his love—their love—aside. *Say it. You owe him that.* "When I left four years ago." She held her breath.

He looked at her for a long time. Just when she was ready to apologize, he said, "I thought I never wanted to see you again. But I could never hate you, Ellie. You're like the puzzle I could never solve. The game I could never win."

He shrugged, but she recognized the hurt that lingered in his eyes, and it pierced her heart. She wanted to apologize, but words would never be enough. Somewhere deep in her soul, she'd known back then that sneaking out was unforgivable, and yet she'd been too scared to stay.

He reached for her hand, and this time, she took it willingly. He pulled her into a hug.

This is dangerous.

Her body remembered the curves of him, the feel of him against her the last night they'd been together four years earlier, when she'd come back needing the security of him and had found so much more. She'd lain in his arms. He was reading, planning in that crazy smart brain of his, and she'd been...memorizing him. Longing to make love to him. It was that longing that had sent her hightailing it out of New York while he slept that night. Now, remembering the ache of knowing that night might have been the last time they'd ever see each other, she drank him in, allowed her body to fall weightless into the safety of him, and Dex tightened his embrace.

She felt it again, the desire to kiss him. The desire to have something more with him, and it scared the shit out of her.

"Thank you, Dexy." She drew back from him, and in his eyes she saw the same longing she felt in her heart. She pried herself away. "You have to meet your friends."

She watched his jaw clench, and at first she thought it might be hurt that she saw in his dark eyes. Then she recognized it for what it was. He stepped back and ran his hand through his hair, then tore his eyes from hers and walked to the door. He was steeling himself against her. She'd hurt him and he wasn't going to be hurt again. She couldn't blame him really. Even she didn't know what she was doing these days. *Or maybe ever.*

"El..."

"Thanks for everything. I'm glad we ran into each other." Christ, she was torn. She wanted him to stay and hold her and she wanted him to leave in equal measure. *I'm a mess, and I'm not gonna drag you down with me.*

"Me too. I've got a huge release in three weeks and almost no time to breathe." He looked down.

Her heart broke just a little. *I've ruined us.*

"But I'd like to see you and catch up. Can I call you?" he asked.

Ellie bit back the lump in her throat and grabbed hold of the security of him. "I'd like that."

Dex opened the door and hesitated, sending Ellie's heart into another flutter of confusion. *Stay. Go. Take me with you.* Somewhere over the last four years she'd buried the truth of how much she'd needed him. How much she'd wanted him. She'd had to in order to survive. As he closed the door behind him, she felt the same sinking feeling in her gut as the last night she'd crawled back out his window as a teenager and the same heart-shattering desperation she'd felt four years earlier, when she'd come back full of need and empty promises and then left when her need for him was too immense and the fear of hurting him—and herself— became all consuming. She'd sucked away his strength to use as her own and then snuck away like a thief in the night. Now, the same gut-wrenching, inescapable pain that had followed her back to Maryland four years earlier returned, and it was, without a doubt, the worst pain in her life.

When she was finally able to force her legs to move again, she went to the bathroom to wash her face. She had to stand beside the toilet to close the door. The tile floor was made of one-inch-by-two-inch blue and white squares, circa 1965. The mirror had a warped haze going on, morphing Ellie's face into even more of a mess. To her left was a small shower. The shower curtain hung lopsided, missing two rings at the top, and the bottom was peppered with specks of mildew. She wondered how Dina managed to live with such filth. Ellie swallowed her distaste. Some of the foster families she'd stayed with had beautiful bathrooms on the main floors of the house, but the bathroom she and the other foster children were forced to use looked much like this one. She washed her face and brushed her teeth. She'd have to shower in the morning, but the idea of climbing into the filthy thing now gave her a headache. Or maybe that was the rum. She wasn't sure. With a shower out of the question, she cast off her bra and slipped into a pair of sweats and a clean T-shirt, then checked the alarm on her cell phone. She climbed onto the couch and pulled a throw blanket over herself. She was asleep in seconds.

Chapter Six

DEX HEARD REGINA and Mitch's voices before he opened the door to his apartment at the Dakota. Prior to opening Thrive's formal offices, they'd worked from his old apartment. When he moved into the Dakota soon after he'd seen Ellie four years ago, he'd converted the third bedroom into a workspace. Both Regina and Mitch still had keys. Dex stood with his hand on the doorknob thinking about Ellie. When he'd hugged her goodbye, finally feeling the comfort of her body against him after all these years, he hadn't wanted to let go. The last time he'd been with her, he'd awoken to an empty bed and a broken heart. That's when he'd forced himself into the numb state his father had unknowingly helped him nurture. His father wasn't one to allow any of his children to wallow. It didn't take many harsh stares or demanding comments—*You're a man; get over it*—for Dex to learn how to turn off his emotions. He'd dulled the pain of missing her. Until now.

The release date pressed in on him, edging thoughts of Ellie to the side. He took a deep breath and went inside. The foyer was as large as the entire living room where Ellie was staying. *Jesus. Stop it.*

"Finally. Did you deliver your damsel in distress okay?" Regina asked as she and Mitch carried fresh cups of coffee toward the office.

Dex rolled his eyes.

Regina set her cup down beside her computer. Her black tank top clung to her ribs, and her hair was swept to one side, exposing the sharp line of her jaw.

Mitch sat in a swiveling office chair and propped his feet up on the desk beside an empty bag of chips. He ran his hand through his disheveled hair. "Wanna spill before we get started?"

"No," Dex said.

"Come on, Dex. You've been on some kind of dry streak with women for what seems like forever; then this chick shows up and steals your ability to function. Spill, or you know we'll get nothing done." Regina settled into a chair and looked at her watch. "Three minutes. Ready? Go."

In an effort to shut them up, he admitted, "She's a friend from when I was younger. She's in town looking for a job." *Or running from something.*

"Old girlfriend?" Regina asked.

Only in my dreams.

"First fuck?" Mitch added.

Ellie would never be just a fuck. "No and no." Dex spun a chair around and straddled it. "What's the final date?"

Mitch and Regina exchanged a glance that sent a

pain through his gut.

"Shit. Same day?" Just another thing to add to his perfectly fucked-up state of mind.

"Looks like it," Regina said.

Dex pushed from the chair and sent it spinning across the hardwood. "Why the hell would they do that? They have just as much to lose as we do." He fisted his hands. "The same day?"

"We can delay. Go out a month later so we're the next big thing," Mitch suggested. In the gaming world, there was always another game on the horizon, which gamers referred to as *the next big thing*.

"Or a few days early to capture the audience first," Regina added.

"If we go late, we piss off our fan base. If we go early, we run the risk of losing out because if anything happens—an error code that everyone is slammed with, or any fucking thing—then they're the next big thing. We need ample time to test the game to ensure it has no glitches. We're nearly there, but nearly isn't good enough." He paced the room. Things were so much easier when he was developing smaller games without so many people relying on him. He'd developed three games to date, none of which had failed, but Dex didn't believe in luck, and he knew that in a world of graphics and codes, anything could go wrong. Fully testing games before releasing them was vital. Thrive had a three-tiered testing process. *World of Thieves II* had gone through two tiers already, which meant it was probably fine, but releasing without completing the testing was risky.

"Preorders are off the charts." Mitch set his feet on

the floor. "If we have issues with our product, we're busted." His eyes searched Dex's. "Listen, Dex, there's no chance of that. We've gone through two beta test runs already, and we're testing right through delivery. The glitch they uncovered sixty days ago was fixed in twenty-four hours."

"You're smarter than that, Mitch." Dex glared at him.

"Listen, we could be screwed either way, so let's just make a decision and go with it." Regina chewed on the end of her pen.

Dex threw his hands up in the air and blew out a breath. "Okay. We play. Period. I believe in our product, and unless you know something I don't, then fuck it. We stay on schedule and release on the same day so our fans remain happy and we don't skip the last testing round. And, Mitch, I want another trailer out."

"We just ran one," Mitch said.

Dex let out a breath. "We need something to feed the fans and build more hype now that we're releasing on the same day as KI."

"Who are you gonna pull to get that done, and what am I gonna do to fill their shoes?" Regina asked.

"Review copies go out next week," Mitch reminded him.

"We've got the conventions but not before the release. We've got a slew of interviews and podcasts coming up." Regina pulled up the calendar on her phone. "You've got a few good ones this week and next."

"The PR department's been hot for weeks building buzz and pitching the game to the press. The forums are going ballistic with excitement, but they're also buzzing for KI's game." Online gaming forums could make or break a game's release. The more positive reviews the game received, the more gamers would seek it out, just as a forum full of negative reviews could sink sales. The next three weeks would be stressful as hell, but the benefit of Thrive was that it was no longer all on Dex's shoulders to design, develop, and market the games. He'd had no life when it was just him shouldering the process every step of the way. Every waking moment was spent working on the games, modifying, coding, fixing glitches, and trying to hype the product at the same time. Looking back, he had no idea how any indie developer remained sane. His issues were different now, and the risks much greater, but at least he was no longer solely responsible. He had a competent staff, some of the best in the business—who had jumped on board of his rising stardom and had remained with him ever since.

Regina looked at her watch. "It's two thirty. Let's hammer out the backup plans again and go over the testing schedule one more time, and we'll be out of here by four."

Dex pinched his brows together. "We?" he teased.

"Well, by *we*, I mean Mitch. I'm staying here tonight." Regina had long ago claimed the guest bedroom for the evenings when she was too tired to go home or didn't want to brave the streets alone at night. Dex didn't mind. After living in a house with five siblings, having Ellie sneak into his room and share his bed as a teenager, and never having a moment of silence at college, he'd never gotten used to an empty apartment. Knowing Regina was in the other room was comforting. And if he was honest with himself, it made him miss Ellie a little bit less.

Ellie.

What the hell was he going to do about Ellie?

His mind ran in circles as he and Regina hashed out the issues while Mitch played devil's advocate, pointing out each of the worst-case scenarios. At four o'clock in the morning, Mitch pulled on his sweatshirt and headed for the door.

"Tomorrow, dude. Office?" Mitch asked.

"I'll be there at some point." He had an unsettling feeling in his stomach. Would Ellie be gone by morning? He had to stop worrying about that shit. She was in the city interviewing for jobs. She was a twenty-five-year-old woman who wasn't there to see him.

Regina stretched her arms over her head and turned toward the hallway that led to the bedrooms. "Good night, Dex."

"Night, Reg."

She hesitated. "Listen, if you want to talk about the girl, I'm a good listener." Her bony shoulders lifted in a shrug.

"I know. I'm good. She's a friend. Nothing more."

Regina nodded. "Okay. I've just never seen you go all...focused on a woman before."

Dex walked past her toward his bedroom, ignoring her comment. What was he going to do? Lie to Regina? He'd never had a woman steal his focus before. And why he was focused on a woman as frustrating as Ellie was beyond him.

"Good night, Reg," he said before closing his

bedroom door.

He opened the window a crack, as he'd done since the very first time Ellie had come to his bedroom in the middle of the night, allowing the night air to clear his mind. He stripped down to his boxers and climbed into bed, trying like hell not to think of Ellie, just a few long blocks away, on some stranger's couch.

Chapter Seven

ELLIE AWOKE TO hot, rancid breath on her face. Her eyes sprang open, and she pushed the man hovering over her away and jumped to her feet.

"What the hell?" she yelled. Her eyes darted to the open bedroom door. Her heart hammered against her ribs, and every muscle tensed. Memories of when she was a teenager came rushing back to her. She snagged her phone from the couch and shoved it into the pocket of her sweats with one thing on her mind. Getting the hell out of there.

"Chill out." The guy from the bar stood before her wearing nothing but a T-shirt, and he was clearly aroused.

"Dina?" she called out.

"Shh." He stumbled backward. "She's asleep," the guy said. He stretched, and his erection bounced against him.

"Jesus. Why are you out here? Get some clothes on." Ellie pushed her feet into her boots. No matter what this guy's excuse was for standing there with his dick out, there was no way it would be a good one. She stuffed her toiletry bag into her suitcase.

"I came out to use the bathroom and saw you on the couch. Dee didn't say anything about a roommate." He yawned, looking entirely too comfortable with his nudity.

"Dina," she snapped. "Her name is Dina." She stuffed her clothes into her bag and zipped it up. This was all she needed. There was no way in hell she was staying here.

"Yeah, whatever. What are you doing?" He took a step closer to her.

"Stop." She held her hand up. "Just...stay there. I'm going to a friend's. Tell Dina I said thanks for everything." She left the key on the counter and walked out the door.

"You don't have to leave," he said before it slammed.

"Fuck. Fuck, fuck, fuck." Ellie hurried down the stairs with her purse over her shoulder and her suitcase *thunking* down the steps behind her. Seeing a naked guy was nothing new to her. Living in the dorms and then sharing an apartment with three women meant seeing more unclothed men than she cared to admit, usually running into them coming or going in the middle of the night on their way to the bathroom or coming out of the shower. But waking up to him so close to her had caught her completely off guard. And after what had happened when she lived on Carlisle Street, her mind screamed, *Run. Get out. Now.*

The night air stung her cheeks. The streets were

eerily quiet, except for the *cachunk, cachunk* of her suitcase as she dragged it along the sidewalk. *Now what am I going to do?* Her interview was in a few short hours, and she desperately needed to shower before showing up, not to mention sleep. She stopped into the nearest diner open at 4:45 in the morning for a cup of coffee, then leaned against the front of the building, both hands wrapped around the cup to warm them. She never saw the hooded man until he was already upon her. He slowed just long enough to snag her purse right off her arm, sending her coffee into the air, and took off down the alley.

"Hey!" She grabbed her suitcase and ran after him, giving up a block later when he disappeared into the pre-dawn darkness. Ellie stomped her foot. "Fuck!" She went back out to the main drag, willing away the tears that threatened to send her legs crumbling beneath her. *Suck it up. You're fine. Figure it out.*

She had no money, no place to stay, and an interview she'd surely bomb on the horizon. She was screwed.

Ellie pulled out her best pep talk. *I made it through ten foster homes, almost being raped, college, and Bruce. I can't give up now. This is a setback. That's it. Figure it the fuck out.*

Dexy.

No. She couldn't do that to him. She shivered from the situation and from the cool air. *I'm not a sixteen-year-old kid in the system anymore.* Her asshole social worker's voice came back to her—*Once the system touches you, you're always a product of the system*—whatever the hell that meant. She'd said it with a slant of negativity in her voice. That damn social worker was the impetus for Ellie to pursue her master's in minority and urban education. Even though she had no idea what she'd meant by "always a product of the system," Ellie had felt the need to prove her wrong. Even if it took forever. Even if it sucked along the way.

Ellie pulled her shoulders back and tucked her pride somewhere deep within her, where she could pull it out when she needed it, but not close enough to the surface to make her stop from going to the only place she could. And maybe even the only place she wanted to.

Chapter Eight

DEX ROLLED OVER to silence the banging noise in his head. He needed sleep, and whatever Regina was doing, she'd better stop. Now.

His bedroom door opened, and Regina's voice filtered into his exhausted mind. "Dex?"

He flipped onto his back and laid his arm over his eyes. "Hmm?"

"Were you expecting someone?"

"What?" He lowered his arm and pushed himself up on one elbow. Regina stood in her tank top and underwear. Without a bra, she had little breast buds, almost nonexistent, her hip bones jutted out above the slim lines of her silk panties, and her straight black hair was now tangled and mussed. Dex had become so used to seeing her in her various states of undress that he had no reaction, as if she were his sister.

"There's a knock at the door. I was gonna get it, but..."

"What? Knock?" Shit. Now what? He pulled himself

from the bed and lumbered down the hall with Regina on his heels. He ran through the possibilities. Mitch? Had a key. Siena? Had a key. Another of his siblings? They'd have called. He looked out the peephole and unlocked the door as quickly as he could.

"Ellie?"

She blushed. "I'm sorry."

He pulled her inside and shut the door. "What's wrong?" He looked her up and down, as if the answer might be written in indelible ink for all to see. He knew better.

She lifted her eyes to Regina and took a step back. "I'm sorry. I'll go. I just—"

Dex looked from Regina to Ellie, then back again. *Shit.* "It's not what it looks like." He glared at Regina as if she'd done something wrong.

Regina folded her arms over her stomach.

"Ellie, come in." He set her suitcase by the door and guided her past Regina and into the living room. "Reg, can you make some coffee?"

"On it," she answered.

Ellie was trembling. She had that faraway look in her eyes again.

"Ellie, what happened? Did something happen with your friend?" The protective urges he'd carried with him whenever she was around came back in full force. Every muscle tensed.

She licked her lips and fiddled with the edge of her T-shirt. Her eyes skirted over his chest, lingering at each of his tattoos. "Nothing happened with her." She dropped her eyes and they locked on his boxers and held just long enough for his body to warm.

Shit. No matter how much he tried, Dex couldn't separate his feelings for Ellie from his need to remain numb and protect his heart, and if she continued to stare at his groin, it would take less than a minute before she'd see just how much he wanted her.

She looked away, and Dex let out a relieved sigh. He watched her survey his belongings. The distressed leather sofa, marble fireplace, expansive hardwood floors, and balcony overlooking Central Park. He could almost see the doors to her emotions slamming and locking as she noted each item. Dex glanced behind him, seeing his apartment through Ellie's eyes for the first time. Exclusive. Extravagant. Even if not furnished as such, with recycled furniture and eclectic pieces that looked distressed, more worn than new. He took her hand and pulled her down beside him on the sofa.

Regina came out with two cups of coffee. "Everything okay?" she asked.

"I'm so embarrassed. I'm sorry I woke you guys up." She pushed to her feet, and Dex tugged her down again.

"Sit."

"No, really—" She tried to rise to her feet again, but he held on tight, pinning her to the couch.

"Ellie, tell me what happened."

She looked at Regina, then lowered her eyes again.

"You know, I think I'll go back to bed. Sorry for whatever happened, Ellie, but whatever it is, I'm sure it'll be okay. Dex is good at fixing things." She flashed a friendly smile and left the room.

"Oh my God, Dex. You should have told me. I never would have showed up," she whispered, whipping her head around toward the hall.

"Would you stop? Regina and I aren't...we don't...she's a friend, and not that kind of friend. We worked until four in the morning, so she crashed here."

Ellie pressed her lips together and raised her eyebrows in a gesture that Dex remembered to mean, *You don't think I believe that, do you?*

"Ellie, come here." He tugged her to her feet, glad to feel her trembling had subsided, and he walked her to the hall. "See the open door? That's my bedroom." He pointed to another door. "See that one? Guest room. That's where Regina stays."

"You don't have to answer to me. I'm not even sure what I'm doing here. I just had no place else to go." She headed for the front door, and he settled a hand on her shoulder. "Don't run, Ellie."

She stood stock-still. Silent.

Dex couldn't believe he'd said it aloud. He'd never called Ellie on her inability to stick around before. She'd stopped. She was still there. *Thank God.* He stepped in front of her and brushed her hair from in front of her face, noting the fear that still hovered in her eyes. He pulled her close and felt her resist. He wondered what it would be like if she didn't resist one day. Her face rested on his chest, and he held her there, fighting against her tension and holding her still once again, until her demons left her and her body melted into his. Only then did he take her hand and guide her back to the couch.

"Wanna tell me about it?" he asked, but he already knew the answer. Her silent head shake confirmed his thoughts. "Just tell me this. Do I need to get dressed and go kill someone?"

She leaned against his chest and shook her head. Her hand pressed against his abs, and despite his best intentions, his body reacted to having her close again. He scooted away before she could notice and crouched to remove her boots.

"Let's take these off." He set her boots on the floor, as he'd done a million times when they were kids. He placed his hand on the couch, and she set hers on top of it.

"Old habits die hard, huh?"

He shifted his eyes from her hand and nodded. The cold, determined Ellie he'd seen earlier in the evening was gone, replaced with the vulnerable girl he'd known as a teenager. Her eyes softened, drawing him in, and he felt his numbness fall away.

"I'm not that girl anymore, Dexy. I don't need to climb in your window."

Of course she'd read his thoughts. He probably had his feelings written all over his face. If he couldn't deny them, how could he expect to hide them from Ellie? She knew him better than anyone in the world did.

"Tonight just threw me for a loop, and I really had nowhere to go." She sat up, and he slid in beside her.

Had he misread her? Or was she hiding again, too? "I know you're not. But, Ellie, clue me in here. You can stay here as long as you need to or as long as you want to, but at least give me a hint as to what's going on."

She stared at him for a long time. Dex's chest tightened as he waited. He'd pushed too hard. He should have let it go. He knew better. Hell, he knew better than to let his heart open to her again. She'd already crushed it twice, but he'd felt it soften with each passing second they were together.

"You have tattoos. Lots of them." She reached up and traced the dragon that wrapped around his forearm. She nibbled on her lower lip and touched a larger, heavily scaled dragon that started above his biceps, its tail traveling lower in a sexy, dangerous sway across his muscle.

"I guess," he said.

Ellie hesitated before reaching for the markings on the left side of his chest.

"It's okay. You can touch them." Every gentle stroke of her finger sent searing heat to him down below. She closed her eyes as she traced the fringe of the tattoo that rode over his shoulder and touched his collarbone. Christ, how he loved her touch. By the time they were teenagers, he'd craved so much more of her than just friendship, and when she'd come to him four years ago, he'd thought they'd finally fall into each other's arms for good and he'd be able to finally show her how much he loved her. But at first she'd just wanted to be close to him. She needed him to hold her as he had when they were teens, and he respected that, because he'd needed it just as much as she had. But when they'd laid together as adults rather than teenagers, the love he felt for her multiplied, and he'd told her how he felt. And the next morning she was gone. He'd thought about what it would feel like to be touched by Ellie ever since, but nothing came close to feeling her delicate fingers trailing along his skin.

She drew her shaky hand back to her lap. "Why did you get so many?"

Because I needed to feel something after you left, and pain was better than nothing. "I don't know. Tell me what happened, Ellie."

She nodded and lowered her eyes to her lap. She drew her brows together, then clenched her eyes shut tight and blew out a breath. When she opened her eyes, she looked at him quickly—for a second, maybe—then dropped her eyes again.

Dex held his breath, unable to believe she might actually let him in.

"I woke up to the guy Dina brought home bent over me, with his awful breath in my face and his...He had no pants on."

Dex pushed away from her, fully awake now. "Did he hurt you? Touch you?" He'd kill the bastard.

"No. I think he was still drunk and trying to figure out who was on the couch, but it freaked me out and brought up all sorts of memo—" She cleared her throat. "All sorts of awful things. So I took off."

Dex pulled her close again. "I'm glad you had sense enough to come here."

"I didn't really have any other options. After I left, some guy stole my purse." She tucked her feet beneath her and leaned against him.

"Jesus, El. Did you call the police?" Dex hated that she was going through this kind of shit. Ellie was such a good person. He remembered one day when they'd been taking one of their silent walks home from the bus stop and she'd seen a cat for the second day in a row, sitting in the tall grass by the creek. The next day she'd saved part of her lunch and given it to the cat. She'd done the same thing every day thereafter until she'd been sent away, at which point Dex began to feed the damn cat.

"No. I figured the guy was long gone, and then the only place I could think to go was here. I promise I'll find another place to stay tomorrow."

"Stay, Ellie. I like having you here." He wrapped both arms around her and brought his legs up on the couch beside them. She nuzzled against him, and fifteen silent minutes later, she was breathing the peaceful rhythm of deep sleep. Dex couldn't remember a time when he'd felt so whole and so scared at the same time. Oh wait. Yes, he could. He remembered it all too well. As he rested his cheek on her head, his heart already wrapped around her again like a cocoon, he knew she might do the same thing to him again, but having her in his arms was so much better than having her only in his dreams. He closed his eyes, willing to put his heart at risk one more time and praying she'd still be there in the morning.

Chapter Nine

ELLIE'S PHONE ALARM sounded at eight in the morning, startling her. She scrambled to pull her cell phone from her pocket and turn it off. Dex mumbled something and tightened his grip around her waist. *Shit. What was I thinking? How could I let us get close again? And why do I want to crawl right back into your arms?* She felt as if she'd slept for two days, even though she'd had only a few hours' sleep, and she knew it was because she was with Dex. She peeled herself from his grip and stepped from the couch. He rolled over and she caught sight of his formidable erection. What was it with New York men and erections? Unlike the reaction she'd had the night before with the drunken stranger, she felt a thrill run through her.

The last time she'd slept beside Dex, she'd asked him if he'd love her forever, no matter where they were or who they were with. She'd thought she meant love her like a friend, but she'd realized as the word left her mouth that she hadn't meant like a friend at all.

Without hesitation, he'd smiled with that cockeyed, sexy grin of his and responded, *You can always be sure of me. Always.* He'd leaned over and kissed her then. A heart-stopping, toe-curling kiss that had scared the shit out of her. She'd felt his arousal against her belly, but he hadn't made a move beyond the kiss, and she'd been too scared to. Dex had been her best friend, and she loved him. *God, how I loved you. I had no choice but to leave you.*

Ellie surveyed the living room. It looked different with the sunlight streaming across the hardwood and the fright of the evening not hovering around her. She saw more of Dex in the room. The leather couch was distressed. It wasn't dark brown but a caramel color with low, thick wooden feet that gave it a homey, broken-in appearance. There were two large television screens and chunky wooden furniture with an enormous computer monitor on the top. She smiled as her eyes danced over stacks of gaming and computer magazines and piles of books.

She warmed at the sight of pictures of his family that were haphazardly placed around the room. She looked over the family photo that sat atop the marble mantel. His father's stern eyes and stoic expression, above his starched white collar, contrasted sharply with his mother's smiling eyes and long gray hair, which flowed wildly over the shoulders of her colorful bohemian blouse. She remembered each of his brothers, even though she'd only met Jack once or twice. They could have been cloned, their handsome faces and dark hair were so similar. But their eyes told different stories. His mother, Joanie, his brothers Kurt and Rush and his sister, Siena, had vibrant blue eyes, while the others' blue eyes were as dark as night. A smaller photo of Dex and Siena when they were little was placed beside a larger photo of Jack, Sage, and Dex. In it, Dex looked to be about thirteen years old. She ran her finger along his lanky body, all elbows and knees at that age. She glanced back at him snoozing on the couch, broad chested and rippled with strength. His tattoos made him look even manlier than he had four years ago. Oh yes, he had grown into a fine specimen of a man.

She went into the foyer and retrieved her suitcase, then wound her way down the hall looking for a bathroom. She passed the closed door where Regina was sleeping and wandered into Dex's bedroom. The bed was unmade, and the room carried a chill. She touched his dresser, a bold, manly wooden piece of furniture with thick legs and solid wooden handles. The top of the dresser was littered with gaming magazines and drawings. A small frame caught her eye, and she picked it up. She should feel as though she was snooping, but with Dex, she never felt that way. She'd come in and out of his bedroom so many nights that it had felt like it was hers as well. That was stupid, and she knew it, and she'd never been in this bedroom. So why did she still feel as close to him?

Her hand shook a little as she studied the photograph of the two of them. She remembered the day the picture was taken. *I remember almost every day we've ever spent together.* She ran her finger over his image, shocked that he'd not only kept it, but framed it and had it on his dresser. *He must think about me as much as I think about him.* Along with the realization came a stab of guilt, which she tucked away, focusing instead on the photograph. Dex had been seventeen and she was sixteen. It was June, just before the end of the school year. Dex had needed a haircut. She remembered teasing him about it. His hair fell over his eyes and he wore no shirt. She was pressed against his chest. *I was always pressed against his chest.* A stranger would never know who was behind that mop of dark hair that his hand was buried in. She could still feel his heart beating against hers, his hand covering her lower back, the other cupping the back of her head, and the way his embrace had felt like he was claiming her as his own.

"REMEMBER THAT DAY?" Dex leaned against his bedroom doorframe.

Ellie started and put the photograph she was holding back on his dresser. "Dex, I'm so sorry. I was looking for a bathroom, and I..."

He smiled and picked up the picture. "It's my favorite. Do you remember taking it?"

She nodded, and he wondered if she felt the same longing for that time as he felt when he looked at it. The picture had been taken two weeks before she'd been sent away. Siena had just gotten a camera and was always taking pictures. Ellie hated getting her picture taken. She'd had on a halter top. Dex remembered thinking how pretty she was and that she never wore shirts like that. She'd turned away, and he'd wrapped her in his arms. Her back was warm and soft, and Dex had wanted to hold her forever. He'd told

Siena to stop, but Siena had taken the first shot—the picture in the frame—and she'd caught the happiness on his lips, the look of love in his eyes. She'd caught his heart on film, and though the next five pictures showed a very different and protective Dex because Siena hadn't listened when he told her to stop taking pictures, he'd kept this one for himself.

Ellie nodded. "Siena was always up for mischief."

"She still is. I'm having lunch with her tomorrow. Want to come?" *Please say yes.* Having Ellie with him last night brought back so many memories and forced the ache of missing her to the forefront. He knew he shouldn't get close, but resisting Ellie was not in his bailiwick of skills.

"I can't. I need to find a job and I need to find a place to live. Oh, and call the bank to cancel my credit card." Ellie ran her hand through her hair, and her fingers tangled in its thickness.

He set the picture down. "What about reporting it to the police?"

"That sounds like a headache. There was nothing but a little cash and one bank card in my purse. I'd better shower." She started to walk past him, and he stopped her.

"Ellie, use my bathroom. The only other full bath is in the room where Regina is sleeping. How are you getting to your interview?"

She shrugged. "Walk, I guess. I'll figure it out." She opened her suitcase and began to unpack her clothes for the interview.

"I'll give you money for a cab."

She spun around. "No. I don't need—"

"No shit. You don't need money for a cab. You'll walk twenty blocks or however long it is to the school. I know you can and will, Ellie. But until you get the bank thing worked out, just take the cab money. You can make breakfast to pay me back." He smiled, knowing she was going to fight with him about the money and almost relishing in it. She was too tough for her own good—and so damned cute when she got ornery.

"I suck at cooking."

"Then you're in luck, because I don't."

She shivered. "It's chilly in here."

He crossed the floor and closed the window. "Old habits."

She narrowed her eyes.

"I sleep with it cracked every night. Always have. Well, ever since..." *Ever since you showed up at my bedroom window that first time.* He realized his mistake as soon as he'd said the words. He'd just given her another reason to run. *Don't get close to Ellie Parker or she'll take off.* That could have been written under her photo in her high school yearbook. The week his mother invited her to dinner, Ellie didn't walk home with him once. It had taken her almost two full weeks to find her way back to him again. But like a fish to water, she'd come back, and then she'd eased into his family's hearts the same way she'd snuck into his.

She shifted her gaze from the window to her toiletry bag, clearly ignoring his comment. *Damn it.* He had enough going on in his life that he didn't need the roller coaster ride that was Ellie Parker. But he'd be damned if every part of his body didn't crave her now that she was close.

"I'll be really quick in the shower, and I can walk, but thanks anyway."

Chapter Ten

AFTER CALLING THE bank and checking directions online for the school, she realized that walking a few miles in heels might be a bit much after sleeping only a handful of hours the night before. She'd swallowed her pride and borrowed cab fare from Dex, ignoring the smirk on his handsome face. He'd wished her luck before she left, and as she walked into the old brick building, she realized that luck hadn't been on her side in months. Maybe even years. Or ever. Although, what else could running into Dex have been?

The halls of the elementary school were bright and cheerful. The school had that unique elementary school smell of paste and cafeteria food. She missed the kids she'd worked with in Maryland, and she hoped they were getting the attention they needed from their new teacher. When Ellie was teaching, she didn't have shivers of doubt. She was confident in her teaching skills, and although school had been a painful experience—Ellie had always felt like a misfit—it was the one place she could prove herself. She'd excelled at schoolwork, earning A's in most of her subjects despite feeling out of place. Grades were all about her. She controlled how much she studied and how intently she paid attention. No one else could take credit for her grades, good or bad.

"Ms. Parker? I'm Principal Price. I'm glad you made it." Principal Price was an older woman with pencil-straight salt-and-pepper hair worn in a severe blunt cut just below her ears. Her smile was forced, which Ellie noted went along with her feigned kindness. She imagined this woman, who was as vertically challenged as Ellie, hovering somewhere around five foot three, had a default scowl that took hard work to mask.

"Thank you. I've heard a lot about your school." Ellie followed her into a small office, which was impeccably clean save for a small stack of files on one side of her desk.

With her nose in Ellie's file, Principal Price said, "On your application you stated that you were moving to New York to return to your roots. Is that right? So you're from the city?"

Was it? Or was it to be closer to Dex? *Focus, Ellie.* "Not the city, just outside. You know what they say…" Shit. Ellie had no idea what they said, much less who *they* were. "Once a New Yorker, always a New Yorker." She pressed her hand to her knee in hopes of settling the nervous bounce that had taken over.

"Tell me about your teaching style."

Ellie had practiced for her interview nonstop on the train to New York, and she rattled off her prepared answers. "While I follow the outlined curriculum for the students, I cater how I teach each lesson to the needs of the children. I work with the kids who need more time or depth to understand a concept while the ones who do understand are working their way through the problem. I find that holding up the entire class for one or two children's needs tends to cause the kids who do understand to lose interest."

Principal Price wrote something on her clipboard.

"Can you tell me about the class? What are the children like? Have most of them gone through the previous classes together, or do you have a high turnover rate in the classrooms?"

Principal Price opened her drawer and pulled out a spreadsheet. She slid it across the desk and Ellie looked it over.

"Our fifth-grade students scored above the national average in every area tested in the spring. Overall achievement was at the sixtieth percentile, ten points higher than the national average of fifty." Principal Price continued rattling off statistics and milestones.

Ellie redirected the question and asked about the morale of the students, hoping to glean a little insight into the children themselves, their behavior, their attitude toward school.

Principal Price referred again to the statistics, reiterating that they had achieved above-average scores.

She tried one last time. "I understand the rankings and achievements, but I'd love to know about the children's personalities, how they interact, if there are any children who need more attention than others.

Anything that I should be aware of with regard to working with them in the most effective teaching manner possible?"

"Ellie, they're children. They come to class to learn, and you'll teach them the curriculum to ensure that they pass the state requirements. I'm sure whatever you did at your old school will be similar in practice to teaching here. The most important thing is that we meet the established milestones."

By the time the interview ended, Ellie couldn't get away from the building fast enough. She'd hoped to find a school that focused on the children as individuals rather than statistics, and Principal Price seemed more interested in the latter.

Her phone vibrated, and she pulled it out to read the text.

How'd it go?

Dex. *Of course.* He was so polite, and attentive, and...so Dex. Her lips lifted into a smile as she typed a response. *Fine, but I didn't like it.*

She wished she could pick up a little something to thank Dex for letting her crash at his place, but buying a gift with his money didn't cut it. The bank had said they'd overnight a new card to her and it should arrive at Dex's place by tomorrow. She had two more interviews lined up this week, and she hoped something panned out. At least once she got her bank card back, she could find another place to stay and not impose on Dex anymore. The thought of staying someplace else left her feeling lonely.

Her phone vibrated again. *Sorry. The next one will be better.*

Mr. Optimism. Dex had a way of always seeing the bright things in life.

She answered. *It's fine. I have two more this week.*

When her phone vibrated, she expected it to be Dex again. It was Dina.

What happened last night? Jed said you took off in the middle of the night.

Ugh. She'd hoped she wouldn't have to explain herself. She texted back quickly.

Couldn't sleep. I left your key on the counter. Thanks for the place to crash.

Dina didn't text back. Neither did Dex. By the time she reached his apartment building, it was one o'clock and she was starving. She noticed the decadence of the gabled and turreted building for the first time. Above her, intricately carved ceilings provided a beautiful canopy, and expensive floors inlaid with mahogany laid the path to the elevator. She felt nervous just walking across the floor. The building took her breath away and made her feel uncomfortable all at once. She pulled the key to his apartment from her pocket as she waited for the elevator and dropped it just as the elevator doors opened. A stunning dark-haired couple walked out.

"Hi," the woman said as she stepped into the lobby, hesitating beside Ellie, who was still bent over, retrieving the key she'd dropped.

She felt her cheeks flush as she stood and dropped the key again. She groaned silently.

"Here, I've got it." The woman picked up the key and handed it to her. "Are you staying here?"

"Yes, with Dex Remington." She watched the couple exchange a glance. Their eyes softened as they turned their attention back to her.

"I'm Josh Braden, and this is my fiancée, Riley. Any friend of Dex's is a friend of ours. If you ever need anything, we're on the sixth floor. Just pop on up."

Ellie shook their hands. "Thanks. I'm only here for a few days."

Josh reached for Riley's hand. "Well, nice to meet you."

She rode the elevator up to Dex's floor. Dex had given her a key to use, and she was surprised when she slid the key in and found it was already unlocked. Her heartbeat sped up. Was he home? She went inside, and the unique smell of him—fresh soap and sheer masculinity— surrounded her. She slipped out of her heels and breathed a sigh of relief.

"Yeah, I know."

Ellie froze at the sound of Regina's voice.

"She showed up here at like five in the morning." Regina came down the hall wearing the same jeans she'd had on the evening before and the tank top she'd slept in. A Twizzler hung halfway out of her mouth as she spoke into a cell phone.

Their eyes locked.

"Mitch, I gotta go. I'll be in soon." She ended the call and smiled at Ellie.

It wasn't a feigned smile, like Principal Price's, and Regina's not-yet-made-up brown eyes looked much kinder than they had last night.

"Hey," Regina said.

"Hi." Ellie wondered why she was still there. "Is Dex here?"

"No. He's at the office." She narrowed her eyes.

"Everything okay?"

"Yeah. I'm sorry to have barged in last night. I just got into town and the girl I was supposed to stay with kind of blew me off, and things got a little nutty after that. But I'll be gone soon." She couldn't help but stare at the tattoos that covered Regina's arms and chest. She wondered what Regina was hiding from. She had read somewhere that people who had many tattoos were hiding behind the body art. She thought of Dex's tattoos and wondered what that said about him.

Regina gnawed on her Twizzler. "Hungry?"

Regina was talking to her as if she were a friend. She didn't know what she had expected, but the question took Ellie by surprise. "Kinda."

"Come on. I'm a killer cook." She walked past Ellie and headed into the large kitchen. She began taking items from the pantry and putting them on the counter. She definitely knew her way around Dex's kitchen. "The kitchen is always stocked. Though I have no idea why. He never eats here."

Do you? Ellie wanted to ask but bit her tongue.

"So you grew up with Dex? What brings you back here?" Regina moved with grace as she mixed flour and other ingredients in a bowl, cracking eggs with one hand and tossing the shells in the sink.

"Work. I taught at an elementary school in Maryland, but..." *I found out my boyfriend was married and didn't want to be known as a home wrecker; then he grabbed me and...* "I wanted to come back home."

Regina nodded. "I've moved so much that being in one place for a few years has been nice."

Maybe she'd misjudged Regina. She was actually

being nice. "Do you want some help?"

"Nah. Just chill." Regina added fresh blueberries to the batter, then poured it onto a skillet.

Ellie was dying to know about Regina and Dex's relationship. She'd believed Dex when he'd said they were just friends, but Dex was hot, and Regina had acted like she owned him the night before.

"You're the girl in the picture, aren't you?" Regina asked.

"Picture?" Ellie knew damn well which picture she was speaking of, but she was too nervous to admit it. Regina and Dex were obviously close friends. She tried to ignore the pang of jealousy that speared her when she thought about Regina in Dex's bedroom. *Cut it out.* Part of Ellie wished she'd never run away four years ago. She could have been the one with Dex all this time. But they weren't that type of friends. *But we could be. Maybe.* The thought took Ellie by surprise. The fact that she didn't immediately discount the idea surprised her even more. *What the hell is going on with me?*

Regina finished cooking the pancakes and set them on a plate. She took a Twizzler from inside a bread box on the counter and shoved it into her mouth. "The one on his dresser in his bedroom."

They might not have been that type of friends, but then there was that picture. *In his bedroom, where any woman who accompanied him in there would see it.* She pushed away the need to figure out what it meant and played it off as if it were nothing. "Yeah. We were kids." *Is it nothing? It doesn't feel like nothing.*

Regina nodded. "Eat while they're hot."

"Aren't you having any?" *Or do you exist on*

Twizzlers and beer?

Regina smiled and held up her Twizzler. "The breakfast of champions. Real food slows me down." They sat at the kitchen table together. Regina put her feet up on the chair next to her while Ellie wolfed down the amazingly delicious pancakes.

"What was Dex like as a kid?"

Ellie didn't have to think for long to retrieve the right words to describe Dex. "He was the kid who always did the right thing even when he was trying to do the wrong thing. He was sweet and...chivalrous." She smiled, remembering the way he'd gone after Siena for taking too many pictures of Ellie.

Regina looked away with a thoughtful expression in her eyes. "I can see that."

"These are delicious. Thank you. I can barely boil water." Ellie dragged the last piece through the thick syrup and popped it into her mouth. She wondered if the Dex she'd seen last night was different from the Dex everyone else saw. She hesitated before asking, "What's Dex like now?"

Regina sauntered to the bread box and snagged another Twizzler. She twirled it in the air before chomping down on it. "I think he's probably a lot like he was as a kid."

"He always had his nose in a book or his hands on electronics," Ellie said. She used to love to sit with him while he tinkered with his computer. She remembered feeling like they never even needed to talk, that just being with Dex had made everything seem better. *Like last night.* A web of confusion tangled her thoughts. Why were all those feelings coming back so strongly?

"And did he used to get this glint in his eye when he had an idea?" Regina asked.

"Like this?" Ellie's eyes widened and the right side of her lips lifted to a cockeyed smile; then she narrowed her eyes and drew her brows together.

Regina laughed. "Yes! That's the one. See? He hasn't changed. Did you graduate from high school together?"

Ellie felt sadness squeeze her heart. "No. I was a year younger than him, and I left before he graduated." She had always wondered what would have happened if she'd stayed. She didn't have grandiose dreams of going to the same college as Dex or anything as romantic, but she'd have liked to have had more time with him. Her stomach fluttered as she realized that the feelings she'd had for Dex when she'd run away four years ago weren't buried as deeply as she'd thought. They were rising to the surface, and this time, she wasn't in such a rush to push them away. She'd missed him. God, how she'd missed him.

"Did you two date?"

"No." The answer fell from her lips so fast it took her by surprise.

"No? *Hm.*" Regina twirled her Twizzler.

"*Hm* what?"

"Nothing. It's just. The way he reacted to you at NightCaps seemed...I don't know. Like you two had been close." Regina took Ellie's plate to the sink.

Ellie cleared her throat. "We..." *Should have been? I wish we were? I was too scared?* "Were just good friends."

"I guess that makes sense. Dex doesn't date many

women. He's always working. We all are, really."

All's fair in love and war. "Did you two date?" Ellie held her breath.

Regina looked over her shoulder, her hands busily scrubbing the dishes. "You're kidding, right?"

Ellie shrugged. She'd already sunk her feet in deep; might as well see how much dirt she could get.

Regina turned back to the sink. "Nah. I crash here a lot, but he and I? We're just friends. Dex is..." She dried her hands and came back to the table. "Dex Remington is a complicated man."

"Really? That's a change, then, because he never used to be. He was always easy to understand when he was younger. He didn't have many needs. I mean, give him his books, a computer, and a quiet room, and he was happy." She wondered how he'd changed.

Regina shrugged. "He's still like that, but he's pretty closed off. He protects himself. Which, given his social status, is probably not that bad of an idea."

"His social status?" Ellie had seen Dex on enough magazines to know he was doing well, but he didn't act like he'd changed very much on the social scale.

"Yeah, you know. Now that he earns millions, everyone wants a piece of him. It's a good thing that he protects himself."

It occurred to Ellie that Regina might think she was after Dex's money. *Great. Now I'm a money-hungry vagrant?* "I didn't realize...Do you mean like protecting himself from people trying to rip him off?"

"He protects his heart." Regina held her gaze.

A direct reflection of my impact on him. She cleared her throat, skipping over that comment altogether.

"Listen, I know what it must look like. A girl from his past suddenly shows up out of nowhere. I'm not here for Dex's money, or to take advantage of him or anything. It was a complete fluke that we even ran into each other."

"Fluke? Or something else?" Regina leaned her elbows on the table again and stared at Ellie.

"What else?" Ellie sat back, too tired to deal with being accused of anything.

"Fate, maybe?"

Fate? "I don't believe in fate." *If fate were real, that would mean I've been fated to a shitty life, making it from one moment to the next on a hope and a prayer.* "Besides, I'm not looking for a man, thank you, and I highly doubt Dex has any interest in that with me." Then again, she'd felt an ocean of emotions coming from him. Her own feelings were coming in with the tide, too. Or maybe they'd always been there but she was finally allowing herself to feel them again. She just didn't know if she was ready to swim.

Regina checked her watch. "I gotta run."

"Thanks for the pancakes, Regina."

"My pleasure." She started for the door, then turned back to Ellie. "I'm glad you're here. Dex seemed happy to see you."

When the apartment door closed behind Regina, Ellie let out a breath she hadn't realized she'd been holding. *Fate. Fate? Could running into Dex be fate?* Ellie's phone vibrated, and she pulled it from her pocket.

Meeting till 10. Will u be up after?

Dexy. Ellie closed her eyes, thinking about what

Regina had said. The last few weeks had been stressful. From the minute she'd found out about Bruce's marriage, she'd been on edge, and not just because he'd slammed her into a wall. She'd blamed herself. There had to be something wrong with her to not have known he was married. The clues were right there in front of her. He "traveled" all the time. He hardly ever spent the night, and if she called him in the evenings, he almost always said he was somewhere he couldn't talk. But for the first time in forever, Ellie had opened her heart to a man. Only she hadn't really opened it at all, had she? She'd opened her legs, but the minute she was back in Dex's arms, she realized there was a huge difference between opening her heart and allowing herself to be physically close with a man.

Fate? She had no job, no money, and no plan. And for the first time in her entire life, she wasn't scared to death about any of it. She walked down the hall to Dex's bedroom and picked up the photograph of the two of them. They'd been so young, so vulnerable, and yet neither had taken advantage of the other's friendship. Ellie pressed the photo to her chest, and she knew the fear that usually lingered in the back of her mind had not appeared because she was right where she belonged. A chill ran down her spine. Not a good chill but a *holy-shit-what-am-I-doing* chill. No one in her life had ever stuck around. Her mother couldn't stay sober enough to take care of her—or even to stay alive. She had never known her father, and every foster family she'd ever been with hadn't wanted to keep her. No one stuck by her.

Except Dex.

Ellie had boxed off her heart with barbed wire, and it had served her well—until Bruce. Fucking Bruce. She would not let one asshole define who she was. If she'd done that, she'd have lost hope years ago. Hell, she'd have given up. No. She'd made it this far, and she was going to have a happy life—even if it killed her.

She closed her eyes and breathed in deeply, then blew it out slowly.

She texted Dex with trembling fingers. *Sure.*

But maybe, just maybe, she had the indefinable, unfathomable *fate* on her side. Dare she let herself believe? Her legs told her to take off. Suddenly, she was fifteen years old again, lying beside Dex in his bed. *Don't leave without saying goodbye.* He'd made her promise. But when he'd come to her house, she'd told her foster family to say she was already gone. She'd watched him out the window. His jaw, too young for whiskers or stubble, was not too young to tremble. His soulful eyes filled with so much pain it killed her to watch. She'd had to turn away, and when she'd found the strength to turn back, he had already gone. She remembered thinking that if she didn't say goodbye, it wouldn't hurt. She'd never been more wrong in her life. And when she'd returned four years ago, she'd forgotten that pain, and she'd done it again.

Her phone vibrated again. She read Dex's message. *Please don't run. Xox.*

Chapter Eleven

THRIVE WAS BUZZING with the news of their release date remaining firm and Dex not backing down to KI's manipulations. The more Dex thought about their release date, the more he believed they were doing the right thing. Dex had never given in to peer pressure. Not in high school when the rest of the kids on his robotics club team had wanted to amp up their robot with materials not included in the approved list and not when he was developing his first PC game in high school. Even Siena had tried pressuring him into being a cooler teenager. And then there was Ellie, with her quiet support, her caring nature, and her belief that every moment counted. She wasn't like any of the other girls he knew in school. Ellie didn't push him to go to parties or dress a certain way. She didn't care that he chose not to play football like his older brothers had or that he never had much to say. Hell, she never asked him for a damn thing. Except once, when she'd asked him to love her forever—and he'd been all too happy to hand over his heart. Which she'd carelessly shattered.

Thinking about Ellie brought conflicting feelings. He was falling for her all over again, and the same old fears prickled his nerves. Would she really be there when he got home tonight? Was he acting like a fool, setting himself up for heartbreak again? Intellectually, he knew he should have learned from experience where Ellie was concerned and treaded carefully. Dex wasn't stupid, at least not academically, but matters of the heart were a whole different game. He'd left pieces of his heart on the lawn of her foster family's house. Crumbles of it formed a path from that house to his, and at the time, he hadn't known how to respawn. If only it were a game and he'd have had a save point in place to which he could retreat—erasing the nights he'd spent with her, the love that had grown toward her. But life didn't come with save points, and his father would allow him no time to dwell on anything— good or bad. *You're either all in or all out*, his father had told him. He'd looked at Dex with that harsh stare of his, dark eyes piercing his already broken heart, and said, *You're better than that, son. You're a man. Suck it up and move on.*

He'd sucked it up, but he'd never really moved on.

"I like Ellie." Everyone had left the meeting except for Regina and Mitch. Regina stood beside Dex as he logged off of his computer.

"Yeah?" He waited for the *but*. Dex hadn't dated much in recent years, or introduced many women to Regina, but the few times he had, Regina had nitpicked them until he lost interest. She'd been right each time. She had a sense about those things.

"Yeah."

He lifted his eyes from the computer screen and put his hand on top of hers. "But?"

Regina turned and faced him, then pushed herself onto the worktable and swung her black Converse, leaning back on her palms. Her eyes roved over his face.

Dex waited for the *but. She's too weird. She's moody. She's too something.* He could come up with a litany of things Ellie was *too* of. Stubborn would top that list, followed by complicated and moody. But all of it made her the beautiful, frustrating package that she was.

"No buts." She narrowed her eyes. "Do you need there to be a *but?*"

There it was. Her need to protect him.

"I don't think so. It's complicated." Complicated didn't begin to scratch the surface. "We're not really like that, Regina. We're friends." Even after how much she'd hurt him in the past, he still wanted more with Ellie. But no matter how much he wanted there to be more, Ellie still had her guard up. And it was probably a good thing, because Dex's ability to safeguard his heart against his love for her was quickly becoming nonexistent.

She slid back onto the floor and touched his arm again—a habit she'd begun when he used to stare at the computer screen and "Uh-huh" her, only half listening to whatever she said. Now he looked up at her raccoon eyes. Regina was a runner, just like Ellie. He'd always known she was, but she didn't physically run. She hid behind her tattoos and makeup. Maybe that was what had endeared her to him. In many ways, she was a lot like Ellie.

"Sometimes friends make the best lovers," she said and headed for the door.

"It's not like that," Dex hollered after her.

"Maybe it should be," Mitch added.

He'd forgotten Mitch was even in the room. He looked around his monitor and met Mitch's gaze. He sat with his feet up on the table, his hands clasped behind his head.

"Listen to Mr. I Will Never Date over there," Dex teased.

"I'll date. You find me a woman who understands my working until four in the morning, getting up at noon, living and breathing Metacritic, and having nightmares about glitches and missed release dates." He scratched his scruffy neck.

"Maybe if you shaved once in a while, you'd find someone who would put up with the rest of you." Dex pushed to his feet and watched his friend turn his attention back to his keyboard. "Why don't you go home? We're no longer a three-person team, Mitch. It's okay to take a night off. The testing team has this under control."

"Nah. Not now, but soon. I wanna check out the forums and see what the fans are saying." He typed something, then sat back with a *whoop*! "Rock it out, Thrive! We can't wait." He scrolled down. "Hurry up!" He clicked on something else. "*World of Thieves II* is gonna blow away KI's game."

"See?" Dex breathed a sigh of relief. "Suit yourself, Mitch. Lock up?"

"Yeah, yeah." He waved him off. "Give Ellie a kiss

for me."

Dex glared at him.

"What?" Mitch threw his hands up in the air. "She's hot. If you won't kiss her for you, I figured you might for me."

"G'night, Mitch." Dex played it cool, sauntering out of the office at his typical relaxed pace, while his insides were churning a mile a minute. He'd thought about Ellie all day. When she'd shown up at his apartment the night before, he'd wanted to take her in his arms and never let her go. He wanted to kiss away the pain and fear he'd seen in her eyes. But one wrong move and she'd be gone. He hadn't been able to keep his distance. He'd fallen back into the guy he'd been the last time she'd seen him. The guy who adored her too much to let her suffer alone. The guy who wanted nothing more than for her to be in his arms, placing no demands upon her, and allowing himself to open his heart, regardless of what she might do to it. But he wasn't a kid anymore, and she was no longer a lost girl. She was confused, and she was going through a hard time, but she was a woman, not a girl. And the feelings he'd been repressing for so long were pushing his friendly facade to the side and quickly moving to something much bigger. Hotter. He had to be careful or he'd get burned.

On his way out of the office, his phone vibrated with a text from Sage.

Hey, bro. You okay? How'd it go with Ellie?

Sage had been the only person Dex had told about the time they'd spent together as teenagers. He'd had to tell someone, and Sage wasn't the kind of brother who would give him shit or tell him to get over her. Sage was thoughtful and empathetic. He'd listened to Dex tell him what he missed about her, what he loved about her, and what he found more frustrating than an interminable glitch in one of his projects. Sage had always been wise beyond his years, which was why Dex had turned to him when Ellie had shown up four years ago. Sage had been there to help him pick up the pieces of his heart again, but Dex had never quite recovered from the desolation she'd left in her wake. *What the hell am I thinking?*

He looked at his cell phone and hadn't a clue what to say. He went with the safe route of tucking away his feelings and sticking to the facts as he texted Sage. *I'm cool. She's staying with me right now. Don't ask. No clue where anything is going.* He didn't even know how to text about Ellie without showing his emotions. Sage's response made that loud and clear.

Dangerous territory. I'm here if u need to talk.

He texted quickly. *Thx.* Dex headed back to his apartment with his shoulders hunched forward to ward off the evening chill, wondering if they'd ever had a chance at something more. Had the hurt through the years stolen any chance of a future together? Could they find their way through the missing years and navigate the circuits of change that had taken place and finally uncover their grown-up selves? And if they made it that far, would they forge a new path together, or would it all be too much? *It's Ellie. It's definitely too much.*

Chapter Twelve

ELLIE PACED DEX'S apartment. She'd never been so nervous in all her life, and certainly not nervous about seeing Dex. She must be overtired. The toll of the trip, a night without sleep, and the uncomfortable interview all coming down on her at once. She'd showered in Dex's bathroom and spent fifteen minutes with the smell of his soap soaking into her skin and permeating her senses. She felt a little naughty relishing in thoughts of him. *Naughty?* She'd never felt naughty in her life. She didn't even know where that feeling came from. And when she put the feeling of *naughty* beside an image of Dex in her mind, it was new. Different. And a little scary. She'd changed her clothes twice—which was two more times than she ever had in preparation for a date with Bruce—finally deciding on her fallback outfit, jeans and a black V-neck T-shirt. Boring? Maybe. Safe and comfortable? Definitely. Now her chest constricted and her nerves twinged. She opened the door to the apartment and went into the hall. She needed air. Something. Anything to escape the feeling of being trapped.

She sighed. *This is stupid. Trapped by Dex?*

She pushed the elevator button. Maybe a quick stroll down the block would ease her nerves. The elevator doors opened, and Dex took a step out, wearing faded jeans and a snug T-shirt beneath an open long-sleeved button-down shirt. Jesus, he was handsome. She looked down at her own clothes and thought about how alike they were—except Dex would never have hurt her the way she'd hurt him. Ever.

His smile faded too quickly. "Are you leaving?"

"No." *Maybe?*

He looked at the apartment door, then back at Ellie. "Come on." He motioned her into the elevator.

They rode down to the lobby in silence and then headed out onto the street.

"Where are we going?" Ellie asked, keeping up with Dex's quick pace.

"You had that look."

She didn't need to see his face to know he was serious, and she didn't need to think about what he meant. Dex knew. He always knew. She pondered how to reply, and before she could conjure up a suitable response, he broke the silence.

"I figured we'd get it out of your system together. You let me know when you feel more settled." Dex shoved his hands in his jeans pockets.

Guilt hovered around Ellie's shoulders like a cloak, heavy and cumbersome. She wanted to say that she had no look. She didn't need to get anything out of her system. She'd outgrown the need to run from feeling trapped, but it would have been a lie. She didn't know if she'd ever get past that feeling. She stole a glance at Dex as he walked beside her as if it had been his plan all along. Was it his plan? Maybe he *had* planned on helping her get her restlessness out of her system. He always did know just what she needed.

"Staring makes some people uncomfortable," Dex said while staring straight ahead.

Shit. "I'm just trying to figure you out."

"Really? Not much to figure out. You needed to escape. I'm escaping with you."

Cars filled the streets and people filled the sidewalks. Ellie moved closer to Dex to let a group of guys pass, and she brushed against his side. Her stomach fluttered. She still couldn't piece together what had changed between them, but there was no doubt that the stirrings she felt were deep and real and more sexual than she'd ever felt before. He took her hand and held on tight. Fingers interlaced, steps in perfect stride to one another.

"What did you do in Maryland when you needed to escape?" Dex asked.

"What do you mean?"

"When you felt trapped." He said it like she knew what he meant.

She knew.

All too well.

"I...what we're doing now. I got out and walked." She slowed her pace and he followed. "But I walked alone."

"You think it'll ever change? Your need to escape?"

She shrugged. She caught a glimpse of his eyes,

shadowed with worry.

"Why do you feel trapped with me, Ellie? I'm the one you used to run *to*."

And the one I ran from. His voice was so filled with hurt, it slayed her. "It's not you. It was never you." Except it was. When she left the first time without saying goodbye, it *was* because of Dex. She loved him too much to say goodbye. And when she left him four years ago, it was because she'd loved him too much to stay.

They continued walking in silence. Ellie's cell phone vibrated. She checked her text, and her heart stopped cold when she saw *Asshole* on the screen. The name she'd given Bruce after they broke up. She'd thought about deleting his number, but she'd wanted a warning if he ever called. She didn't want to accidentally answer a call from him. She read the text. *I miss you.*

"Something wrong?"

Everything. She'd ended things with Bruce under no uncertain terms. She'd made it clear to him not to contact her again, and there was no way she'd respond to his stupid text. She turned her phone off and shoved it back in her pocket, then upped her pace.

"Ellie, I know you said you're not the same girl you were before, but you sure as hell act a lot like her."

She tried to free her hand from his, but his grip was too tight.

He pulled her into an alley, away from the eyes of strangers, and he looked down at her with the most intense stare she'd ever seen on him. His body wasn't touching hers, and yet she felt heat radiating from him.

He wasn't pushing into her, but she felt the curves of his body, ached for them. What was wrong with her? She didn't ache for men. And here she was, staring into Dex's eyes, which were caught between angry and sad, and all she wanted to do was climb beneath his skin.

He took a step forward. Her back met the brick wall.

"Level with me, El. I can't be another pit stop. I won't be another pit stop." He breathed so hard, his chest expanded before her.

"You were never a pit stop." *Why am I whispering?*

"No? What was I? You showed up four years ago, climbed into my bed, and ran away two days later. What do you call that?" He searched her eyes, and she knew he was looking for the truth.

The truth hurt.

The truth sucked.

She lied.

"A mistake," she said.

He narrowed his eyes. "No. That was anything but a mistake. No fucking way." His voice grew louder. "No, Ellie." He stepped away from her and released her hand.

"I don't know what you want me to say, Dex. I came here four years ago because I missed you." The truth poured out of her. "You were all I thought about for all those years, so I tracked you down and came to see you. I needed...I needed to be sure of you." She crossed her arms and looked away. She felt like she was in a bubble that might pop at any moment. Just a few feet away, people passed by without noticing that her life was spiraling out of control and she was barely hanging on.

"You left me." He narrowed his eyes, and they bored right through her. "I told you I loved you, and you left me."

He'd let her back into his life without any questions about why she'd left without saying goodbye as a teenager. She could hardly believe it then, and now she felt like a complete heel, and she was petrified that he'd be the one to send her away this time. But she wouldn't lie to him again. He had to know the truth, no matter how embarrassing.

"I couldn't stay. I'd have messed up your life and continued to screw up mine. I needed to make something of myself in order to be something for you." Tears pressed at her eyes, and she closed her lids tight against them. When she opened her eyes, he was still staring at her, waiting. He was always waiting. "You didn't need me hanging around like a needy child."

"So you made the decision for me? Like I was unable to determine what was best for myself?" His face was red, his eyes more angry than she'd ever seen before.

"I needed to become a self-sufficient woman, whatever the hell that means. You deserved someone so much better than me."

"You've been self-sufficient since the fifth grade, Ellie."

His voice was so soft, thick with love, but she didn't miss the hint of hurt that rang like a constant reminder of what she'd done.

"Is that why you didn't make love to me that weekend?" he asked.

"You never tried," she whispered.

"How could I?" He turned away, and when he drew his eyes back to hers, they were filled with honesty. "I wanted you so much it hurt, but you weren't a sure thing, Ellie. You're like a...I'm not sure what. Something that's there one minute and gone the next. I needed to be sure. I thought it would go one of two ways. You'd make a move, letting me know it was safe to love you, or..."

"Or I'd leave." She wanted to wrap her arms around Dex and tell him she didn't understand why she ran away and that all she'd ever wanted was him. It had always been him. But she hadn't even realized it until this visit, and she couldn't move her arms, and when she opened her mouth again, no words came out.

He closed the gap between them and planted his palms on either side of her head, pressed against the brick wall. He'd caged her. Trapped her. One powerful leg outside of each of hers. He had to know he was making her sweat, kicking up her pulse to panic mode, inciting her flight response in a major way. He had to hear her breathing as if each breath was drawn through a kinked hose.

"I just needed to be sure of you," she repeated.

"You can always be sure of me, Ellie. Just don't break me. I can't go through it again. Twice just about killed me." He lowered his unshaven cheek and brushed against her face. "Be sure of me."

He smelled familiar. Safe. Masculine. He smelled of the only love she'd ever known. She reached up and touched his cheek. Her heart swelled. He grazed his lips over hers. Testing. Tasting. Sending heat down her center. Dex leaned his forehead against hers. She stole his breath as he exhaled, craving the taste of him. She wrapped her hand around the back of his neck and pulled his lips to hers. He kissed her gently, a soft, loving, long-awaited kiss that had her falling to pieces, melting bonelessly against him. One strong hand swooped around her waist and pressed her to him, rescuing her from her body's defeat. He buried his other hand beneath her hair and pressed his body to hers. She clawed at his hips, pulling him closer, taking what she needed, deepening the kiss and stealing the breath from his lungs. His hips gyrated against hers. She met his efforts with her own, her mind a heady mess of want and need—tangled by tentacles of guilt that infiltrated and squeezed the desire, creating pain where there had been pleasure.

He drew back, and they both gasped for air. He searched her eyes, but his feelings were so raw, it was too painful for her. She didn't want to think. She wanted to feel. She needed to feel him against her, to hide her pain within the emotions she drew from him. Ellie grabbed at him again and pulled his lips to hers. She swept his mouth with her tongue, following the dips and delicious curves of the edges of his lips, which she'd thought about for so long. He drew back again, and she sucked in air once more, needing him to enable her to breathe.

"No," he said in one long painful knife to her heart.

She opened her mouth to protest and no words came out. She clenched her jaw and covered her face.

Dex took a step back. "I love you, Ellie. I've always loved you."

She dropped her fingers. *Love. You love me? No one loves me.* "You love..." Her voice trembled. "Saving me."

He stepped back, narrowing his dark eyes until they appeared almost pitch black. "No." He shook his head. "You don't need saving. You've never needed saving. You needed to be loved. And now you just need awakening. You need to see that you're loved, to feel it, and to love back, Ellie."

She couldn't stop shaking. From the kiss or from the fear that coursed through her, she couldn't be sure, but every breath took a bumpy ride as it was pulled from her lungs.

"Why?" She swiped at a lone tear that streamed down her cheek. "Why would you want to be with me, Dex? Why do you love me? I hurt you. I'm bad news."

He stepped forward again. "You're not bad news. You're scared. You need love. You're fucking frustrating, but, Ellie, you're the best news I could ever get. But..."

She held her breath.

"But I won't survive you walking away again. One more time and I'm done. I'm a strong man, Ellie, but I'm not Superman."

Done? Of course he'd be done. Ellie was surprised he hadn't cast her aside already. Then again, Dex would never do that. She looked at the pain in his eyes and her certainty faded. *Oh God. Maybe I've hurt you so badly that one more hurt would really push you to be done with me.*

I'm scared as hell. Don't give up on me. Please don't give up on me.

He folded her in his arms and held her tight. His

lips met the top of her head. For the first time in her life, Ellie didn't want to run. She'd given in to the fear that had consumed her and had propelled her forward four years ago. Now, as the fear came rushing in, she fought against it. She had to. Thoughts of Dex had drawn her to New York. She knew that now as clearly as she knew that Dex was worth fighting for—even if the only one she was fighting was herself.

Chapter Thirteen

DEX FELT AS if he'd been put through the washer and spun dry. His body ached with desire for Ellie. Desire he'd repressed for all those years, muddled with the all-too-clear memories of when she'd left and the torturous weeks of trying to pull himself together afterward. He'd sworn he'd never put himself in the same position again, and as he unlocked his apartment door and watched Ellie walk in before him, he knew that no matter what happened four years ago, or what might happen tomorrow, she was the woman for him.

Quite possibly the only woman for him.

He followed her inside and silently took her hand. They went to the balcony, and instead of sitting on a chair, Ellie slid her legs through the iron railing and sat on the cold concrete overlooking the park. Dex sat behind her, one leg on either side of her, and wrapped his arms around her, pulling her close. He closed his eyes and felt her heartbeat through her back. He knew the chance he was taking, allowing himself to feel for her again. To love her. Hell, he couldn't help *but* love her.

"Do you ever wonder what would have happened if I had grown up in a normal house, with a normal family?" she asked.

All the time. He'd never admit that to her. Admitting that would be like saying there was something wrong with her for not having had a normal upbringing. "No. If you had, you probably wouldn't have spent time with me."

"Sure I would have. I just wouldn't have been so...unhinged." She let out a long sigh and leaned back against him.

He turned her face so he could see her eyes. "You've never been unhinged. Just a little lost." He pressed a kiss to her cheek. "Tell me about Maryland, Ellie. Tell me about why you're here."

She took a deep breath, and he felt her weighing her answer. When she didn't respond, he changed the subject. Anything to keep her in the present. He was so afraid she'd fall back into her need to run. Was he stupid to want her to stay? Would she ever stay? Was she even capable of staying in one place when she wasn't forced to?

"Tell me about what you want to do as a teacher."

She pulled her legs from between the railings and sat cross-legged facing him. Her eyes held a spark of hope, and when she spoke, her voice was markedly more animated. "There's so much I want to do. The interview I went on today was really disheartening. The low-income schools are really just scrambling to keep up. They have no money, they have minimal resources, and the worst part was that today, every time I asked about the kids, the actual children, the answers came in statistics and school-wide goals and percentages." She looked away and shook her head.

Dex wanted to pull her back against him, to feel her body against him again. He reached for her hand just to remain physically connected to her.

"Do you remember when we were in elementary school, if there was a kid who had trouble, they had a person who came into the classroom to help them, or the teacher would spend a few extra minutes making sure they understood?"

"Sure." He caressed her arm, from wrist to elbow. He loved listening to her and hearing the excitement in her voice, but he needed to touch her.

"Well, that doesn't happen anymore. Now there are more kids from low-income families, and they're often from troubled families. They face the additional challenges of poverty and are sometimes several years behind their peers. Many times one parent has been in trouble with the law and they can't afford the things they need, so they go without or their older siblings work to help the family, or in many cases, steal and get into other types of trouble."

She stopped talking and looked at his hand, which was now caressing her other arm. She smiled and took his hand in hers, drawing his eyes to hers, distracting him from touching her.

"Those kids need a different way of learning altogether. Where each child in an upper-income school has a laptop and programs available, the lower-income schools have half as many."

This was the Ellie Dex knew so well. The take-charge, pull-it-together-and-make-it-work Ellie. *If only you could be that way with your personal life, too. Maybe one day, if I love you enough. If you feel safe enough.*

"And what's the solution?" He knew she had a solution. She always had a solution, even if sometimes that solution was running away.

"I don't know. But I know that I don't want to work somewhere that the kids aren't the primary focus. I don't care about statistics and meeting the school's goals as much as I care about the individual children finding their path to learning what they need to learn. I know that as a teacher, the other stuff should be vitally important, but it's their learning that I want to be a part of. At the end of the day, I want to know I've done everything I possibly could to help them, not everything I could to ensure the statistics are met. That will come with successful learning, but I don't think it needs to be the focus." She fiddled with a seam on her jeans.

He wanted to fiddle with her jeans. He suppressed the urge to run his hands down her thighs.

"I know it's a little Pollyanna of me, but I've done some research and there are government programs that offer grants to develop educational software programs for kids. I can't help but believe that there would have to be a way to make the resources they do have—even if they only have half as much—work for the entire class. Software that would have elements for teaching grammar, math, and even history in some kind of fashion that would make it fun for kids to use."

"Like...some kind of MMO where the kids share the

platform and instead of games they're using educational software?" Dex's mind clicked into high gear.

"I'm not sure what an MMO is, but the idea is shared computers, shared software, somehow..."

"An MMO is a massive multiplayer online game. It enables lots of kids to play the same game at the same time. But you don't have to go that direction. It's just a cool idea. Maybe something with its own platform." His mind was spinning down a developmental path, moving way too far ahead of the idea stage Ellie was playing with.

"Platform?" Ellie shook her head.

"Yeah, a system, like Xbox or PlayStation, only you use it for educational purposes instead of gaming. Anyway, the software runs on the platform. I'm just thinking out loud here, but as you conceptualize the software, it's something to consider. Kids can share the platforms." He saw the confusion in Ellie's eyes. "You know what? I'm getting way ahead of myself. I'm sorry. This is your baby. Let's just focus on the grant end of things."

"I know it's a long shot, but I can't believe that entire schools of children aren't being taught all they can be because of limited funding. What does it say about our world if kids are statistics and their futures depend on the resources available to them?"

Dex laughed a little. "But that's exactly what our world is, El. You know that. And it's not just that. Hell, I feel like even what I do hinders kids and their learning."

"How so?"

"I love gaming; you know that. But lately, there's this strange thing that goes on in my head. I feel like I'm achieving everything I always dreamed of, and I'm making millions of kids...gamers...happy, but I'm also feeding into the sedentary lifestyle that comes with gaming that I really despise. Kids are becoming couch potatoes. Hell, they were couch potatoes when we were young. Remember? I spent hours in front of my computer, too. I don't know why it bothers me so much, but it's like now they're not socializing in person. They don't even flirt in person anymore. Foreplay is all done on phones and message boards. It's crazy. We're all so plugged in these days, which is great, but...I don't know. I guess I feel like kids are spending all their time playing games instead of experiencing life, and it's been bugging me, which is kind of stupid, because I don't do much besides gaming, either."

"Yeah, but you can't really change everyone else," Ellie said.

"I know, and I'm not sure what you're proposing, but it's something I'd like to think about. Helping the educational side of kids' lives as much as the entertainment side seems like a meaningful thing to do."

"I'm not sure what I'm proposing either. I just know that I want to be part of something that helps solve the problems, not a part of pushing the issues aside in order to meet a statistical need."

Dex brushed her hair from her shoulder. He grazed his lips over her neck, then kissed her softly. "That's one of the things I admire most about you. You've always wanted to help others."

"I've...I've never been in a real position to help anyone," she admitted.

He loved hearing the hitch in her voice, knowing his touch was getting to her. "You helped me."

She laughed and playfully pushed at his chest. He caught her hand in his, locking eyes with her. He brought her hand to his lips and kissed each finger, then trailed kisses up her wrist.

"When...Oh God, Dex." His name was a heated whisper. "When have I ever helped you with anything? You've always been there for me, but you've never needed anyone."

"That's where you're wrong, Ellie. Have you really forgotten all the times you pulled me through?"

She shook her head and pulled her hand from his grasp. "You've got it wrong. It was the other way around."

No way in hell did he have it wrong. When his father said things to him that made him want to crawl under a rock, she was there to lift his spirits up. In high school, when he was lost in development of his first computer game, she sat right by his side at a time when other kids ignored him or left him alone because he seemed aloof or too much of an egghead. She didn't make him feel weird. In some ways, she was *his* savior. He knew if he reminded her, she'd shove it under the carpet, like it was no big deal, or maybe over the edge of the balcony altogether. It *was* a big deal, but Ellie had never been very good at acknowledging her feelings, until earlier, in the alley. Dex wasn't taking any chances of breaking the moment. He let their silence carry her statement away.

"My new bank card should arrive tomorrow and I have another interview, so hopefully I'll get a job and be able to start looking for a place to live."

The thought sent a pain through his gut. "Stay. Even if you get a job, there's no reason to rush into a year-long lease somewhere."

Her gaze softened. He could get lost in her eyes. "Dex, I'm not sure I'll ever be what you want me to be."

He clenched his jaw. *Damn it. Will it always come down to this?*

"I don't know if I have it in me."

"Damn it, Ellie. Why do you even say those things? You have what it takes to love someone. But maybe you just don't want to love me." He looked away, afraid he'd say something else he knew he would regret.

"You know, you're the only man I'm sure I have *ever* loved, Dex. But you want a woman who knows how to stay. You want a woman who can deal with issues head-on."

"Wait. What did you just say?" He locked eyes with her.

She drew her brows together. "That you want a woman who can deal with issues?"

"No. Rewind. Before that."

Her eyes glazed over again.

"I'm the only man that you've ever loved. You said it and I heard it. Did you mean it?" *Please tell me you meant it, for Christ's sake.*

"Dex." Her eyes begged him not to make her answer.

His body tensed. "Tell me, Ellie. Did you mean it?"

Her eyes widened, then narrowed as contemplation washed over her face. She drew in a long breath and inched her mouth into a firm line.

"Jesus, Ellie." He pushed to his feet. "What the hell is all of this? I know it's been a long time, but what we had then and what we have now...It sure as hell feels real."

She looked down.

"I know you love me, Ellie, and you know you do, too. Whatever it was that made you run from Maryland back to New York must have hurt the hell out of you. I get that, okay? You know that if anyone does, I do. But I can't do this over and over again. When I saw you in that bar, my heart stopped. I wanted to run, Ellie, because of everything you've already put me through, but I wanted to be with you more than I wanted to run. And now? Now I'm just fucking confused."

Ellie rose to her feet. "Don't you think I'm confused?"

"No, I don't think you're confused. I know you're confused. But unlike you, I want to fix my confusion. I'm standing right here, six inches from you, and I'm all ears."

She nibbled on her lower lip, and he knew she wasn't going to say a damned thing.

"Great." He felt his heart shatter once again, just like it had twice before. He was an idiot. A fucking loser. Ellie Parker was never going to change, and unfortunately, he wasn't sure he knew how to change his goddamn heart. "I need to clear my head. If I go for a walk, are you gonna take off before I get back?" He swallowed the lump that clung to his throat.

He saw it in her eyes. She was sliding back into that silent place. *Goddamn it.* "Ellie." He reached for her. She took a step backward. "Ellie, I'm sorry. Don't go reticent on me, please. This is so hard. I'm trying. I'm really trying to stay with you, to stay with us, but I don't know what you expect of me. I hurt, Ellie. Every fucking time that you clamp down on your feelings. Every time you shut me out, it's like a gunshot to my heart. A man can love a woman for only so long without it being reciprocated. On some level you must know that." *Just as I know it's a fucking lie. I'll always love you.*

She nodded.

The silent nod. Fuck. He couldn't walk away from her. It would only push her to take off again. He knew she would, and he wasn't ready to take that chance. But damn it, he didn't want to stand there looking at the woman whom he was sure he loved more than anything in the world, which was fucking crazy because she didn't know how to love him back.

Chapter Fourteen

ELLIE FISTED HER hands. Her gut twisted. She couldn't let Dex walk out of her life. That was *her* job. She walked out, not Dex. Dex never left. She watched him turn away and step into the living room.

Get him. Don't let him go. She was frozen in place by disbelief.

He crossed the floor and headed for the foyer.

No! Don't!

She couldn't stop him. She couldn't promise she wouldn't leave. She wanted to promise—God, how she wanted to promise. Anything to keep him by her side— but she didn't know how. How could she make a promise she wasn't sure she could keep?

The door opened, and she listened as the latch closed and locked behind him. The sound started deep in her belly and grew to a low, agonizing moan. It took a second for her to realize it was coming from her own lungs. "No!" She sprinted out the door and pushed the elevator button again and again. "Come on. Come on."

She pushed it again. "Hurry. Hurry."

The elevator doors opened, and she flew inside and pushed the button for the lobby. "Hurry up. Come on." He'd be long gone by the time she reached the ground floor. The elevator doors closed as if they had rheumatoid arthritis, slow and painful. She watched the numbers light up as it descended to the lobby. The doors began to open, and she turned sideways and pushed herself through and flew out the front door of the complex, smacking right into the wall of Dex's chest.

"Ellie?"

"Don't go. Dex, please. Don't go." She gasped for breath, clinging to his shirt. "Please."

"I couldn't. I got out here and had to turn back. I was just coming back in."

She couldn't think past her thundering heart. *You were coming back. You're here.* "You didn't leave," she panted. She ran her hands up and down his chest, making sure of him.

Dex took her hands in his and brought them to his lips. He pressed soft kisses to her fingers, then lowered his mouth to hers. Ellie released all of her fear, and all of her emotion, and let her heart take over. She kissed him like he was the very strength she needed to survive, and in many ways, he was. When he pulled back and looked into her eyes, she knew she'd do whatever it took to learn to stay.

She poked him in the chest. "Don't do that again."

He flashed his cockeyed grin. "Are you kidding me? Look at the reward I got for leaving. If I'd known I'd get a kiss like that, I'd have left every time I saw you."

She poked him again, and he grabbed her finger and pulled her into another delicious kiss. Ellie pressed so close to his body that she thought he must be able to feel the blood flowing through her veins.

In the elevator, words tumbled from her mouth. "You can't leave. Two people can't leave. Someone has to be the strong one, and the other person—the one who leaves—has to be able to count on them to...to...goddamn it. To not give up on them."

He closed and locked the apartment door behind them, and in one swift move, as if he was afraid to delay—afraid she might disappear into thin air—he wrapped his arms around her and took her in another insatiable kiss.

"I..." He kissed her again. "Won't ever..." He brushed his lips over the line of her jaw. "Leave you."

Ellie closed her eyes, pushing away the litany of what-ifs that sailed through her mind, and gave into the desires that she'd been suppressing forever. She slid her hands beneath his shirt and ran her fingers along the firm ridges of his muscles, the delicate lines of his chest, and up and over the arc of his shoulder.

He groaned. "God, I've wanted this forever." With his hands on her cheeks, he kissed her again, his tongue loving every crevice of her mouth. He tilted her head just enough to open her mouth a little further and deepen the kiss. He slid his lips to her chin and kissed along her jaw, then nibbled at her earlobe, sending shivers up her spine. He pulled her shirt up and off, exposing her black lace bra.

"Ellie." He said her name like it was golden, something to be cherished, before lowering his lips to the crest of her breast.

Never had she been loved the way Dex loved her. Bruce had taken her as if he were in a hurry. She pushed that thought away and concentrated on the smooth, hot strokes of Dex's tongue, which were slowly stealing her sanity. He unhooked the front of her bra, freeing her breasts and cupping them in his hands with a low groan. He brought each nipple to a firm peak with the pads of his thumbs before lowering his mouth to each and bringing Ellie so close to coming apart she could barely breathe.

Without a word, he took her hand and brought her to his bedroom. She pulled at his shirt, and with one arm, he reached over his head and flung it to the floor. Ellie sucked in a breath. She'd seen Dex without a shirt on, had slept against him last night, but experiencing him while every nerve in her body was on fire brought a whole new level of exhilaration. Her body ached to know what he felt like inside her. She brought her mouth to his nipples and smiled as they pebbled beneath her tongue. She planted kisses down the center of his body—and oh what a fine body it was— between his hard abs, to the dip at the waist of his low-slung jeans. He tangled his hands in her hair and drew her back up, taking her in another greedy kiss, a kiss so deep and passionate that her knees weakened.

He unbuttoned her jeans and drew them down, then freed himself from his pants, kissing her as he pulled them down, groping her breasts, touching every inch of her body, making her crave more of him. He lowered her to the edge of the bed and pushed her legs apart, settling himself above her.

"Condom," she whispered.

"Not yet." He kissed her again, his whiskers pressing into her cheek and upper lip. An intense combination of pleasure and pain shot through her. She arched into him, and he slowed the kiss to a sensual, affectionate sharing of emotions.

She moaned when he lowered his teeth to her neck, then gently sucked the sensitive skin until her legs tingled with the force of a thousand needles. His hard length pressed against her belly. His back felt so good beneath her palms, strong and virile. His lips moved down her neck to her breastbone, where he sucked and licked until she was panting for more.

"Dex," she begged.

"Not yet." He lifted his head and met her gaze. "Just in case you show up only once every four years, I want to love you like you deserve to be loved. I want to love you so you want to come back."

She heard the pain behind his words, and she buried her hands in his hair and drew him up to her, kissing him hungrily. "I always want to come back." *I do! Oh my God. I really, truly do!*

"Then I want to love you so you're begging me not to let you leave." He moved back down her body and slid his fingers into the thin thread of her thong just below each hip. "God, you're beautiful." He kissed the curve of her hip, first one side, then the other, before pushing her thighs apart and lapping at the sensitive skin beside the tiny swatch of fabric that covered the part of her that was throbbing with desire. She arched up, desperate for more contact. He slid his finger beneath the fabric and stroked her. She couldn't stifle the whimper of pleasure. Years of pent-up emotion tumbled forward. She sucked in a breath at the contact, and he let out another sexy groan, nearly sending her over the edge. He moved the fabric to the side and licked her gently. The first swipe of his tongue sent her arching up. He held her hips down to the mattress, pinning her beneath him, then slid her thong down and tossed it aside.

Now completely naked, she lay beneath him, her eyes closed, as she memorized the feel of his big, capable hands sliding down her hips to the outside of her thighs, the feel of them as they slid beneath her ass. He lifted her up, giving himself better access to drive her insane with that crazy talented mouth of his and heightening all of the tension she'd been repressing. Just when she was on the verge of coming apart, he slid his fingers into her and her hips rose off the bed, his name sailing from her lips like a prayer. He licked and thrust, sending shocks right through her. She clenched the mattress in her fists and gritted her teeth as he teased to her peak and held her there, then brought her down slowly, until every tiny pulse felt like the last and the next sent another shock of heat through her.

She grabbed at his shoulders. "Dex." His name was one long, hot breath. "Dexy, please."

In one swift move, he flipped her body over and inched up her legs, kissing the curve of her ass, then dragging his tongue up over the arc of her cheek to the dip beside her spine. His touch was so erotic, so full of love, that she wanted to stay right there forever, surrounded by the safety of him. When his chest pressed against her back, the initial shock of skin against skin caused them both to suck in a breath. She lay beneath him, completely trusting in him, without an ounce of fear of what he might do. He ran his hands up her sides, then kneaded her shoulders and the base of her neck. He trailed soft kisses down her arm, and the remaining tension in her limbs fell away.

He nuzzled against her neck and whispered, "You can be sure of me, Ellie." Then he sealed that promise with a kiss. Gathering her thick hair in his hands, he moved it to one side; then he nipped at her neck. "Be sure of me. Take me for granted. I'll never leave you."

She closed her eyes, accepting his words, relishing in them, and wishing reality would never creep back in.

He slid beside her, his hard length pressed against her side. He turned her head gently to face him and took her cheeks in his hands. He looked deeply into her eyes, and she felt her heart open even more. "I love you, Ellie. I always have, and I know I always will."

I love you, too. She kissed him, unable to get her mouth to function in any other way, and when he pulled away, she knew he needed to hear it just as badly as she did. She forced her lips to form the words. "Dexy, I've always loved you." The words reverberated through her. She clung to them, never wanting to lose the feeling of the truth as it settled into her bones.

His eyes narrowed and filled with so much raw emotion that she thought he might cry, which would only make her cry. Instead, he took her in his arms and kissed her until the air in his lungs became hers. He reached into the drawer next to his bed and grabbed a condom from the box. She stifled the gut-wrenching sadness that shifted through her—the wonder of how many women had shared his bed.

Dex slid the protective sheath on and searched her eyes again. She slid her eyes away, knowing he'd see right through them.

"Tell me, Ellie," he whispered.

She closed her eyes. She couldn't, wouldn't ruin their moment with nonsense. She'd walked out on him four years ago. He had every right to be with anyone he wanted.

He cupped her chin and drew her eyes to his. "Tell me."

"It was just a little spike of jealousy."

He smiled. "Jealousy? Really?" He kissed her lips. "I like that."

She pushed his chest and turned away again, embarrassed.

"Hey." He positioned himself above her, pinning her with the intense emotions in his eyes. "Only you. I've never loved anyone but you."

"Love." *Dex loves me.* In her heart she'd always known he loved her, but lying beneath him, his heart beating against hers, his lips so close she could take him in another passionate kiss, it felt different. Bigger. More consuming, and she felt her heart open and drink him in.

"Love, Ellie. There's been a few others. Lust, whatever, but never love. I've only ever loved you."

THERE WAS A fine line between loving someone and smothering them, and with Ellie, Dex knew that line to be almost indistinguishable—and always fluid. He saw her smile fade after he'd told her he loved her, and he knew she anticipated him asking her the same question. Dex didn't want to know if she'd had many lovers before him. She was with him now, and as far as he was concerned, that was all he needed to know. The women who had shared his bed had been few and far between. He'd been too busy working, and his heart had always belonged to Ellie. Hell, he knew it always would.

She cupped the back of his neck and drew his lips to hers. God, he loved it when she did that. She kissed him deep and hard, like she never wanted to stop, and he let her lead, because damn, she was a good kisser, and if she'd let him, he'd kiss her for hours before ravishing her body again. Her hand slid down his side, and she pressed against his lower back, sending a rush of heat through his groin.

She whispered against his lips, "Dexy."

His name came off like a plea, and he took her in another greedy kiss as nerves got the better of him. He'd thought of Ellie day and night forever. What if they didn't fit together as well as he'd hoped? What if she wasn't fulfilled?

"Dexy."

Her voice pulled him out of his worries, and the love and trust he saw in her eyes coalesced. He cast aside his worries and settled his hips above her, then slid inside. Deep. They both gasped a breath at the first stroke of their love. As Ellie's head fell back with a gratified grin on her lips, he felt his heart swell. She met each of his thrusts with a lift of her hips and a slight gyration that sent a shudder right through him. Jesus, how could he have worried? Being with Ellie was a thousand times better than he'd ever dreamed—and boy had he dreamed. Her legs fell open, allowing him to thrust deeper, to push harder. To fill her so completely he would never want for more. Sexy little moans slipped through her lips, urging him faster. He felt her inner muscles reaching for him, tightening to hold him in. Her eyes closed, and her lips parted. God, she was beautiful. He settled his mouth over hers and forced himself to slow his pace, drawing out their lovemaking. He felt the muscles in her legs tighten and knew she was climbing toward the edge. She clawed at him, urging him deeper, faster, whimpering with need, but he kept up the torturously slow pace. He didn't often get to see the Ellie he was with right then, the unguarded woman whose face was a mask of pleasure. Her hard edges and thick barriers had been cast aside, replaced with a softer, more feminine, vulnerable side.

"Ellie," he whispered.

Her eyes fluttered open.

"Look at me, El." He kissed her again, and her eyes drifted closed again. "Look at me." He needed to know she saw him and that she was thinking of him and not allowing herself to sneak away to her silent place. He wanted her to remain right there forever, with that hazy lust in her eyes and her feet digging into the mattress, her fingers clawing at his back.

"More," she whimpered.

He felt her inner muscles pulsate just before she closed her eyes and his name spun from her lips as she clutched at him, breathing in short, hampered breaths.

"Yes. Yes," she called in one long whisper.

Dex followed her over the edge, his body

shuddering against her. Years of love carried his sweet release on and on. Sweat glistened off their bodies as they both gasped for air, satiated, spent, and together.

Finally together.

Chapter Fifteen

SUNLIGHT STREAMED THROUGH the curtains and streaked across Ellie's body as she lay on her side against Dex. He knew last night was a gift, something to be treasured but not counted on. He'd heard his phone vibrating in the middle of the night and he hadn't wanted to separate himself from Ellie. He knew that whatever it was, it would get him riled up, and for just one night, he wanted to be fully hers. He had his whole life to be owned by the PC gaming business. He had no idea how long he had with Ellie.

Ellie's alarm sounded at seven thirty. She stretched her arms above her head and pushed her butt back, grazing Dex's thighs. She stiffened—so did he. She whipped her head around and Dex felt a slow smile grace his lips. He'd expected her to startle.

She was Ellie, after all.

"Hey," she said in a raspy, sexy voice that sent a jolt of lightning to his groin.

"Hey."

"Did you sleep?" she asked.

"A little." He ran his finger down her cheek, figuring he had about sixty seconds before she bolted from bed. He'd spent all night preparing for her quick retreat. He accepted that he couldn't hold her back from whatever she needed to do. Even if that meant leaving him. Even if it would kill him to let her go. When she rested her head on his stomach, he drew his eyebrows together in confusion. She kissed his stomach and slid her hands up along his chest. *Christ.* He had no hope of hiding his desire.

He'd waited so long to love her, to touch her, and to be loved by her. Last night he felt like he was the luckiest man on the planet, and when he woke up and she was still beside him, he allowed himself a moment of revelry before remembering not to count on her. Now he fought against himself. He *wanted* to count on her.

Her eyes scanned his face. He watched, waited, telling himself not to be disappointed or hurt. Easier said than done. She lowered her lips to his chest again, and he had to run his hands through her hair. God, he loved the way her thick hair felt tangled between his fingers, the wild way it wiggled at the ends, like spiral curls that were too tired to hold their coil. He loved the way it framed her face when she hovered above him—like last night. Holy hell. Just thinking about it got him hard again.

He had to stop noticing things about her. *Dangerous territory.*

She inched up his body and placed her soft, perfectly bowed lips on his. He closed his eyes, breathing harder now, trying not to give in to his desires. Ellie was like a frightened deer. She might think she wanted to poke the bear, but when he reared up, she might take off into the woods and never look back.

"Open your eyes," she whispered.

He did, and damn if her blue eyes weren't a breath away.

"I'm not running," she said. She held his gaze. Her voice was serious, strong. But Dex knew better than to fall into her all at once. He'd done that and been burned. This time he had to try to keep his armor intact.

She reached beneath the covers and wrapped her fingers around the length of him. "Mmm."

His armor didn't stand much of a chance. Her lips found his stomach again, and she dragged her tongue down his body, then sucked her way lower. Dex closed his eyes again, felt her hands press on his thighs.

"Open your eyes," she whispered. She locked eyes with him, hovering above him. "I don't plan on running, Dexy."

That was more than she'd given him in the past, and he clung to it like a security blanket.

When she lowered her mouth and took him in, he groaned. He'd never last with the promise of staying on her lips and her hot, wet mouth driving his thoughts to her naked body. She dropped lower, licking his balls and pulling a growl from deep within his lungs. In the next breath, she was straddling him, and she slid down upon him.

"Good God, Ellie." His eyes flew open. "Shit.

Condom." He reached for the box in the drawer but not before she moved expertly up and down every inch of him, drawing him closer and closer to the edge. He grabbed her hips and stilled her. "Don't move."

She smiled and fought against his strength.

"Ellie, you're playing with fire."

"I'm on the pill." She pushed against his hands.

"Why didn't you tell me last night?" He was pressing her hips down, afraid to let her move. He was too close to falling apart.

She shrugged. "Just being careful, I guess. I didn't want you to think I was some kind of tramp for being on the pill."

"I could never think that of you."

"I've only been with two guys and we always used condoms. The pill was my backup. I didn't want to take any chances."

"I always use them. No diseases. I'm clean. But you couldn't have known that. Why would you chance it with me?"

"I trust you. You'd never put me in danger." She leaned forward to kiss him, and he stilled her again.

"You seriously cannot move. I'll lose it."

Her eyes narrowed with pleasure. She nuzzled into his neck, easing down onto his chest. Her soft breasts pressed against him, and she licked slow circles at the edge of his collarbone, then sucked the sensitive skin.

"Ellie," he whispered.

Clearly enjoying the control, she curved her lips into a mischievous smile and gyrated her hips as she'd done last night; then she took him in a hungry, deep kiss. Her hair fell like a curtain around them, brushing against his cheek. She arched up and rode him fast and hard, forcefully taking his hands from her hips and cupping them over her breasts. Dex gritted his teeth against the mounting need to come. He sat up, pulling her legs behind him, and rubbed his thumb over her nipple, then took the perfect mound into his mouth. He reached around her and grabbed her ass, helping her efforts.

"Dex," she whispered. Her eyelashes fluttered, her head fell back, and she grasped his shoulders, calling out an indiscernible cry of pleasure as she tightened around him, drawing out his release. They were chest to chest, Ellie's body trembling from aftershocks and Dex's body soaking them up. They crumbled, breathlessly, to the mattress, clinging together like they were afraid of losing each other.

"Who are you and what have you done with my Ellie?" He stroked her hair, unable to calm the worry that she still might leave.

"I think she's working on sticking around."

LATER THAT AFTERNOON, Ellie left her second interview feeling even more disheartened about finding a job, but at the same time she was counting her blessings. Her bank card had arrived safely and the thief hadn't accessed her account. She'd been out only the cost of her cheap purse and wallet and forty bucks in cash. Not that she didn't need the cash, but she wasn't going to let anything steal the euphoria of the evening and the morning she and Dex had shared. She knew better than anyone that she couldn't change the past. She could only focus on the future. And at that very moment, she was working hard to convince herself that Dex could be part of her future.

She'd always known that she loved him, but when they became one, in that first second of intimacy, she'd felt as though her entire world was becoming whole. She'd never particularly enjoyed sex with the few men she'd been with, and since girls in college had always talked about how great sex was, she'd figured it was her. That she really was incapable of enjoying intimacy. But with Dex, she didn't have to try. The emotions she had toward him were as real as the ground beneath her feet. And while it scared her, it also gave her hope.

She texted Dex, as much to show herself that she could move forward as to bring a smile to his lips.

How'd your interviews go? He'd had two podcast interviews to hype his upcoming release, and she knew he'd do great. Dex always did well. When he set his sights on something, he accomplished it. He was a strong, honest, driven, and good man. Now she knew just how *oh so good* he really was. Her phone vibrated.

Great. You?

She texted quickly before flagging down a taxi. *Okay, but same thing as last time. Kids don't seem to be the priority. Keeping funding is the priority.* She didn't like how negative that sounded, so she deleted it and texted instead, *Okay. I have another one Thursday.*

When he texted back, she stared at it for a long time. *Having lunch with Siena and my mom. Are u sure u can't join us?*

Ellie wanted to make an effort with Dex, but she wasn't sure she was ready to face his family. His family was close. It was one of the things she loved about them. Surely they knew how much she'd hurt him in the past. How could they ever trust her with Dex? How could Dex ever trust her with his heart? How could she ever trust herself with him? Panic prickled her limbs. She took a deep breath and clutched her phone in her palm. If she was ever going to move forward with Dex, she had to take a step.

Tomorrow. I'll take the step tomorrow. First she needed to work on herself. Maybe it was her turn to make a difference in someone's life. Maybe Dex was right to believe in her.

She texted him back before heading into town. *Want to check out ops at Dept of Ed for grants. Catch up after?*

He texted back a few minutes later. *Meet at home 2 nite?*

Home. And just like that, she'd fallen back into the safety of him.

Chapter Sixteen

DEX WALKED INTO the café and scanned the tables. Joanie Remington rose to her feet and opened her arms. The wide sleeves of her colorful bohemian top hung loosely like the sleeves of a robe and her skirt nearly swept the floor.

"Please don't tell me that you only have twenty minutes." Despite her stern words, the smile on her lips told Dex that his mother missed him. Her gray hair flowed in thick natural waves over her shoulders and down her back. At five foot eight, she stood nearly shoulder to shoulder with Siena, who had also risen from her seat to greet Dex.

"Hi, Mom. Sorry I've been so busy lately. You know how releases are."

"That I do. They're like giving birth. Painful and exhilarating," his mother said.

He hugged Siena and tugged playfully at her long brown hair. He'd never get used to men ogling his sister, and in her boot-cut jeans, white blouse, and colorful necklaces, she had at least four sets of male eyes looking her way.

"Sit down before the ogling husbands start getting in trouble," he teased.

Siena rolled her eyes. "Why do you look so happy?"

"What?" Dex pulled out a chair and sat down. They were in a quiet corner of the restaurant. He could always count on his mother to find the perfect spot to be able to talk. That was her thing. Talking. She claimed to be able to look into her children's eyes and see through to their...hell, he didn't know what, but she always knew if they were telling her the truth or not.

"I don't know. Usually you've got that nonplussed, I'd-rather-have-my-nose-in-a-computer look, but today you look happy." Siena was two minutes younger than Dex, and at five foot nine and thin as a rail, with naturally full breasts—a combination as rare as it was beautiful—she had taken the modeling world by surprise at a very young age and was now one of New York's most sought after models.

Getting into a discussion about his private life—the one that had him confused as hell—was not something he was up for. He ignored Siena's comment.

"Dex, tell me how you are." His mother leaned forward. "Every time I call, I get your voicemail or you're in a meeting. What's happening with that other company? I heard you were releasing on the same day as them. Is that smart? Didn't you once tell me it wasn't the best path to take?"

"You really do listen to everything we say," he teased.

"I'm your mother. Shouldn't I?" She arched a brow.

"I guess. Yeah, we're going out the same day. I don't want to play with my fans' expectations. They expect the product, and I want to deliver. We've been working on this for three years. Delaying is just a tactic, and not one I want to play with." He ran his hand through his hair and draped an arm across the back of the chair, thinking of Ellie.

Siena's phone vibrated and she scooped it off the table and read it. "Oh, yes!"

"What?" her mother asked.

Siena texted as she spoke. "Remember my friend Jordan? The makeup artist? She just texted and said they're going to move forward with that article on Sage sometime this year. But she doesn't know when."

"Why is a makeup artist interviewing Sage?" Dex asked.

"No." Siena swatted the air, then finished texting. "There's a gallery that's hosting a show for him and Mom, and Jordan has been talking to one of the mags that she does some makeup work for about doing an interview. I don't have all the details, but it sounds like it's a good thing."

"Mom?" Dex asked. "You're doing a show with Sage?"

"Apparently so. I'm not sure why they want me to do it, but it's a family theme featuring a few different artists." His mother flagged down the waitress. "It should be fun. If nothing else, it'll give me time with Sage and your father a chance to put on his Sunday best and be proud of us. You know how he likes that."

They ordered lunch, and Dex texted Ellie under the table. *Thinking of you. D.* He set the phone on the table.

"Who are you texting?" Siena asked.

"Mitch," he lied.

"I love Mitch," she said with a dreamy look in her eyes. "He's so...not like everyone else."

"He hasn't had a date in a long time. Maybe you should hook up with him." Dex raised his brows in quick succession.

"I didn't mean it like that," Siena said. "Besides, I think Regina has a thing for him."

"Maybe in Mitch's fantasies. You're really out of touch with them." He laughed.

His phone vibrated, and Siena snagged it before he could. She read the text and held the phone to her chest, her eyes wide, a smile on her lips. "Well, well, well. Who were we texting? Sure doesn't look like Mitch."

"Siena." He reached across the table and Siena leaned back with his phone.

Their mother looked at them and shook her head. "Siena, give your brother his phone."

"Who's Ellie?" she asked.

His mother caught his gaze. "Ellie?"

"Ellie," Siena repeated. "Dexy said, *Thinking of you,* and Ellie said, *Me too, you.*"

"Ellie." His mother raised her eyebrows. "I haven't heard that name in years."

Dex reached across the table and yanked his phone from Siena's hands. He texted back, *Will text after lunch. Xox.* Then he shoved his phone into his pocket. He'd worn a white-and-blue-pinstriped button-down shirt, untucked, with the arms folded up to the elbows. Dex leaned back in his chair again and knew by the annoyed expression on Siena's face that he appeared too relaxed for her to enjoy teasing him.

The waitress brought their lunches, and Dex took a big bite of his turkey sandwich, hoping they'd drop the conversation.

"Dex, Ellie?" His mother folded her hands on the table and watched him chew.

When he was done, he let out a breath and ran his hand through his hair again and said, "Ellie Parker."

"Ellie Parker. Ellie Parker." Siena tapped her chin. "Oh my God. Ellie Parker? The foster girl?"

"She's not *the foster girl*. That's a really asshole thing to say." Dex felt the muscles in his neck tighten.

"Well, excuse me." Siena poked at her salad with her fork.

"Dex, isn't she the girl who broke your heart?" his mother asked.

I'm gonna kill Sage. "The one and only," he admitted. He didn't even try to make up excuses for Ellie or lie to his mother. Ellie had hurt him, and for all he knew, she'd hurt him again, but he was willing to chance it. He respected his mother's opinion, and if Sage felt she needed to know about what had happened a few years back, then he had to have had a good reason—although that didn't dampen Dex's annoyance at Sage for not telling him. Siena? She'd always be his little sister—even if only two minutes younger—and along with that came the innate ability to ignore her opinions.

"Wait a second. Dex, that's the light in your eyes." Siena looked at their mother with her mouth set in a perfect "O." "Is she here? Are you seeing her?"

"Siena, leave him be for a minute." His mother looked at him and tilted her head.

"Really? Since when do I have to report to you two about my dating life?" He took another bite of his sandwich.

"Well, considering you don't usually have much of a dating life, I think it's only fair that you share the dirty details," Siena said before plucking a cherry tomato from her plate and popping it into her mouth.

"Dexy, as I recall, you were really taken with her for a very long time." His mother reached across the table and touched his hand. "You're a smart man with an enormous heart. Tread carefully, sweetie, okay?"

"Taken with her? Just because they were friends as kids?" Siena asked.

His mother lowered her eyes, and in that moment Dex knew that his mother knew more than she was letting on, and he wondered what that might be.

"Okay, so you're...what? Dating her? Doing her?" Siena asked.

"Siena," their mother chided.

He let out a breath.

His mother met his gaze and held it. She patted his hand again. "Do whatever your heart tells you to. She was always a nice girl. I don't like how hurt you were, but she didn't have an easy upbringing."

"See? She *was* the foster girl," Siena said.

"Damn it, Siena. That was the situation she grew up in. It wasn't who she was, and it certainly isn't who she is now."

"Dex, chill. I didn't mean it like that. It was just a reference, like saying you're a gamer. Jeez, I'm sorry,

136

okay?"

He pushed his plate away and looked at his watch. "I've gotta take off in a few minutes."

His mother shot a look at Siena.

"What? It's not my fault." Siena put her napkin on the table. "I actually liked her a lot. She was quiet and sweet, and she put up with you and your boring tinkering stage. I never had an issue with her, and I'm sorry that I called her the foster girl. I won't do that again, Dex. Really. I'm sorry." Her phone vibrated again, and she read the message and immediately began gathering her purse and jacket. "Oh crap. I'm sorry, guys, but my agent needs me in his office." She kissed her mother's cheek, then hugged Dex's rigid body, letting her hand linger on his shoulder for an extra few seconds. "I'm sorry, Dex. Call me and we'll all hang out. Okay?"

He nodded.

"My life with my children is so hit or miss," their mother said. "Siena, call me and we'll go shopping or something when you can."

"That sounds like fun. Thanks, Mom. Love you."

His mother watched Siena walk away, and then she shot Dex the same look she had when he was a teenager and she didn't buy what he'd told her. The look that said, *I'm your mother and I have eyes in the back of my head.*

"Wanna talk about it?" his mother asked.

"Not really."

She nodded. "You know, I remember when she used to come to the house. She was a watcher. She'd watch you and Siena, and you could see her mind

137

calculating when it was safe to talk, or sit, or move. She was a sweet little thing, and she understood you, Dex. She knew you better than most of us did."

Why did he suddenly feel like he wanted to climb into his mother's lap and be hugged? "Yeah?" was all he could manage.

She nodded. "There were times when your father would say something harsh to you and you'd carry it close to your chest for hours. Until bedtime in fact. And I'd worry about you. Oh, how I'd worry. You were such a sensitive boy, and you took everything your father said to heart. Still do." She shook her head.

His father knew how to cut him to the core, though Dex knew he never meant to hurt any of them. As a four-star general, he was trained to be severe. Their father had given them backbone and muscle; their mother had saved their hearts.

"I used to worry that something would happen between you two. Something irreversible." She looked at him without judgment. Her tone was kind and motherly, not patronizing.

"It wasn't like that between us," Dex admitted.

"No. I realized that after a while. She was with you all the time, Dex, and that doesn't surprise me. You were two peas in a pod. Both hurting for different reasons. Believe me, if I could have taken her from that house and raised her as my own, I would have."

Dex leaned across the table. "You knew what went on at her house?"

"Oh, Dex. Anyone who was involved with my children got the full motherly investigation. I visited her foster parents. Befriended them as best I could.

They were a mess. The best thing that could have happened was for her to be placed in another home. Even though that was the worst thing for you. And I do believe it was. The separation crushed you. I don't think I'd ever felt so sad for one of my children. Well, other than when Linda died, of course. Gosh, that was awful for Jack. Just awful, and those next two years..." She shook her head, her eyes serious. "Thank goodness he found Savannah."

Dex's oldest brother Jack's first wife had died in a car accident, and Jack had blamed himself. He'd pretty much disappeared from their lives for nearly two years. Then he'd met Savannah, and he'd found his way back to them once again.

"How is Ellie? I've often wondered what became of her."

"She's doing well, Mom. She's got a master's in minority and urban education, and she has great ideas to help low-income kids." He scrubbed his face with his hand. The admission hung on his lips. *I love her, Mom. I really love her.*

"She was always smart. You could see that by looking into her eyes. Dex, how is she otherwise? Some kids who go through the system have a really hard time getting close to people, letting them in." She picked at her salad while Dex pieced together an answer.

"You know, with me she's always been...I'm not sure how to describe her. She..."

"Is she still climbing in your window?" she asked with a tender smile.

Dex furrowed his brow. "You knew? Why didn't you ever say anything?"

"Dexy, you needed her as much as she needed you, and it wasn't like you were two horny teenagers jumping each other's bones. You treated her like she was precious china. And she..." She glanced thoughtfully out the window, her eyes soft, a smile on her lips. "She adored just being with you. You were her hero."

Hero? Ellie was more of a hero than he was. She'd overcome so much in her life. "I'm not anyone's hero, Mom, and we never did anything, but I'm not a saint. I wanted to before she left, but I wouldn't have put her in that position."

"I know. You were creatures of comfort, and you each provided what the other needed. You didn't need sex with Ellie. You needed the safety of each other." She tapped the side of her head. "I kept my eyes open. I worried as you got older and she became more beautiful, but I never figured you to be the kind of boy who was driven by sex. You've always been driven by your heart."

"Okay, this is getting uncomfortable." Dex took a gulp of ice water.

"You boys are so macho, but when it comes to matters of intimacy, you get all childish. I'd love to see her, if it gets to that point, and if not, then I'm glad you found each other again anyway. The way she left last time was heartbreaking, and I'd hate to see you miss out on love forever because you and Ellie never got together or you never figure out how to get over her."

The way she said *last time* confirmed that Sage had filled her in on Ellie's visit four years ago. Dex's phone vibrated with a message from Ellie. His chest tightened.

Part of him was waiting for the *Dear Dex* text telling him that she'd made a mistake. He couldn't shake the feeling that she might leave at any moment, despite her intentions not to. He read the text. *Met someone at Dept of Ed. Going 4 interview. Wish me luck!*

He breathed a sigh of relief and texted back. *You'll do great. Xox.*

"Ellie?" his mother asked.

"Yeah."

"Dex, I don't want to pry, but you had that look in your eyes just then. You're worried she'll leave again, aren't you?" She touched his hand.

Dex didn't answer. He couldn't. Being with Ellie for a night or a week or a day was better than not being with her at all, and talking about it would only make the fact that she might leave more real. His Adam's apple took a slow slide up his throat as he swallowed the worry.

"She might. And at some point you have to trust, Dex. I know she's the one who made it hard for you to trust all those years ago, and in a strange way, she's the one you probably need to trust the most right now."

Dex nodded, mulling over the awful truth of her statement. Ellie was the reason he'd guarded his heart. But she was also the only woman who had ever made him feel as if he had one.

Chapter Seventeen

MAPLE ELEMENTARY SCHOOL was nothing like the low-income schools Ellie had been interviewing with. At Maple Elementary, the teachers dressed comfortably, in jeans and T-shirts or skirts and blouses, whatever made them feel the most confident. While she was at the Department of Education talking with one of the specialists about the grant process, the specialist had told her about Maple, a privately funded alternative-education school. An hour later, she was in the office of the school administrator, Blythe Wagner, discussing her ideas.

Blythe was a short woman with a friendly smile and thick, light brown hair secured with a leather barrette at the base of her neck. She wore a pair of boot-cut Levi's with a loose-fitting cream-colored, short-sleeved sweater. She was naturally pretty, with blue eyes and pale skin. Her face was devoid of makeup, save for a thin application of eyeliner. She and Ellie hit it off right away.

"I like your ideas, Ellie. They're fresh and certainly viable given the right funding opportunities." She leaned her elbows on her knees, perched beside Ellie on a comfortable couch in the main office of the school. "Would you be willing to teach and work through the proposal process in your spare time? We don't have the funding for overtime. It's a lot of work. Grants are not easy to come by, and the kids have to come first. Their learning can't be sidetracked by what may or may not become a project—even if it's a project that, in the long run, will help them."

Ellie felt her eyes widen and tried to gain control of her emotions. Blythe was already talking as if they had a real chance of winning an educational grant and developing educational software was a real possibility. *A project.* Ellie would give anything to see the concept of the software come to fruition. She'd gladly work overtime without pay if it meant working with a technical team that could develop the software. She couldn't have hoped for a more supportive administrator, but she had to make sure she wasn't overselling herself.

She cleared her throat. "I...um...I have no technical writing experience, only teaching experience."

"Yes." Blythe nodded. "I'm well aware of that."

"And I don't know anything about proposal writing. I've taken technical writing courses, but this is just an idea, a concept. I mean, my expertise is working with children, not developing the actual programs." Her heart beat a mile a minute. She couldn't believe everything was happening so fast, and she wanted to lean over and hug Blythe for even offering the opportunity. Most of all, she wanted to be sure Blythe knew exactly what her skills were. She didn't need to fail at her first job in New York.

"Think of it this way. If successful, you'll be the brains behind a program that just might change the way children are taught." Blythe sat back and smiled. "We'd have to find a technical staff to work with. An affordable one."

I wonder if Dexy could help.

Blythe continued. "We would need your guidance to bring the program to fruition. You'll be able to outline it, drive the development in the right direction, and make sure the kids would be getting what they need, without the technical aspects. But there's a bigger-picture concern we need to address. You were with your last job for two years, which is a fair amount of time, but for our kids, we hope for more. They have enough instability in their lives. There's security in knowing that the teachers they trust and rely on are here year after year. No one can promise to stay in a job, and we understand that, but we do like to know where our employees stand with their three- and five-year goals."

Ellie took a deep breath and wondered if she'd unknowingly walked through a patch of four-leaf clovers. Between coming together with Dex and finding her dream job, she felt like the luckiest girl on the planet.

She'd already explained that she'd grown up through *the system*, and Blythe had seen that as a benefit. *You'll understand what some of our students have been through. That makes you even more relatable to them.* She might as well lay it on the line with her. *Sort of.*

"I left Maryland because I found out the man I was dating was married."

A deep V formed between Blythe's eyebrows. "Oh." She nodded as if she understood, but Ellie knew there was no way she could.

"I'm not someone who dates married men. In fact, if you want the truth, I'm not really someone who dates at all. I've been focused on school, then on my career, and when I met him, he told me that he was a traveling sports agent. I actually didn't agree to date him until he'd asked me out four or five times over the course of a month. It's a little hard for me to trust. Anyway, I know this is more than you need to know, but I need you to hear it. We dated for a few weeks, and I began to let my guard down and trust him, and that's when I found out that he was married."

"That sounds very painful," Blythe said in an empathetic voice.

"It was. More so because I realized that there was a woman out there who hadn't had any idea what he was doing." Ellie paused, worried she was being too open, but Blythe was leaning forward, nodding, as if she understood completely, so she continued. "I left Maryland because I didn't want any part of the situation. It was a rude awakening for me, and I didn't realize why I came back to New York until recently, but my best friend is here, and I needed to regroup." *I needed Dex.* "I'm committed, even though it might not seem that way given my short tenure in Maryland." *And my history of taking off.* "But I can assure you, what I want more than anything is to make a difference with underprivileged kids. I want to instill the belief that they can do whatever they put their mind to. I want to help them avoid falling into the path of becoming a product of their environment. I want to help them be more. So much more."

Blythe's lips lifted into a smile, though she was shaking her head.

Oh no. I was too honest.

"Ellie, where have you been hiding?"

THE STREETS OF New York felt completely different than they had when Ellie had arrived. The breakneck pace of the people and the congestion on the roads now offered excitement rather than annoyance. They carried an aura of hope and forward motion instead of appearing as impediments between Ellie and her destination. She was about to text Dex when she had an idea. She had never been to his office, and though she knew he was probably busy, she also knew how much it would mean to him to have her publicly claim their relationship. Showing up to give him the news in person seemed not only a meaningful thing to do, but also, it made her heart soar. There was no one else on earth she'd rather share her excitement with than Dex.

A quick Google search located his office, and forty minutes later she walked through the doors of Thrive Entertainment. From the distressed metal sign above the desk reading LIVE, PLAY, THRIVE! to the mismatched furniture, the office felt very Dexish. The wide-planked hardwood floors were heavily scuffed, which made her smile because only Dex would pay to have scuffed floors installed in the middle of Manhattan.

Her nerves tingled as she approached the reception desk, feeling overdressed in her skirt, blouse, and heels and wishing she had her favorite boots to ground her. It had seemed like such a great idea to show up unannounced, but now that she was there, the idea of popping in felt a little presumptuous. As much as he wanted her to stay and as much as Dex might love her, it didn't mean that he wanted his entire company to know about them. The young man behind the desk wore a black T-shirt with THRIVE! imprinted across his narrow chest and a pair of black jeans. He had on a thick studded leather wristband, and his short, dark hair stuck up in thick, gelled spikes.

"Hi." Her voice came out just above a whisper. She cleared her throat and forced herself to speak louder. "I'm here to see Dex." *Whew. Okay. I did it.*

"Sure." He looked at his computer. "And you are?"

"Ellie Parker." *Bad idea. Truly a bad idea.* She should just turn around and walk out. Tell him never mind.

"Let me buzz him. I don't see you on his schedule."

"No, I'm not. Um. It's okay. I can talk to him later." She turned to leave, and the young man's voice stopped her.

"Hold up, hon."

She closed her eyes and feigned a smile before turning around.

"I already buzzed a message through the system. If you wait one sec, I'm sure he'll respond quickly."

"It's really okay. I don't need to—"

"Ellie."

She turned toward Dex's voice and watched him cross the floor, arms open, looking drop-dead gorgeous in his jeans and button-down shirt. His eyes locked on hers and sent her stomach on an instantaneous roller coaster ride. Then she was wrapped in the warmth of him, and his lips were on hers for a split second, in a very appropriate, quick, claiming kiss. She felt her cheeks flush when they drew apart, his hand clutching hers.

"Sam, this is my girlfriend, Ellie Parker."

Girlfriend? Girlfriend. She tasted the word...and liked it. "Hi, Sam."

"Ellie, it's a pleasure. I'll just put your name on the *always-allow-in* list." Sam winked at Dex.

"You know it. Thanks, Sam." Dex led her through the office, which was open, like an enormous loft, and lined with workstations. There were no interior walls, no cubicles, and more computers than she could count. Every employee was dressed casually, sporting a wide variety of denim, leather, and tattoos. An orange couch was tucked in the far corner of the space beside three oversized chairs and faced three enormous television screens. At least they looked like television screens, but they appeared to be fed by computers.

Dex raked his eyes down Ellie's body as they walked. "Wow, you look hot. I'm surprised to see you." He squeezed her hand.

"I do?"

"Smokin'."

She tucked that compliment in the secret Dexy compartment in her heart, right beside the memory of his voice telling her he loved her. That he'd always love her. "I'm sorry for just showing up like this. I wanted to give you my news in person."

He stopped cold. His eyes darkened. "Please tell me you didn't come here to tell me you're leaving, because it's not true what they say about public spaces. I would totally make a scene here."

She knew he was only half kidding. "No. It's great news." She saw Regina approaching from the far end of the room.

He let out a fast breath. "Good."

"Dex." Regina touched his arm. "Small problem." The tattooed head of the viper that ran across her collarbone poked out from beneath her tank top. The hoodie she wore dipped low in the back, weighed down by the hood, and Ellie caught another mass of colorful tattoos that crept up the back of her neck. Regina smiled at Ellie. "Hey there, Ellie. Nice to see you."

"Hi." She didn't know what to make of Regina. The thick makeup and tattoos, combined with the harsh stares she'd given Ellie the night they'd met at the bar, contrasted sharply with the kinder woman who had made her breakfast and just flashed a sincere smile in her direction. Had she chosen a more visual path for her own walls and worn her mistrust on her sleeve, she wondered if it would have helped her deal with life in the long run. Regina seemed comfortable in her own tattooed skin, while Ellie, even after twenty-five years, was just beginning to get used to hers.

Everyone has walls to hide behind and secret insecurities. Some just hide them better than others. She glanced at Dex, his jaw muscles twitching, his hand still embracing hers, and she knew his heart was tortured by her as much as it loved her.

Regina turned back to Dex. Ellie noticed the way she held on to his arm, and she felt a flash of jealousy, which she quickly pushed away.

"KI pushed their date back a week. Just announced it. They're going out after us." Regina tightened her grip on Dex's arm as he flexed his fist.

"Shit. Okay, meet in five, conference room." He tugged Ellie toward his office. "I'm sorry, El, but this is critical. Can we talk fast?" He closed the door behind them and took her in his arms, then kissed her deeply, rendering her brain cells useless. Her hands found his hips and she pressed into him, her body instantly responding with a sharp ache of need down low. The parts that he'd awakened last night wanted to come out to play. *Stop it. Stop it. Stop it.*

When they drew apart, she blinked several times, trying to regain control of her breathing. Damn, he knew how to steal her worries—and replace them with pure and luscious lust.

"What's your news?"

"How can...?" She drew in a deep breath and let it out slowly. "How can you do that? Jesus, Dex. Your kisses are like aphrodisiacs."

He pressed his hips to hers again. "Yeah?"

"Yeah," she said in a dreamy whisper. *Shit. Concentrate.* She took a step back. "You stay there," she teased, holding her palm up. "I got a job. A really great job."

He opened his arms again. "That's great, El. What school?"

She held her palm up to ward him off. "Don't touch

me until I get this out, because you make me babble like a lovesick fool."

He wiggled his eyebrows. "I do. Hmm..."

She laughed softly, then continued. "Maple Elementary. It's a privately funded alternative education school."

"Sure. I know them. My mom has spent time there, teaching kids art, I think."

"Really? Oh, Dex. I loved the woman who interviewed me, Blythe Wagner, and their vision is so close to mine. She'd even like me to work on a proposal for the educational software I told you about. It'll take extra hours, which I won't be paid for, but I know I can do it."

"This is great news. I knew things would work out. You're too smart and too passionate about education and kids not to have found someplace where you can make a difference. See, fate really does play a part in our lives."

Fate? That word was coming up a lot lately, and Ellie found herself giving it a little more serious consideration.

Chapter Eighteen

DEX HEADED INTO the conference room with a full heart. He knew how much courage it took for Ellie to come to his office. He also knew it meant she was really trying with regard to their relationship, and that thought chipped away at the anxiety that had been prickling his mind for the past twelve hours. He half expected her to bolt from his life, but his mother's words had really hit home. *She's the one you probably need to trust the most right now.* Maybe his mother was right. He needed to put his faith in Ellie instead of expecting the worst.

The full conference room, the strained faces, and the quiet that came over his employees when he entered the room pushed his thoughts of Ellie to the background and brought the issues with their release date to the forefront.

Mitch's voice broke the silence. "We should wait to release."

Dex stood in the doorway, mulling over the

ramifications of delaying the release date. *Angry fans. Bad press.*

"They're doing the *next big thing* rollout. We can't win. I knew we should've gone out later. One week after they launch, we should release. I suggested that two weeks ago," said Mike Talen, one of their programmers.

"What do we gain by doing that?" Dex asked.

Mike looked around the room, as if someone else might offer up the answer. Dex crossed his arms and waited for him to respond.

"We become the *next big thing*," Mike said.

"How about going out a month after instead of a week? We can see what they roll out and tweak our system to beat it?" Regina suggested.

Dex walked around the room and felt the eyes of his employees trailing him. He'd been thinking about Ellie's project—and Thrive—ever since she'd first mentioned the idea of writing a proposal for a grant to develop educational software. He'd even mentioned it to Mitch, and Mitch had been excited about the possibility. The idea had sparked Dex's interest for more than just the intellectual challenge of developing such a program. It offered a way to balance out his misgivings about the gaming industry. With his and Mitch's design and development skills and a few key staff members pitching in, they could make a kick-ass educational software program that felt more like a game than a method for teaching.

As he surveyed his employees, he saw a team of loyal, dedicated, hard-working, intelligent people. A bright and worthy team he had personally selected.

The decisions Dex made today would affect every person in that room, plus the ones who worked for Thrive but weren't present. Dex didn't take these obligations lightly, but then again, no matter how relaxed he looked on the outside, he never took anything lightly—ever. Expanding development into new areas would potentially provide security for his staff, if the expansion didn't cost them too much of their game-development time. The idea was a tricky one, and testing the viability of it on a small scale was inspiring. Even if it meant that he put his own capital into the initial development and prototypes, together— with his team and Ellie—they could potentially change the face of education for low-income kids. The idea renewed his enthusiasm and bolstered his confidence.

"Who here believes in our product?" Dex raised his hand. "Show of hands."

Every person in the room raised their hand.

"Great. You can put your hands down now." He circled the far end of the conference table. "Who here thinks our product is better than KI's?"

Again, the same show of hands.

"What's the chance of error on the release?" He looked at his programmers. "Statistically speaking? Percentage?" Dex already knew it was near zero, but he wanted to make a point.

"You're not an indie developer anymore, Dex. Chances with our team are safely two percent or less," Mike said.

"He's right. I've looked over the beta testing. We've nailed it." Regina gnawed on the end of her pen with a nod.

"And what do we lose by postponing?" Dex had circled the room and stood at the front of it again.

"If their game kicks ass and we don't leave enough lead time after they release, users might not jump as quickly to check our game out and we could lose a huge market share," Mitch said.

After a minute of silence, Dex asked, "What about our fans? Do we not create these games for our fans? Isn't that the whole damn reason we're in this business? To bring games to the fans that they'll stay up all night playing?" *Pissing off their mothers, girlfriends, wives, teachers. Shirking responsibilities and letting their muscles atrophy.*

"They'll get over it. Companies delay all the time," Mike said with a wave of his hand.

Dex set his palms on the table and narrowed his eyes, dragging them slowly across each and every face in the room. "They'll get over it." He let the words sink in, then pushed from the table and crossed his arms, speaking louder. "They'll get over it." He stared at Mike. "They'll fucking get over it?" Dex took a slow stroll to Mike's side of the table. "Let me ask you something, Mike. If you waited three years to buy something you wanted, and you found out it was going to take a month longer in production, how would you react?"

Mike shrugged.

"Really?" Dex lifted his brows, feeling the eyes in the room boring into him. "Because if I had to wait a month for anything, I'd be pissed. And as a teenager, I'd have bashed the company on as many forums as possible. Even if I went back to those same forums a month later to retract what I'd posted, those initial posts still exist. Our rep is tarnished, and rightly so."

He took a deep breath and let it out loud and fast. "Our product is ready. It's rolling out to reviewers, and we have buyers standing by. I didn't set out to let people down. I set out to create the best damned games I possibly could, without the bullshit excuses that I hated as a kid. And to a kid, any reason to delay a game release is a bullshit excuse. That is what Thrive Entertainment is all about. Making our fans happy. Live. Play. Thrive. They can't play if we're holding up the release to play marketing games."

"But, Dex, it's been shown that the second game out can make a killing," Lisa, a thirtysomething blonde and their financial marketing consultant, pointed out.

"How close to breaking even are we with preorders?" Dex asked.

Lisa shook her head. "More than two million preorders. We're long past clear, and we've broken preorder records. There's no failing unless our game fails."

Dex nodded. He held up his palms toward the ceiling, then weighed them like two sides of a scale. "Let's see. We believe in our product. We've tested the hell out of it. We can make fans happy." He lowered his right hand. "Or...we play scared and piss off fans, maybe sell more, maybe not." His right hand dropped lower. "Seems to me it's a no-brainer."

"Dex." Regina crossed her arms and leaned back in her chair. "It's a risk."

"It's a calculated risk, and it's the one we're taking. If we cower to KI's bullshit, it says we don't believe in our product. I believe in our product."

And I believe in Ellie.

Dex took one last look around the room and said, "So that's the game plan. Let's go out there and make it happen. Regina, I'm taking off." Dex had created his world. Now it was time to make something more of it. He could use this world he created for fun or for good. *I'm choosing both.*

"Wait. We have the podcast at six and a marketing meeting at eight." Regina shot a look at Mitch.

"Yeah, I know. I've got something I need to take care of. Mitch, you take the podcast. Reg, you can handle the marketing."

Dex headed out the door—and toward his future.

Chapter Nineteen

THE APARTMENT WAS quiet when Dex walked in. Too quiet. He called Ellie's name. She hadn't answered her phone and now the silence caused his stomach to feel funky. He found the empty envelope from her bank card and her cell phone on the table by the front door. Her black boots were on the rug beside the table. *She'd never leave without her boots. Why am I even thinking that way?* Shouldn't today have proven to him that she wasn't going anywhere? At least not right now.

"El?" He walked through the empty living room and dining room. Her cell phone vibrated, and he picked it up on his way back to the bedroom. *Asshole* flashed on the screen. *Asshole?* He smiled. That was *so Ellie.* He didn't have to wonder long to figure out who Asshole was. Ellie could have used that term for any guy who pissed her off. A boss. *A boyfriend.* The thought made him cringe. He squelched the urge to read the text when he caught sight of Ellie through the halfway-open bathroom door, dancing in her lacy black underwear and T-shirt. He tossed the phone on the bed and stepped closer. The sound of her humming caused his ears to perk up. He watched her through the partially open door. Her hips swayed as her shoulders moved from side to side in a seductively slow dance. Damn, she was hot. The hair dryer was beside the sink, and the scent of her sweet perfume filled his senses. His body heated up, and when she threw her hands up above her head and did a sexy little shimmy, he just about lost it. Christ almighty, she was his midnight fantasy come true.

He couldn't have stopped himself if his life depended on it. He stepped into the bathroom, and Ellie started; a yelp slipped from her lips. He took her in his arms and captured the balance of the fright—her panting breaths—in his mouth. She smelled fresh and feminine, and her skin was so damn soft as he slipped his hands beneath her T-shirt. When he met the bare skin of her breasts, a deep growl escaped his lungs.

She was totally in sync with him, loving him right back with her hungry kiss. She tugged the earbuds from her ears, and he lifted her up to the countertop, pushed her shirt up to her shoulders, and shoved his hips between her legs. He could barely hold back. He wanted Ellie. All of Ellie. She buried her hands in his hair and drew his mouth to her breasts. He gratefully obliged and stroked her nipples with his tongue until she writhed against him. *Fuck, she's so hot.* She drew his lips back to hers and kissed him hard and deep, and as she drew back, she licked his bottom lip, then took it in her mouth and sucked it, letting it go slowly through her teeth. Dex groaned, unable to form a coherent thought. He grabbed her ass and pulled her to the edge of the counter, then rubbed her through her damp panties. She settled her teeth on the tender skin of his neck while her tongue worked slow strokes over his already-heated skin; then she pressed his hand firmly between her legs.

"Ellie," he whispered. He pulled at her panties, and she lifted up, giving him access to draw them down; then he lowered his mouth to her and loved her until her body shook with tiny pulses of pleasure.

"Dex. Please. Please," she begged.

He ripped open his jeans, and they dropped to his ankles. Their eyes locked, and she leaned in to him, kissing him again. Knowing she tasted herself on his lips nearly made him explode. He grabbed her hips and drove into her. She gasped a breath against his lips, unwilling to release her grip on the back of his neck, and then kissed him again. She was so wet, so hot; he wasn't going to last. Shit, he wanted to make love to her for hours. He wanted to keep her in his arms forever, breathe air into her lungs, and fill her heart with happiness so she never had reason to feel sad or alone—or leave him again. He'd waited so long to be with her, and now his body trembled with a mixture of desire, anticipation, and worry that he refused to acknowledge. He needed more of her—to drive the fear away. Far, far away. In one quick motion, he lifted her off the counter. Her legs clung to his waist; her breasts pressed against his T-shirt, her lips against his mouth. She used his biceps for leverage and met each thrust with a slide of her own.

He carried her to the bed, still buried deep inside

her, and they tumbled down together. She smiled up at him and his heart swelled. He pushed her hair from her face. "God, I love you."

Ellie grabbed his hips and whispered, "Dexy, go slow."

He obeyed, and she did that incredibly sexy thing with her hips again, that little move that stroked him—and her—in the spot that sent them both spiraling toward the edge, and as her eyes fluttered closed, she whispered, "Now." He surged up, penetrating deeper. She clawed at his back, and her inner muscles squeezed every inch of him in erotic contractions, pulling the come right out of him. He nuzzled against her neck, teeth clenched, grunting through his own earth-shattering release.

Chapter Twenty

THEY LAY ON their backs wearing only T-shirts and gratified smiles. The murmur of a vibration rattled beneath Ellie. With one arm, Dex hoisted Ellie against his side and grabbed her phone from beneath her.

"Sorry. I tossed your phone there. It was buzzing when I walked in, and then I saw you and..." He licked his lips.

She moaned. "You kill me." Ellie kissed his chest and made no move to look at her phone. Today had been too perfect. She didn't want to chance seeing another text from Bruce and clouding her happiness. She snuggled against Dex. "Something changed for me today. For the first time in forever, I feel like lots of good stuff is happening at once."

He kissed her forehead. "Your life is going to be nothing but good things, El. We just had to find our way back to each other."

She leaned up on her elbow and looked into his eyes, remembering the first time she'd snuck out of her house. It wasn't just Dex's kindness that drew her to him that night. She'd seen something else in his brooding, shadowed eyes. A hidden unhappiness that tugged at her heart. She'd braved the darkness, following the sidewalk to the next street down, then turned and went to the Remingtons' address. She couldn't remember what had compelled her to look it up two weeks earlier, but she had felt the need to do so. That night she stood outside his house trying to figure out which window might be his. She'd peered into the three bedroom windows she could reach, and though the first and second were dark, she'd found him in the third. She had no idea how long she'd watched him. Fifteen minutes? An hour? She'd been mesmerized by his ability to lie still for so long. Absorbed by whatever he was reading. Her mind was always running in ten different directions, trying to determine a way out of the hell that had become her life. If she wasn't lovable enough for her own mother to sober up and reclaim her, how could she ever expect anyone else to? By the time she got to the foster home on Carlisle Avenue she'd already become jaded by the system. She'd known her foster homes were temporary, and something about Dex had seemed permanent. Even then.

Through the window that night, she watched Dex in the dim light of the reading lamp. He was lying on the twin bed, which looked too small beneath his lanky frame, wearing only a pair of cotton boxers. She'd been twelve the first time she stood outside his window. He was thirteen. They'd known each other for almost two years. Even at her young age, she'd seen more in Dex than just a boy on the cusp of growth. His legs were thin and long, his muscles yet undefined. He set down the book and pressed keys on a keyboard beside his bed. The monitor came to life and illuminated his handsome face. Back then his cheeks were smooth, still too young to have sprouted hair. His jaw and nose were still buffered with the last bits of youthful tenderness, less angular, and his eyes—those piercing midnight-blue eyes—called to her even then. She'd been standing on her tiptoes in her jeans and oversized sweatshirt. It was October, and the leaves were damp from a light evening rain. The toes of her sneakers had slipped out from beneath her, and as she grasped the windowsill in an effort to remain erect, her knuckles had rapped against the glass. She remembered the metal-on-metal sound of the window as it slid open and the look in Dex's eyes when he saw her clinging to the sill.

"Hey," he'd said.

"Hey." *Gulp.*

He hadn't said another word. He'd held his hands out for her to take hold, and when her hands touched his, she didn't think. She scaled the wall, holding on to his hands and using her feet to walk up the bricks. She put her arms around his neck when he reached for her, and when he helped her down from the sill, inside his room, then took her hand and led her to the bed, he knelt down and took off her shoes without a word. She remembered watching him move around her like he'd been waiting for her his whole life. He'd looked at her and smiled with the right side of his mouth. And then he'd sat back on the bed against the headboard in the same position he'd been in when she'd arrived, and he lifted his arm. She'd crawled in beside him, one hand on his bare belly, the other against his side—in what would become their nightly position—and she'd closed her eyes. That was the first night she'd slept, really allowed herself to forget the world and fade away, in all the years she could remember.

Dex's hand on her cheek pulled her from the memory.

"Hey, you okay?" he asked.

She laid her head on his chest. "Better than okay."

"What were you thinking of just then?" He ran his fingers through her hair.

"You." For the first time in her life, Ellie wondered if she should return to their old neighborhood and face what had driven her to sneak out for all those years. Find some closure.

"That's good, right?" He flashed that crooked grin she loved.

She pushed the thought from her mind, unable to deal with anything that heavy right then. She wanted to focus on what she had now and the hope that was growing inside of her for a future...with Dex. "Yeah," she whispered. "Dexy?"

"Yeah?"

"I was thinking. You have misgivings about what PC games do to kids, and I know you love making them, but what about balancing those misgivings by helping kids in another way? Would you ever consider helping us make that software program for kids? I mean, I know it's not your thing, but—"

He lifted her chin so she was looking into his eyes. "I've thought about it since you mentioned it to me. I even talked to Mitch about it. Yeah, I want to."

She sat up and pulled the blanket over her lower half. "Really?" Excitement prickled her limbs.

"Yeah. I was thinking, most educational software programs *feel* like educational programs. The way you explained what you had envisioned the first time you told me about it, it made me think of a multiplayer platform. So I took that idea a little further. We could develop educational software that feels like a game. Obviously, it can't be like *World of Thieves* or have weapons or those types of elements, but we can use the same type of premise, set the program in a made-up world with cool characters and reading prompts, match prompts, whatever educational elements you need. You'll have to guide us on that end, but it's totally doable."

"You really have been thinking about it."

"I'll always make games, but I worry about what's going to happen ten years from now. I mean, now that both guys and girls are gaming all the time, if you look down the road, their kids will grow up doing it, too. Soon no one will play sports or go to museums, or hell, even leave their houses."

Ellie wrinkled her brow. "A little overdramatic today?"

"Maybe. A little *over* everything today. But I do want to be involved with something that will help kids. So yeah, whatever you need. I'm in."

She sighed and tumbled down beside him again.

"You're waiting for the other shoe to fall and clunk you on the head." Dex touched the top of her head.

"You can tell?"

"I can always tell." He leaned over her and lifted up her shirt, exposing her stomach. Dex drew a heart on her skin with his index finger. "Nothing's gonna clunk you."

Her phone vibrated again, and she groaned.

"Just answer it," he said.

"I don't want to."

He stared at the phone, and guilt speared her heart.

"Who is *Asshole?*" Dex's voice turned serious. He held her gaze, and when she tried to look away, he shook his head. "Ellie, we owe each other honesty. I will never lie to you, and I don't think I could stand it if you lied to me. Not after all these years and everything we've been through."

She closed her eyes for a breath. *Tell him. Don't ruin this.* She covered her eyes with her arm. "If I tell you, you can't judge me, because it's not my fault. And you can't look at me, either."

"Ellie."

She shook her head, her arm acting as a barrier between the hurt she knew would fill his eyes and the embarrassment that would fill hers. And if she dared tell him the whole truth, he'd go ballistic. She knew this about him. He'd go to the ends of the earth to protect her. But he couldn't slay the demons that haunted her heart if he didn't know what they were. He wouldn't morph from sweet, loving Dexy to man-on-a-mission without a reason, and right now she needed sweet, loving Dexy. *Just this last time.* It wasn't a lie, really. She was going to tell him the truth, omitting only one tiny piece of information. *Tiny, my ass.* Okay. One big fucking chunk of information that she wasn't ready to relive.

"Okay, fine," she relented. "I came to New York because I found out the guy I was dating was married." She held her breath and pressed her arm to her eyes.

"And?"

She dropped her arm and sat up. "And? Really? Married, Dex. Do you know what that means? Do you know what that makes me?" *Jeez, do I have to spell it out to you? T. R. A. M. P.*

He laughed. "Feisty, aren't we?"

She pushed his chest. "I'm not a home wrecker. I had no idea he was married, and I'm thoroughly and utterly mortified to have been part of the whole mess."

Dex took her hand. "I'm sorry. That does suck."

"It does."

"So you left Maryland because of that? Did you know his wife?"

Ellie shook her head, and guilt drove her eyes shifting downward. Not telling Dex the truth was harder this time than she'd anticipated. She had seen trust in his eyes, and now, as she stole a glance at him, she saw empathy that she didn't deserve. She had just begun to find her footing with her students, her roommates, and then, hell if it wasn't swept out from under her by that asshole. That was enough of a kick in the ass. Her life was just beginning to settle around her again. She and Dex were finally making headway as a couple. She couldn't take another kick in the ass, not now.

"No. He traveled a lot, and I never put two and two together."

"How'd you find out?" He inched nearer to her and held her close.

Ellie knew he wasn't going to let her retreat into herself. "He was in the shower, and when his phone rang, I answered it." Her eyes filled with tears. *Damn it. Do. Not. Cry.*

"Oh, Ellie." He pulled her close and stroked her back, kicking that damn guilt into high gear.

"She was so hurt, Dex. I mean, I could feel this woman's pain through the phone, and it was one of those times when nothing needed to be said. I knew the minute I answered and heard a female gasp on the other end of the phone. She said something like, *Is he with you?* And I stuttered, then apologized. Profusely. Jesus, I had no idea." *And then he hurt me.*

"I know it feels horrible, but you can't really blame yourself if you didn't know."

She closed her eyes until the tears subsided. Each tear seared her heart with pain at hiding the rest of the truth. "I've told myself that a hundred times, but then I talked to one of my roommates. She'd just gotten her degree in psychology, so it was free therapy. She asked me if I thought maybe I'd chosen him because he was safe. She said I wouldn't ever have to get close to him because some part of me knew he was married." She gripped Dex's hand. "Dex, I swear to you, I had no idea. I know I'm fucked up, but I'd never be that person. No way. You know me." She searched his eyes and saw that he did know her, probably better than she knew herself. And he trusted her—right at that moment, she wished he wouldn't.

"I honestly can't see you getting close to anyone in

the first place, married or not." He brought her hand to his lips and pressed a kiss to it. "Or maybe I just wouldn't want to think about it. Does he still contact you?"

She nodded.

"Does he know where you are?" The softness left his face, bringing out the harsher lines, the muscles in his jaw. The protective Dex.

"I don't know. I think he knows I came to New York, but of course he'd have no idea where I am." *Would he?* No. There was no way he'd be able to track her.

"Ellie, if he's in New York, I wanna have a talk with him."

He dropped her hands, and Ellie saw his biceps jump beneath his tattoos. His eyes slanted dangerously.

"No, Dex. I don't want to feed this creep's...whatever it is. He's probably just not used to being turned away. His wife's already been hurt. I just want to forget about it all and move on." Her phone buzzed again, and she reached for it.

Dex snagged it. "May I?" He held up the phone.

"Read it? Yes. Respond? No." She watched him as he scrolled through the messages. His chest expanded as he read, his shoulders pulling back, muscles strung tight. He pressed his lips together in an angry line. When his eyes finally met hers, they were anything but loving. "He knows you're in New York."

"'Kay." *Shit.*

"He wants to see you." He didn't even blink.

It occurred to her that Dex was weighing her reaction just as she had weighed his. "Okay."

"Okay?" He glared at her.

"Not okay, like I'll see him. Okay like, whatever. No way." She pulled the covers up to her chest.

"Ellie, do I have to worry about him hurting you? Is he that kind of guy?" He put his hand on her leg, and she hated herself for stiffening beneath his touch. "Hey," he said softly. "I'm on your side, El."

Oh God. Oh God. Oh God. She couldn't breathe. She needed fresh air. She pushed to her feet, and Dex grabbed her hand.

"Don't."

"I need fresh air."

"Please. Just this once, try to stay with me. Talk this out with me."

Her leg bounced up and down. Dex had that damn look in his eyes again like she was tearing his heart out. She wanted to stay with him—more than anything in the world, she wanted to. She lowered herself back down to the bed. Now the entire mattress shook with her jumpy leg. She nibbled on her lower lip.

"You don't have to tell me who he is, and I won't try to find out, but I do want you to promise me that if he does anything that worries you, you'll tell me. I need to trust you in this, Ellie."

I can't trust myself. How can you trust me?

Dex had known Ellie for more years than anyone else in her life. He was a quick study, and she knew that not reaching for her was killing him. Dex was a hugger. She was a hider. When she looked at him, she wanted more than anything to be a hugger. To be his hugger. For moments she'd been able to slip into that world, as she'd done in the bathroom and in the silence when they cuddled so many years ago. But at times like this, when discomfort needled her nerves and she was pressed to the wall to expose her most vulnerable points, it was harder than hell to fight the visceral need to flee.

"You told me that I could always be sure of you, Dexy, and I am trying so hard to be that person for you, too." There it was. Plain. Simple. Honest. *Almost.*

Chapter Twenty-One

MIDNIGHT FOUND THEM eating pizza on the living room floor while outlining their ideas for the educational software. Ellie watched Dex staring intently at their notes. He looked the most content when he was creating or planning. She would like to think that he looked the most content when she was in his arms, but she knew that at those intimate times, while he was happy, he worried that she'd leave again. She was working on that. She was thinking of the way he'd come home midafternoon and made love to her when he lifted his eyes from the notebook and smiled.

"You had a meeting tonight, didn't you? When you texted earlier, you said you had a late meeting." She remembered it explicitly.

He shrugged. "I wanted to see you."

"You blew off your meeting to see me? But I had just been to your office."

Dex ran his hand through his hair and sighed.

"Did you think I wouldn't be here?"

"No. I can't make you stay, El. I know that. I can only hope that you want to stay."

"I do."

"I believe that you do. But that's not why I blew off the meeting. I realized today when we were deciding on our release date that what you were doing mattered. It mattered a hell of a lot more than the gaming empire I built, and—"

"That's not true."

"Hear me out. I'm proud of what I've done, and what I do, but as I said earlier, I've also been really conflicted about it. This afternoon I felt driven to do something about it. You made me feel that way. You're willing to work extra hours and put yourself out there with no promise of extra income or anything other than knowing you're doing something of value for kids."

"In case you haven't noticed, I don't have much besides time or ideas to give to anyone."

He sighed. "Ellie, when we were growing up, you gave me everything I needed even though your own heart was bleeding. You inspired me then, and you inspire me now to do something about what I've been feeling. I can and will continue with my gaming, but, Ellie, I've got the technical skills you need to make your dreams come true. With your brains and vision and my technical abilities, we can do this."

"Oh, Dexy." He had the most generous heart of any person she knew, and it drew her from where she sat on the floor to his lap. She ran her fingers through his hair and forced herself to say what she felt so strongly that her heart ached. "I so love you."

He leaned his forehead against hers. "Thank you," he whispered.

He stayed in that position for a long time. There was no mistaking how much it meant to him to hear her say she loved him outside of a moment of passion. When he lifted his head, he said, "Wow. All it takes is a diatribe about helping kids? I'll remember that."

Ellie knew he was making light because the moment was so heavy it threatened to draw tears from both of them.

"We'll do this together, Ellie. Just keep your promise about that asshole, okay?"

"Yeah. I will." Guilt pressed in on her and she had to ease it, if even just a little. "Dexy, I have to tell you something else." Before he could react, she said, "He wasn't very nice to me. I don't want to talk about it, but I wanted you to know."

He nodded. "You don't want to talk about it?"

She shook her head, silently praying he'd give her the space she needed.

"I had lunch with my mom and Siena today."

She saw something wash over his expression too fast for her to read. Relieved that he wasn't pushing her, she went with it. "You...yes. How did it go?"

"Do you know that my mom knew that you used to sneak into my bedroom?"

Ellie covered her face. "Oh God. She must hate me."

"You're kidding, right? No one could ever hate you. She actually really liked you. She said we needed each other. And...she said I had to trust you."

She leaned against the couch beside him, completely thrown by this. She said *he* had to trust *her*?

That's what she'd seen in his eyes. Contemplation. Confused but unwilling to rock this particular boat, she dodged the issue. "Do your parents still live in the same neighborhood?"

"Yeah."

"Maybe one day we should go back there. Just so I can get some closure for the time I spent there." She'd been thinking about that neighborhood a lot lately. Ellie was well aware of her trust issues, and she knew where they all stemmed from, though she wasn't sure they didn't begin much earlier than the episodes that she remembered.

"Anytime you want."

Dex's phone vibrated. "Regina." He read the text. "Podcast was great. Mitch did well. Are you okay?" He touched Ellie's leg and spoke as he typed. "More than okay. Thanks for covering tonight."

"You never told me what you decided about your release. Are you releasing on time?"

"Yeah. Thanks to you for that, too." Dex didn't elaborate. He leaned over and kissed Ellie with one of those toe-curling kisses again.

"You have to stop doing that or we'll never get anything accomplished." She took a deep breath.

"Can't. Sorry." His phone vibrated again. "Reg again. She says to tell you she said hello." He touched her hand. "Looks like you made a friend."

"I can sure use a few of them about now. I'm going in to fill out forms tomorrow and meet the staff at Maple, and I start teaching Monday. I'm hoping to make a few friends there, too. It'll be good to be working with people who understand low-income issues and put kids before statistics. It's like a whole different world."

"I know." The way he looked at her told her that he really did get it. Of course, he *got* all things Ellie. He handed her the notebook. "So, is this what you had in mind?"

Ellie looked over the technical specifications and arched a brow at Dex. "English, please. Speak slow because I'm still in lip-lock land."

He laughed. "Basically, you want to produce a platform that can be shared among the kids, and you want it to be at least forty percent less expensive per child than computers. Meaning that if schools have enough money for only half their students to have laptops, then a multiuser platform—let's use Xbox as an example—would allow them to team up for almost the same cost, and each child would be able to participate and learn through these shared platforms. The software would run on the platform. Does that make sense?"

"Yeah, something like that." It was so nice to be taken seriously. The first two interviews she'd had left her feeling like she was asking for the impossible. Blythe had boosted her confidence, but Dex, who had the knowledge and skills to make this work, gave her hope.

"And I would take it one step further and allow for several users on one platform with the option of a multiuser program where they are competing in levels of educational games. Or we can go with split screens so each person can move along at their own rate."

Ellie sat up on her knees. "Yes. That would be ideal. Then the kids who had more trouble wouldn't feel left behind, but they'd have the option of learning from the others if they shared the program." She gathered her hair and laid it over her shoulder. "This is so exciting, Dex."

"These are only the bones, El. We'll need finite details on the software you want to create and explicit goals, paths to learning, all sorts of things."

"There are already tons of educational programs out there for kids. I really was hoping this could be something completely different. Not the kind of thing where kids feel like they're learning, although they have to learn, of course. But gearing it toward real-life issues and settings. Real life for low-income kids, which is very different than real life for middle-income or high-income families whose kids probably have every system under the sun anyway, so they may not have interest in this type of system. But for kids who aren't as privileged, getting to learn on a system that is geared toward what they recognize and feel safe around might just do the trick. I guess I need to do more research and talk with the staff, of course, and even talk to some of the parents to ensure we're hitting our mark." She caught Dex staring at her.

"What?" She felt her cheeks flush.

He shook his head. "You. Everything. I've missed you, Ellie. It's been way too fucking long. Best friends should never be apart for that long."

Best friends. She liked the sound of that. Almost as much as she liked being called his girlfriend.

An hour later, Ellie and Dex had showered and climbed into bed. Dex in his boxers and Ellie wearing one of Dex's T-shirts. A cool breeze whispered across

Ellie's skin.

"I'm right here." Ellie snuggled against him as she lifted her chin toward the open window. "I think you can close it."

"Just because I let you into my heart doesn't mean you can control my window," he teased. "It reminds me of you. I'm not sure I even know how to sleep with it closed anymore."

Dex held their notes in his right hand, and he draped his left arm over Ellie, pulling her close. A small reading light cast a yellow glow over the notebook, which Dex was once again studying. Ellie watched him for a moment and then was lulled into the rhythm of his heartbeat against her ear and the cadence of his breathing. She closed her eyes, and the last thought she had before drifting into the most blissful sleep of the last four years was, *I'm sure of you. And you can be sure of me, too.*

DEX'S PHONE VIBRATED at two in the morning. He started awake and snagged it, hoping it wouldn't wake Ellie. *Siena?* Why was she texting so late?

Sorry about today. Dex rolled his eyes. That's what was so important at two in the morning?

He texted back. *No worries, but don't ever say that again. You do know it's 2, right?* A minute later she texted back.

Who r u kidding? You work from midnight till morning.

He smiled as he typed his response, knowing it would make Siena squeal. *Not when Ellie's here.*

He silenced his phone, knowing she could text all

night, and a second later she did. *Yay! Happy 4 u. I'll bring the camera next time I see you 2. Haha.*

He smiled at her response, then set the phone aside and curled his body around Ellie. He made a silent deal with God and the devil and anyone else who would listen that he would do anything if it would keep Ellie in his life. Then he closed his eyes and held on tight.

Chapter Twenty-Two

ELLIE SPENT THE next few mornings at Maple Elementary getting to know her coworkers and preparing for her first day with the students. Dex worked long hours in preparation for his release, and they came together in the evenings as if they'd been living together forever. They worked into the night, putting their thoughts for the educational software and platform to a coordinated proposal of technical and educational specifications.

Late Saturday morning, Ellie sat beside the glass balcony doors, the heat of the sun warming her legs. She rubbed her hand across the warm area on her thigh. She heard Dex talking on Skype while playing a game on his computer in the other room. His laugh sent a shiver down her back. When she looked at him, she swore she could feel blood pumping life into her heart. She loved knowing he was right in the other room and realized, as she sat listening to him laugh and then curse at his game, that she'd begun to feel things again—emotions she'd hidden from forever, and she wondered how she had gotten along without him for so long.

A knock at the door drew her attention. Before Ellie reached the foyer, Regina and Mitch walked in with four cups of coffee and a bakery bag.

"Hey, Ellie." Mitch handed her a cup of coffee. He flinched and shot a look at Regina. "Oh, Reg, we shouldn't just walk in anymore. Sorry, Ellie. We're not used to the big guy having company."

"She's not company. She lives here," Regina corrected him with a stern voice.

Ellie froze. Regina had been so nice the other morning that her comment took her by surprise.

Regina elbowed her. "Relax. It's the only way to clarify to him that you two are an item." She pointed to her head. "Thick."

Ellie let out a breath.

"I'm not thick up there. It's down below you have to worry about." Mitch winked.

Regina rolled her eyes. She handed Ellie a Danish. "Is he in the office?"

"Yeah. Come on back."

They joined Dex in the office, where he was no longer on Skype but sat before three glowing monitors. He was playing *World of Thieves II* on one and watching a podcast on another. The third was set to a game-review site. He didn't turn around when they came in.

"I'm leveling up. Give me a sec," Dex said.

Leveling up. How many years had she heard him say that when they were younger? Ellie had spent hours sitting beside Dex while he played video and PC games. Had she paid attention, she could have memorized them, but games had never held her interest. It was the intensity with which Dex played that intrigued her. He didn't just play the games; he seemed to live them. She used to love the way his muscles tensed and his eyes lit up when he played. And listening to his voice as he'd narrate while he played, explaining the storyline, or his hooting and hollering when he did something amazing in the game, had always soothed her, made her feel like she was part of his world.

Earlier that morning, when they'd made love, Dex had told her that he wanted a million lives with her. As corny as it was, it had made her heart soar, because in Dex's gamer mind, things didn't get much better than that. A little thrill chased the memory up the back of her neck.

Mitch took off his sweatshirt and tossed it on a chair. "Ellie, you don't mind that he plays games?"

She shrugged. "He's played ever since we were kids. Why would I mind?"

Regina poked Mitch in the back. "See, not all women mind."

Mitch plopped into a chair in front of another computer. "Right. Well, I haven't met the ones who don't. They don't mind for a day or two, but then they're all, *You never pay attention to me.*"

Regina took a pack of Twizzlers from her back pocket and stuck one in her mouth. She wore a long-sleeved shirt that clung to her ribs and a pair of jeans littered with holes and cinched across her hips with a thick leather belt.

"How would you know? You never even date." Regina turned on her computer.

"What? I date," Mitch retorted unconvincingly.

"Right. Then you're just not looking hard enough," Regina said.

"Ellie's off-limits," Dex added before cursing at his game.

Ellie stood behind him with her hand on his chair, watching the figures on the monitor battle their way up a treacherously steep cliff. Lightning streaked the dark sky around them, and as they made their way to the top of the rocky ridge, his character made two forceful thrashes with his sword and then one final thrust through his opponent's chest, sending his opponent staggering backward, blood spurting from his muscular chest. Two heavy chains crossed the long leather vest he wore, dripping with blood and *clanking* as he stumbled toward the jagged ridge. His arms pedaled backward as he teetered on the edge of defeat. Dex's character took three determined steps forward and landed a hard sidekick to the man's chest, sending him spiraling over into the dark abyss below.

Dex's arms shot up in the air with a *whoop*. "Yes! The master wins again!" He pulled Ellie into his lap. "Watch." He held her around her waist as the screen exploded in a flurry of flashing colors before going completely black and then coming back to life with his character walking through an elaborate iron gate. His powerful legs carried him through massive wooden doors of a stone castle. The words RETICENT HOLLOW were carved above the arched doorway.

Ellie gasped. She gripped Dex's hand, his words

whispering through her mind. *Don't go to your silent place. Don't go reticent on me.* He pressed her hand to his cheek, then kissed it with a wink and a nod. She watched his character take the stone steps two at a time to a dark room. In the center of the darkness was a woman, her arms wrapped around her knees, her head bowed. He stepped closer, and she raised her head, revealing beautiful blue eyes and thick dark hair. The characters stared at each other for what felt like interminable minutes. The sound of two heartbeats melding into one echoed from the speakers. The character reached for the woman as the heartbeats faded in the background to a whisper of a pulse. A tear tumbled down the woman's cheek as she rose to her feet and fell into her savior's muscular arms. "You can always be sure of me," he said.

The edges of the screen faded to black, closing in slowly until all that was left was a tiny circle of the savior's back and the sound of their hearts beating on.

Ellie's body stiffened. Her heart stilled.

"That's the stupidest line ever," Mitch said with a laugh.

"I think it's kind of romantic," Regina said.

Ellie looked into Dex's warm blue eyes. *Oh, Dexy. And you can always be sure of me.* He smiled at the same time she did, the secret words of their love passing silently between them. He pulled her close and nuzzled against her neck. "Always," he whispered.

She could barely breathe past the lump in her throat. He'd memorialized their love. The love she'd almost thrown away. Jesus, maybe fate was real after all. She took a few deep breaths and pushed to her shaky legs before she began to bawl like a baby.

"Okay..." She cleared her throat. "On that note, I'm heading out to get a new bag." Ellie touched Dex's shoulder, and he pulled her into a deep and passionate kiss. A kiss that pushed that lump away and replaced it with security—and embarrassment. "Dex," she whispered, heat creeping up her cheeks.

"What?" He flashed his crooked grin, which clearly said, *I can't help it if I want you every minute.*

She was surprised to see that Regina and Mitch were intent on reading something on Mitch's computer screen, as if they hadn't even noticed the kiss that sent her heart reeling.

"Forums look good. Same old shit from KI touting their stuff as more dynamic, faster game play, ripping ours, but fans are coming to our rescue." Regina pulled out another Twizzler and put it in her mouth.

"I'm gonna run." Ellie wondered if they could hear the quiver of lust and embarrassment in her voice as strongly as she could feel it.

"Hey, El?" Regina called after her.

"Yeah?"

"We don't judge. No worries, okay?"

Blushing again, she nodded. "Thanks. I'm not used to—"

"Sucking face in public. Yeah, we get it, but really, we're both happy for you guys. I was starting to worry that Dex was gonna be one of those thirty-year-old guys who lived alone with his nose in a computer twenty-four-seven." She arched a brow in Mitch's direction.

He reached over his worktable and swatted her.

THE BRISK AIR stung Ellie's cheeks as she walked down the street. A sense of calm had washed over her during the last few days, and as she headed toward the shops, she felt pride blossoming inside of her. She'd not only stayed with Dex, but the urge to flee was no longer swirling inside her mind like an ever-present Tasmanian devil. She might be a master at telling herself things would be okay, but she was no master at ridding her body of the storm of worry that followed her thoughts like shadows. Today that shadow was almost gone as she put one foot in front of the other, feeling, wanting, needing Dex in every part of her life.

She took the subway to Greenwich Village. Ellie had read online about a thrift shop that looked like it had a few bags that she not only liked but could afford. Her other option was a street vendor, and she'd happily go that route, but the less expensive the better until her paychecks started rolling in.

As teenagers, she and Dex had gone into the city a few times. One of her favorite memories was when they'd spent the afternoon walking through the Village. Dex had always carried himself with quiet confidence, and she remembered that when they'd come to the Village she'd felt safe with him, much like she did now, while living with him. *Living with him.* How the hell did that happen? The word *fate* whispered through her mind and brought a smile to her lips. She thought about how she'd ended up at Dex's apartment. Dina hadn't reached out to her again, which was probably a good thing. She realized that Dina was probably a more typical twenty-five-year-old in that way than she was, but Ellie didn't care. She'd given up aiming for *typical* a long time ago. Everyone had their comfort zone, and she had always tried to remain in control of hers. Dex pushed her to the brink in that regard, but somehow when he did it, it wasn't so hard to deal with.

She gazed in the thrift shop window, thinking of Dex and the ending of the game he was releasing into the world. *Reticent Hollow.* He hadn't forgotten about her after she'd gone away. *What have I done to deserve him?* A familiar voice interrupted her thoughts, snaking its way toward her and searing her nerves like a hot bullet. Her body froze and her pulse soared. *Fuck.* She spun around looking for Bruce and caught sight of him two stores away, his arm around a tall blond woman. Ellie hurried inside the thrift shop, thinking of the annoying texts he'd sent her over the past week, claiming he'd missed her and that they weren't "done." She hadn't answered any of his texts, and now, knowing he was right there in New York, she almost wished she'd stayed in Maryland. No, she didn't. She wouldn't trade being with Dex for anything. She hovered behind a rack, watching out the window until he passed. What the hell was he doing in New York? Was that his wife? *Shit.* This was the last straw. Her veins burned with anger. She watched his handsome profile move slowly past the window. Short brown hair, wide jaw, penetrating eyes—which she couldn't see from her angle but she could damn well picture. Why were all assholes gorgeous? Bastard. Her hands fisted, and sweat formed on her brow despite the cool air.

"Can I help you find something?"

Ellie started. "Oh. Um. No, thanks. I'm...just looking." *Hiding.* She started for the door, planning on hightailing it back to Dex's apartment, but when she reached the door, she froze. She'd already run. She'd left her job behind, a job she'd really enjoyed, with kids she cared for. She drew her shoulders back, refusing to be forced back into the person she'd been when she was younger. Fuck him. She came for a purse, and she was going to find one. *I didn't know he was married. He's the asshole, not me.* She bit her lower lip as she tried her damnedest to convince herself and draw courage from her silent pep talk. *He can't hurt me anymore.* After a deep breath, shaky as a leaf in the wind, she turned back around and headed for the bags.

She weeded through a pile of bags, unable to concentrate. Her army-green jacket, which had been comfortable when she'd left the apartment, was now too hot and bulky. She took it off and held it under her arm. Her black sweater felt stiff and prickly. The bags were all ugly. Damn it. He'd ruined her entire day. She thought of calling Dex, but what would she say? I saw the asshole with some woman? He didn't approach her, didn't even seem to see her. She needed to get a grip. And she needed to get the hell out of the Village before he *did* see her. Ellie headed out of the store with her head down and made a beeline for the subway.

Chapter Twenty-Three

AT THREE O'CLOCK Dex began to wonder when Ellie was coming back. He, Regina, and Mitch often worked through the weekend afternoons and into the wee hours of the next morning, but now that Ellie was back in his life, he wanted to spend as much time as possible with her. It was Saturday night, and he wanted to take Ellie on an actual date. He pulled out his cell and texted her.

Miss you. Back soon?

He turned back to the program he'd been working on. "Hey, where can I take Ellie on a date?"

"When?" Mitch's eyes never left the computer screen.

"Tonight."

"Why go out? You can have crazy wild animal sex here," Regina teased.

"Just because all you think about is sex doesn't mean Dex is the same way," Mitch said.

"Right. When's the last time you saw me go on a

date? Sex is the last thing on my mind." Regina lowered her chin and stared at Mitch.

"I don't know what you do with your free time," Mitch said without looking at her.

"You two are my free time." She sighed. "That's sweet, Dex. You really like her, huh?"

Dex stood and stretched. "You might say that." He started to walk out of the room and hesitated in the doorway. "I'm getting a drink. You guys want anything?"

"Pizza?" Mitch asked.

"Veggie burger," Regina said.

"Why don't you guys call Jay's and have them deliver? I don't want anything." He left the room and pulled out his cell. He called Ellie. His call went directly to voicemail. He tried to quiet the panicked voice in his head that immediately jumped to her leaving town. He wouldn't allow his mind to go there, but hell if it wasn't a struggle.

The door opened a few minutes later and Ellie walked in. Her eyes jetted around the room in the old unsettled way that he hadn't seen over the last few nights.

"Hey." The fine line between loving and smothering was a tightrope walk, and Dex felt like a two-hundred-pound bull, wanting to ask why she looked so haunted and why she had her phone turned off. Instead, he stuck to the safer subject. "Did you find a bag?"

"Yeah, at a street vendor." She held up a backpack. "I figured it couldn't be stolen if it was on both arms." She set it on the table by the door.

He folded her in his arms and held her, reading her body language. He'd become a master of reading her silent signals. When she was scared, her body trembled. Uncertainty caused her muscles to tense. The need to escape made her leg bounce, and wandering eyes translated to her being stuck in the midst of it all. She put her arms around him and pressed her cheek to his chest. He'd expected her to be tense, to take the time she usually needed to accept his comfort. Why did this quiet, warm need scare him even more? He eased his hold on her, but she held on tight. Something had happened. His muscles tensed.

"Hey. You okay?" He stroked her back.

She nodded but tightened her grip around him.

Dex's mind spun in ten different directions, none of them good. Either something had happened when she was out, or she was battling some internal demon that had reared its ugly head. One would piss him off; the other would break his heart. He kept his silence and let her draw whatever comfort she needed from him. When she finally peeled herself away from him, he felt a rush of cold where she had been.

She looked at him and smiled, but it never came anywhere near her beautiful, haunted eyes. "God, I needed that."

"Glad I could help." *Tell me what's wrong.*

"Are you guys still working?"

He saw it then. She'd flicked a switch just as she'd done a million times before. Whatever she was dealing with, she wasn't about to reveal it. Damn, she was frustrating.

"Yeah, but I'm done. I wanted to take you out

tonight."

Her lips curved into a smile—a real smile this time. "Like a date?"

"Yeah, like a date."

"What do people do on dates in New York? You already know I'm a sure thing, and you know I can't hold my liquor, so..." she teased.

"It depends on what mood you're in." He searched her eyes and saw a flash of something that he couldn't read.

"You want the answer I'd give anyone else, or do you want the answer I'd only give you?" She crossed her arms and leaned against the wall. Clearly constructing her own protective barrier.

"What do you think?" At least she wasn't shutting him out completely. He watched her weigh her words before answering. She held his stare and set her jaw. Her arms tensed. She drew in a deep breath, and Dex fought the urge to pull her close again. He waited, hoping she could take this step.

"I'm fighting off the need to kill someone."

Shit. Not what he was expecting. Dex's breath came faster. "What happened?"

She shook her head.

"Ellie, you made me a promise." Goddamn it. If some asshole hurt her, he'd kill him.

"I did, and there's nothing to report other than a few annoying texts. I turned my phone off." She looked away, and he knew there was more.

"And?" When she didn't answer, he pushed harder. "Ellie, did he say something I should worry about? If you told me who he was, I could put a stop to it."

"No. I can handle this. I'm not a child, and while I appreciate you standing up for me, I don't need you to handle this for me. It's my mess, and I can deal with it."

"You're the most frustrating woman I know. Frustrating and..."

"And?" She crossed her arms and pinned her eyes on his.

"I don't know. I'd say clueless, but you're anything but clueless. You know exactly what you're doing, and that's what makes this whole thing so frustrating." His nerves tightened like guitar chords; the muscles in his arms twitched. He hated when she was right. Ellie thought she was strong—and she was—but he also knew she was sweet, and vulnerable, and feminine, and goddamn it, he wanted to fix this shit, and fix it now. His father would never sit back and let bad things happen to anyone he loved. But his father would never have consulted his mother on how to handle things either. He glanced at Ellie's stern face, and the need to be strong was written in the tension in her cheeks and eyes. He could no better dissuade her from that strength than he could treat her the way his father had treated him so many times. His father's love had sharp edges. Dex's love was molded by his mother, flexible and full of empathy.

"Fine. Whatever. I'll give you frustrating." Her lower lip trembled in an unexpected show of vulnerability. A crack in her armor.

He took her hand. "Laser tag."

"Laser tag?"

"Yup. You said you needed to kill someone. I say, let's go do it."

"Did someone say laser tag?" Mitch called as he walked down the hall toward them.

"Laser tag? That's your big date?" Regina was two steps behind Mitch.

"We're going to release some pent-up energy." Dex looked at Ellie and hoped he was doing the right thing by not pushing her to reveal all the shitty details of the texts.

"Mind if we go?" Mitch asked. "I could use a little killing action myself."

"Jesus, you Neanderthal. They're going on a date, not having a birthday party." Regina shook her head.

"Come with us. It'll be fun." Ellie smiled up at Dex. "Do you mind?"

As much as he wanted to romance Ellie, that idea had gone out the window the minute she'd clung to him like she needed to refuel her will to survive.

"Totally fine with me."

"Rock on!" Mitch said. "I'm so gonna blow you away." He shot a dark look at Dex.

Dex laughed as they grabbed their jackets and headed out the door. "In your dreams."

"Listen to them. They act like we don't even count. We're gonna take your chicken asses down," Regina said.

"I've never played laser tag," Ellie admitted. "You guys have all that experience of playing those shooter games. I knew I should have paid better attention for all those years."

Dex had a feeling that Ellie would be a natural at blowing people away. If she could shoot as well as she could walk away, she'd be a master at it.

Chapter Twenty-Four

LASER TAG WAS nothing like Ellie thought it would be. She'd anticipated feeling stupid running around in the dark with a fake gun and trying to shoot her friends. She thought she'd feel guilty taking them down, but it turned out that she felt empowered for the first time in her life. Knowing she wasn't really killing anyone helped, of course, but she pictured each of the other players as Bruce. Her finger hovered over the trigger and her eyes narrowed as she listened for the sound of feet moving, heavy breathing, and the unique rustling of plastic guns against bodies. Ellie had spent her whole life in the background, observing people and situations, strategizing, biding her time until the ripest moment became apparent. She'd been preparing for laser tag her whole life. Who knew?

She closed her eyes and listened. In here, Dex had a certain walk, a hunkered-down sneak that she noticed the minute he put the weighty vest on. He'd bent his knees and walked with purpose, with a stealthy slant.

She heard the sounds of him now, his gun knocking against his muscles, his hard and heavy breathing. She held her breath as the sounds came closer, and when she felt his presence, she opened her eyes and pressed the trigger.

"Damn." Dex watched the lights on his vest go black.

Ellie whispered, "Sorry." She took off in another direction, her heart pounding, mind soaring. This was the most fun she'd ever had. The dark arena made it easy for her to feel free, even if she couldn't forget seeing Bruce or reading his texts that claimed they *weren't through*. What did that mean, anyway? *The asshole.* Why did he have the power to make her so angry?

She rounded a corner and aimed at Mitch's vest. Just as she tagged him, Regina tagged her. "Aw!" she hollered, then laughed, a deep, hearty belly laugh that tore through her with such force that she fell back against the wall. She covered her mouth, realizing that she'd lose the game if she played like a dork. But, damn, that laugh felt good.

They played a second game and then headed back toward home. They were covered in sweat and laughing as they climbed into the taxi.

"NightCaps?" Mitch suggested.

"El?" Dex asked.

She loved that he consulted her. "Sure, but no rum and Coke for me."

"Lightweight," Regina said. She handed Ellie a Twizzler. "Power food."

Ellie took the Twizzler, and sitting between Regina

and Dex, she felt...happy. Markedly happy. She wondered if the euphoria she was feeling was what normal people felt every day. People who hadn't grown up in a string of different houses, always feeling like an outsider, on the defensive, ready to bolt. *That's it. I don't feel like an outsider with them. I feel like I'm part of their group. Part of their family.* The idea of family warmed her soul, even if it wasn't a nuclear family. She'd take a family of friends that she could count on over no family any day of the week.

NightCaps was packed. Dex slung an arm over her shoulder as they made their way to the back of the bar, where Regina slipped into a booth just as a couple vacated it. Dex took Ellie's hand in his and said, "This is where it all began."

Ellie shook her head. "No. It all began back on Carlisle Street." Actually, even that wasn't true. It all started the day she was taken from her mother and placed in the foster system when she was just five years old.

"What are we drinking?" Regina asked.

"I can't be trusted when I drink, so whatever you order for me, please don't let me have more than one." Ellie put her hand on Dex's leg. He covered it with his own and pulled her close.

"I won't let you get too blitzed," he promised.

"Yeah, I'd trust that face." Regina rolled her eyes. "Dex said you have an idea for educational software on its own platform. Sounds really cool, and if you need help, I'd love to be part of it."

"Me too," Mitch said.

"Who's gonna do the Thrive work?" Dex acted

insulted, but Ellie could tell by his smile that he was only teasing.

"Your forty-seven other employees," Mitch said. "We're offering to help, not take over. Besides, look at all our free time. What else are we gonna do? Sleep?"

"You guys work harder than anyone I know," Ellie admitted.

"You should have seen Dex before he opened Thrive. He literally worked for eighteen hours each day. He worked from the moment he woke up without a break." Mitch nodded at Dex. "When I met him, which wasn't long before he opened Thrive, he was surviving on fast food and coffee."

"Remember how we all used to crash in Dex's living room?" Regina laughed. "Trust me on this, Ellie. Waking up in the same room as these two guys after two days of not showering is not pleasant. I don't know what it is with men. They eat, sleep, work, and showering doesn't even come into play."

"Dex showers," she said, remembering earlier that morning when they'd shared a shower and he'd washed her body. Then loved it until she could barely remember her name.

"Maybe now, but when he was in design mode?" She waved her hand in front of her nose. "Whew."

"Okay, enough." Dex flagged the waitress down and ordered their drinks. "Did you eat today?" he asked Ellie.

"A little." She looked at Regina. "Do you guys want to share something? I probably shouldn't drink on an empty stomach."

They ordered appetizers, and Dex's phone

vibrated. He checked the text.

"Hell yeah. We just broke preorder records." He let out a *whoop*. "Time to celebrate."

"We are on fire. You were right to release on time, Dex. Ballsy move, but a good one. No need to kowtow to KI." Mitch held his fist up above the table, and Dex bumped it with his own.

"Isn't it crazy, Ellie, that the guy you knew in high school is now one of the most successful game developers in the United States?" Regina leaned back and stretched an arm across the back of the booth.

Mitch looked at her. "Don't make a move on me, tattoo girl."

She pushed him.

In the days they'd been together, Ellie had been so wrapped up in finding a job, getting over Bruce, and trying to figure out how to be a *normal* person in a relationship that Dex's career success hadn't even crossed her mind. Just another thing that made her weirder than the next girl.

"When I think of Dex, I see the spindly, sweet-eyed teenager who made me feel safe for the first time in my life. He could be a garbage man or the president, and I probably wouldn't notice. And I definitely wouldn't care." She felt her cheeks flush and realized that she'd just revealed her heart to Dex's closest friends and admitted something that she had yet to admit to herself.

Dex kissed the side of her forehead.

"Jesus, Dex. Where were you hiding her all this time? And please, Ellie, can I clone you?" Mitch asked.

"Believe me, you don't want to. I'm like a walking

earthquake. You know if I'm around things will turn to chaos, but you never really know when."

"Hey, that's not true," Dex said firmly.

"Oh, yes, it is." Ellie nodded.

"Why?" Regina asked.

The waitress brought their drinks and appetizers, and Ellie sucked down a mouthful of her rum and Coke to ease the sting of the conversation.

"Why do you feel like you're an earthquake?" Regina ignored the harsh stare Dex was giving her—the one he made no move to hide from Ellie. "You're smart, you're really nice, and you're obviously really into Dex. Why do you feel like that?"

Ellie sighed. No one had ever taken the time to discuss why she felt like she did; they'd just accepted it. The same way she did. Or they flat out denied it, like Dex did. "Wherever I go and whatever I do, something always falls apart. Look at when I came to New York. I'm here less than a day and my friend abandons me, I wake up looking at some strange man's junk, and then my purse gets stolen. That stuff doesn't happen to anyone else that I know. I'm like black-cloud Ellie."

"Stop. You're not anything like that." Dex squeezed her hand.

Flat-out denial.

"But those aren't things that you did. Your girlfriend was a flake. The guy was...what? Drunk? Stupid? And your purse? Well, you are in New York." Regina nibbled on a mozzarella stick.

"When's the last time all that stuff happened to anyone you know?" Ellie asked.

They exchanged shrugs.

"My point exactly." Ellie's leg began to bounce beneath the table. "I'm gonna go to the ladies' room. I'll be right back." She laid her jacket on the bench and headed for the narrow stairwell. She locked herself in a bathroom stall and breathed deeply.

She heard the bathroom door open.

"Ellie?"

Regina. "I'll be right out." She flushed the toilet without going and came out of the stall. Regina was sitting on the sink with a Twizzler hanging from her lips like a cigarette.

"Hey," Regina said. "Sorry if I made you uncomfortable. Dex just about ripped my head off."

"You didn't." She washed her hands and concentrated on keeping her leg still.

"All I was trying to say was that maybe if you didn't think of yourself as chaos, chaos wouldn't find you." Regina lifted her brows.

"Do you really believe that stuff?" Ellie dried her hands and leaned against the wall. "I mean, it's not like I want my life to fall apart every few weeks. I want to live a normal life."

"Well, that's the first issue. Your expectations are off-kilter. There is no such thing as a *normal* life. Life is what it is. Sometimes it sucks and sometimes it's great, but most of the time it's just kind of there."

"You know what I mean. I want to leave the apartment in the morning and know that my ex-boyfriend isn't going to text me and make my skin crawl. I want to know that I can love and be loved." *Oh my God, why am I telling you this?* "I want what you guys have. That peace of mind to know that you'll always be there for each other without ever having to say it." Ellie covered her face with her hands. "I sound like an idiot. I'm sorry."

"But I've seen you with Dex, and I've seen the way he is with you. I think you have that. Why would you question it? Don't you feel it?" Regina crossed her arms and studied Ellie.

"Because people like me don't have the same luck as other people." *People like me.* God, how she hated saying that, but it was true. Foster children were like every other kid on the outside, but inside, she'd always felt more defensive, less self-assured than her peers. Except when she was with Dex. When it was just the two of them, she felt no judgment and no different.

"People like you? Ellie, you seem like a regular woman with really great ideas."

"Great ideas, maybe. Regular? No way. I'm the proverbial product of the system."

"Wait a second. You're a fossie?"

"A what?" Ellie took a step backward.

"A fossie. A foster kid. No one else called us that, but I had to come up with a cute name to make it bearable. I grew up in foster homes. My mom was a total whack job and my father was a thief. In and out of jail. So..." She waved her arms. "I had the pleasure of belonging to no one."

"Really?" Being a foster child had always made her feel like the only card in a deck without a match. Regina's admission made her feel like she'd finally found one.

"Yup. Since I was seven. Six homes in eleven years." Regina ran her hand down her arm. "I guess we all wear our pasts in different ways. I throw it in people's faces and you...hide from it."

Ellie pushed herself up on the counter beside Regina. "So you do understand what that was like."

"Sure. There are zillions of kids who went through the system. You're far from alone. And that whole can-I-be-loved thing? That's the most consistent issue that I've heard. Our parents fucked up, so we think it's our fault. Well, I've gone through enough therapy to understand that it's not our fault. Our parents made their decisions. We just tagged along for the ride, and sometimes the ride crashed and threw us into another lane." Regina jumped down from the sink and stared into the mirror, then shifted her gaze to Ellie and patted her leg. "If there's one thing I know, Ellie, it's that Dex doesn't love easily. Ever since I've known him, he's protected his heart like he's been hurt before and he needed to keep it caged up and safe. Then you waltzed into his life and the man's cage turned to dust." She reached into her back pocket and pulled out a Twizzler and swatted Ellie's leg with it. "Girl, that man has love written all over his face. All you have to do is let yourself be loved."

Ellie had heard that a million times from social workers or foster parents, and never had it hit her like a ton of bricks the way it did when Regina said it. Something about hearing it from another woman who had gone through the system, coupled with the fact that Regina knew Dex well and she saw what Ellie had felt coming off of him in waves, made the truth of what Regina had said more real.

"Thanks, Regina. I needed to hear that."

"Yeah, well, don't thank me yet. Because if you hurt him, then I'm gonna have to kill you, and that's not something I look forward to. Jail and all that? What a waste of a life." She yanked Ellie's hand. "Come on. Lover boy awaits."

Chapter Twenty-Five

IN THE BAR, Regina grabbed Ellie's wrist. "Dance with me."

Ellie groaned. "I really suck at dancing." She caught Dex's eye and silently pleaded for him to save her. He rose to his feet, and she thought she'd been saved, but when he reached her side, he leaned down and whispered, "I can't wait to see your moves."

Mitch followed Dex onto the floor, and before Ellie could wrangle herself away, Dex's hips were gyrating dangerously close to hers, his jeans pressed tight against him in all the right places as all of his body parts moved in perfect sync, with some sort of seductive dirty-dancing action going on that made Ellie tingle all over. His dark eyes captured hers, and when he lowered his mouth and settled it over hers, she closed her eyes and let her body do what came naturally. She felt his hands on her hips, and the sweet rum combined with the heady swell of love in her heart moved her body in perfect rhythm with his.

"Damn, you're sexy," he whispered against her cheek. His hands roved up her back, and he pressed his hips into her.

"Hey, this is a dance floor, not a bedroom," Regina said, waggling her finger at them. "I thought you couldn't dance?" she said to Ellie.

"Dex brings out a whole side of me I never knew I had." Ellie secretly loved to dance, but she had been dancing in public only a handful of times. Dex ran his hands beneath her hair and up the back of her neck, causing a full-body shudder. When the song ended, he closed the gap between them and took her in another deep kiss. Her desire to bolt forgotten, she snuggled next to him in the booth.

"Wow, you guys are great together. Unlike left-foot Charlie here." She pushed her shoulder into Mitch's.

"Hey, at least I try."

Regina smiled at Mitch. "You are kinda cute when you're trying to be sexy." She sucked down her drink and flagged down the waitress, who brought out another round.

Ellie's phone vibrated in her jacket pocket. She dug it out and sighed.

"It buzzed while you were in the bathroom, too," Dex said.

She read the text and noticed that the previous text, also from *Asshole*, had already been read. "Did you read it?" She wasn't sure how she felt about that. She'd never read his texts. *I answered Bruce's phone.* The thought gave her pause. *Why would I answer Bruce's phone but not read Dex's texts?* The answer came like a breath of fresh air. *Because I trust Dex.* And then the realization hit her. Hard. *He doesn't trust me.*

He hadn't answered her question. The table fell silent. Ellie was aware of Regina and Mitch sharing a glance, though she didn't look to see how it translated.

"Dex?"

"Yeah, I did. I figured it was that guy, and I was worried."

She nodded, mulling over the implications. "And what did you find out from the text?" She'd read it. She knew exactly what he'd found out.

"What you should have told me."

Their eyes locked. Ellie's stomach twisted. She'd managed to fuck up her life again. She knew she should have told Dex about Bruce's text, but all he'd asked was if it was her he'd seen by the thrift shop, and she didn't want to worry Dex over something so innocuous. *Damn it.* She should have told Dex about seeing him in the first place.

"I didn't think it was that big of a deal. I knew you'd want to talk about it and it would become a big deal, and I just want it all to go away." She reached for his hand, but he pulled away. "You're mad? You were just dancing with me and you were fine. That's a terribly delayed reaction."

"I was waiting to see if you'd tell me. I want to trust you, Ellie, but if you don't trust me enough to tell me when things are going on, how can I trust you?"

"Um, we're gonna go to the bar for a bit. Move, Mitch." Regina shoved Mitch out of the booth.

"I wanted to tell you, but I couldn't."

"Ellie, what's going on? Do you want to see this guy?"

"No," she said angrily. "That's not it at all and you know that." She pulled back, giving space to the anger that was growing between them. The ugly, unexpected, goddamn anger that was spearing her heart and shattering their wonderful evening.

He leaned closer to her, his eyes dead calm, his voice a seductive thread of hope. "Then why, Ellie? All I asked for was honesty. Is that so hard? Or does honesty rank up there with staying in one place?"

"That's just mean." *And too damn close to the truth.*

"No, babe." He ran his finger down the line of her jaw, and she wanted him to follow it up with a kiss despite the hurt in his eyes and the ache that ran through her entire body. "The truth isn't mean. It just is." He didn't shift his gaze. He waited. Too damn patiently.

Ellie's heart raced for a whole different reason than it had earlier. She thought of what Regina had said, and she thought of how much she loved Dex, and finally, the truth came out loud and clear. "I just want it to go away. If you start something, it will never go away. I want to wake up and be done with it. I hate worrying when my phone rings. I hate that I see the same worry in your eyes with every text. I wish I could go back three months and never accept that date with him. But then I think...no, I don't wish that at all, because if I didn't accept that date, I wouldn't be here now, with you." She moved closer to Dex, though he made no move to accept what she was saying. He sat up straighter and leaned against the wall.

"Whatever my fucked-up life has been and whatever that asshole put me and his wife through, even though it sucked, it brought me here. Right here, Dex. With you. Can't you see that I am trying? I want what we have—the love, the closeness, being with my best friend day and night—but I'm not you. My fucking moral compass doesn't always tell me to shoot straight. Sometimes it says to jump over the hurdles that are too big or too scary. Or sometimes to avoid them altogether, but you have to know that I'd never want to be with someone else."

Dex's stoic expression killed her. She breathed faster, feeling like the air was being sucked from the room. He couldn't possibly believe she'd want to be with someone else. *Could he?*

"Dex?" Her voice was a thin thread.

He tore his eyes away, and it felt like he'd scraped her heart with sandpaper. He ran his hand through his hair.

"I don't honestly believe you want to be with anyone else. But when you didn't answer your phone this afternoon and then you came home looking like something awful had happened and I knew you were keeping it from me, what was I supposed to think? All I know was that I had that sinking feeling in my gut that made me feel like I was drowning, just like when you left last time."

"But I told you I wouldn't leave." Even as she said it, she knew it wouldn't hold enough weight. She'd left last time, and she knew how hard it had been for them both to get over that hurt. She saw it in his eyes, and if she was honest with herself, even as he loved her in the shower, on the bed, every moment he was with her, she felt the worry and mistrust hovering behind all that emotion. Lurking. Waiting to come forward like a ghost and slip in like a barrier between them, whispering, *I knew you couldn't stay.*

He reached in his pocket and threw a wad of cash on the table; then he took her hand and pushed her gently out of the booth. "Come on." He crossed the floor to Regina and Mitch. "Hey, I paid, but we're gonna take off."

Mitch nodded. "You guys okay?"

He looked at Ellie, and her first inclination was to run. Sprint out the front door as fast as she could and jump on a train to anywhere just to outrun the pain of her life falling apart—again. In the next second, she gripped Dex's hand tighter, and she knew she never wanted to let go.

"Yeah, we're good."

Ellie wondered why he lied. They headed for the door, and Regina reached out and grabbed hold of Ellie's arm, tugging her away from Dex, and for a split second, Ellie wanted to fall into her arms and cry.

Regina held on to her so tightly Ellie worried she was upset that she'd hurt Dex. Regina lowered her head so only Ellie would hear her whisper.

"You deserve to be loved. Do you hear me?"

Ellie didn't answer. She couldn't push anything past the lump that formed thick and resistant in her throat.

Regina yanked her closer. "Did you hear me, Ellie? You are not a product of the fucking system. You deserve to be loved, and if you have to fight for it, then that's what you do. Fight for this with everything you've got." She tugged her against her bony chest and hugged her.

Ellie felt the beating of Regina's heart against her chest. She shot a glance in the mirror behind the bar and caught a glimpse of the wicked stare Regina was giving Dex. It had been a long time since Ellie had an ally, and now the lump in her throat anchored her feet to the ground as tears of thankfulness pressed against her lids. She gripped Regina's wiry waist, hoping her eyes would convey the thank-you that wouldn't push past the goddamn lump.

I deserve to be loved. I deserve Dex.

Dex reached for her hand and yanked her away from Regina. He narrowed his dark eyes and glared at Regina as he dragged Ellie out the door.

Chapter Twenty-Six

FRUSTRATION BUBBLED WITHIN Dex's chest and gut. He stifled the desire to release years of suppressed frustration and tell Ellie exactly how she was driving a knife through his heart. Ellie clung to his hand like a lifeline as he pulled her to the street and flagged down a cab. They climbed in, and she looked at him with her beautiful blue eyes, sadness and worry fighting for top billing. Damn it. He needed a shield to protect himself from the love he had for her. He looked away, feeling his nostrils flare and his chest constrict. He gave the driver his parents' address.

"Why are we going there?" Ellie asked.

"Because. That's where this all started, and that's where we're gonna figure this out." He stared straight ahead, the muscles in his neck twitching with the need to look at her. Dex had always been in control of everything in his life—except his feelings for Ellie and their relationship. In every other aspect of his life, he knew where he was going and he knew how he was going to get there. Now he was completely, one hundred percent fucked. He knew what he wanted, but he was not even remotely in control of how to get there—or what it would take to remain there with Ellie. Always with Ellie.

They drove in silence for a long time. Forty minutes, maybe fifty with traffic, he wasn't sure, but it felt like forever, and it gave him time to think. People had always come in and out of Dex's life. Friends from college, colleagues in the gaming industry, girlfriends, buddies, but very few had remained on the fringe of his every thought like Ellie always had. As they drove toward his parents' neighborhood, he wondered if she was on his mind because she was unobtainable. The whole wanting-what-you-can't-have thing, but then his mind revisited the last few days. Ellie was here. Present. With him. *She is trying.* She got a job and was putting down roots. With him. She wasn't running away. No, he decided. She wasn't unobtainable. At least not anymore.

"Dex?"

He looked down at their hands. How many nights had he held her hand? How many nights had he been afraid to move for fear of waking her and having her crawl out the window? Dex loved Ellie's small, feminine hands. He loved the way the curve of her palm felt against his, the way her fingers were so slim he could barely tell they were laced between his. He loved when they touched his chest and roamed lower, loving him in ways that could only come from her heart.

"Yeah?" he answered.

"How did we come to this? Over a text? I don't

understand what's going on, and I need to."

"So do I," he answered solemnly. He still couldn't look at her, though he felt her eyes boring into him, trying to read his expression, which he hoped was unreadable. He'd always thought he was as good at caging off his emotions as Ellie was, but the truth was, she read him like a book. She knew when he needed her, and she knew when he loved her.

Do you feel both now, Ellie?

The driver's deep voice broke the silence. "Where would you like me to drop you off?"

"The corner of Carlisle and Marlboro, please." The tension brewed in his stomach and filled his limbs with heat. He didn't know what led him here tonight, but he assumed he'd figure it out.

That's how Dex handled everything in life. He acknowledged the issue, studied it, then calculated possible solutions. When there was an impediment, he found its weakness and worked past it. Ellie's weaknesses were his undoing: honesty and staying power, or lack thereof. To work past those weaknesses, they needed to acknowledge them and understand where they stemmed from. On nothing more than a hope and a prayer, Dex paid the driver and stepped from the cab.

"You want me to wait for you?" the driver asked.

Dex glanced at Ellie as she stepped from the car and shivered against the night air. "No, thank you. We're good."

He watched the cab drive away. Ellie wrapped her arms around herself.

"Why do you keep saying we're good when we're

obviously anything but good?" she asked.

He didn't answer. He reached for her hand, and she slid her hand under the back of his shirt and pressed her palm against his skin. His heart ached for her. He'd give anything to turn back, go home with Ellie and climb into bed, then love every inch of her and pretend tonight never happened. Forget they needed to fix anything and just be happy loving her. But Dex's mind never forgot, and he needed more. He wanted more— of Ellie. He wanted all of her. Forever. He would never have that until her past became *their* past.

They walked up Marlboro Street, and he tucked her under his arm to keep her warm. They walked to the top of the hill, and Ellie stopped three doors from her old foster home.

Dex waited. It was almost midnight, and the houses were dark. He looked down the street and wondered what Ellie must have felt walking alone at night to his bedroom window. Funny, he hadn't thought about it back then. He'd just been glad she'd come. Now he wondered how he could have let her brave the streets alone at night to be with him. She had courage even then.

She'd always been brave.

Braver than him.

It took courage for her to risk what they had by keeping the fact that she'd seen her ex, and that she'd received the text from him, a secret. He knew she loved him. He could feel it through to his bones, but there was something there, tethering that love, keeping it just out of reach.

"Why didn't you tell me about the text?" he asked.

"I told you—"

"I'm not buying it. You could have told me and asked me not to act on it. I would have listened. What is it, Ellie? What makes you keep secrets?" He felt her hand fall away from his back, then heard it slip into her pocket. *Fuck.*

"Come on." He began walking toward her old house. Ellie didn't follow. He turned back. "Come on, El."

She shook her head.

Without getting upset, and with no frustration in his pace, he returned to her. He always came back to her. He held his hand out. She looked at him, then at his hand. He nodded and reached farther. She reached toward his hand, hesitated, looked up the street, then took his hand in hers.

"I'm right here. Be sure of me," he said.

"But you're scaring me. I don't know if I should be sure of you or not." Her voice held a thin thread of doubt, and her honesty sliced through his heart.

Dex couldn't find the right words to heal the hurt that filled the space between them like an open wound. Instead, he brought her to his chest, hoping that somehow the love he felt for her would come through. She wrapped her arms around him and held on tight.

"Be sure of me, Ellie. I'm not a leaver. I won't leave you."

"But you're afraid I will," she said just above a whisper.

Her body trembled, and he felt his resolve slipping away. He drew back again. The leaves on the trees shuffled as a breeze swept up the hill.

"I am," he admitted. "Terrified."

"Me too," she admitted. "I don't ever want to leave you, but I'm terrified to walk up the street. I'm terrified that no matter how much I want to stay, uncovering these ghosts will send my legs running in the opposite direction and I won't be able to stop myself."

"I'll stop you."

"Oh, Dexy." Her eyes burned with tears. "I'm terrified to ruin your life. I'm terrified that you'll decide I'm not the woman you think I am."

He closed his eyes against the sadness that welled there. Then, under the guise of a deep breath, he pushed away the sorrow and brought her hand to his lips. He kissed each of her delicate fingers, then took her face between his palms and said, "I know the woman you are, and I love the woman you are. But if we're gonna ever be a real couple, a forever couple, we have to deal with this shit head-on. I'm not giving up, but I'm not setting myself up to be hurt again either. I can't do this alone, Ellie. You're either all in or all out." *Christ. I sound like my father. Maybe he wasn't just being a prick after all.* "No matter how much it hurts for either of us, we have to deal with whatever keeps dragging us backward so we can move past it."

She took one step, and that was enough for him to know she wanted the same thing as he did.

In the driveway of her foster home, her mild trembling turned to full-on shaking. He took off his jacket and wrapped it around her, tensing his muscles against the cold air. Then he took her hand and walked her around the back of the rambler to the window that had led to her bedroom. She looked down, to the left, behind her, but not at the window.

Dex led her to the hill beside the house, where they sat in the grass facing the window. He put his arm around her and held her in the silence. "What happened in there, Ellie?"

"You already know."

"No. I know there was yelling, but what made you sneak out and come to me?"

"You did." She looked at him with trust, and love, and sincerity, but none of it helped him to understand what had really driven her down the dark street and to his window.

"I don't understand. We barely spoke back then."

"I saw in you the same sadness I felt. You had buried secrets that you didn't want the world to see, just like I did." She snuggled closer to him, and he buried his nose in her hair, inhaling the now-familiar scent of her shampoo.

"Tell me, Ellie. I want to move past this. I need to understand. We can't have anything without trust, and if you have to keep secrets, then we'll never amount to anything."

The silence stretched between them, contorting to tension. His muscles tightened. He opened his mouth to ask her again, and she stopped him with a hand on his thigh. She squeezed his leg as she spoke.

"He used to tell her that she was shit. He said she was like her mother, that all women were like their mothers."

"Who, Ellie? You?"

She shook her head. "Margie. My foster mother. She used to cry at night. He'd yell; then she'd cry. All

223

night long she'd cry, and in the morning she'd have these big red circles under her eyes and her nose would look swollen, but she was cheerful, like she was the happiest woman in the world. Then he'd come into the kitchen and kiss her cheek. *How are my girls?* he'd say to us. It was like they had an on-off switch that they flicked at night and then again in the morning."

"And did he say those things to you?" Dex asked.

"He didn't have to. It's not hard to figure out how I'd end up with someone hollering that all women were like their mothers every night. But the worst part was her. Can you imagine what a mess she must have been? And she tried so hard not to let on."

"That must have been awful, but why would that cause you to keep secrets? Why are you afraid to really let me in?"

She ran her finger in circles on his thigh. Doodling without a pen. He felt the difficulty in the simple movement. Just when the silence stretched to the point of discomfort, she said, "I was hoping I wouldn't have to go this far, which is why I led with the fights." She blinked up at him. "They fought because of me."

He pulled her closer.

"He used to come into my room at night."

Dex held his breath. In the back of his mind, he'd always wondered if there was more to her distrust. He'd kill the bastard.

"I think she knew. He never touched me, but he'd come in and…" Her hand stilled, and Dex covered it with his own. "He'd touch himself when he thought I was asleep."

Tears sprang to Dex's eyes. He tightened his grip

on her to keep himself from hauling the bastard's body out of bed and slamming his head into the brick wall. He clenched his eyes shut, not wanting to upset Ellie any more than she already was.

"And then you'd come to me?" His voice cracked.

"After the first few times, I started locking the door, but he'd take it out on her. The yelling went on and on, so I..." She looked away, and he leaned his head against hers, feeling his heart crumble for her. "I just pretended to be asleep." She sucked in a breath. "And then...then when he left my room...I'd go out the window."

"Why didn't you tell me?" He could have told his father, who surely would have done something. How could that bastard get away with that? Dex clenched his teeth, fighting the urge to curse a blue streak and tear into the fucker's house. He had to hold it together. If they had a chance in hell, he had to be strong for her. He'd take care of that pig, but first he had to take care of Ellie. Jesus. How could anyone do that to her?

"How could I tell you? I couldn't admit it to myself. I couldn't even tell the social worker when she placed me back there." Tears streaked her cheeks, and he felt her lean away.

Dex pulled her into his lap and held her. "I'm so sorry." Tears broke free and tumbled down his cheeks. He buried his face in her chest, holding her as their tears fell for the pain she'd held in for so long. "You didn't deserve that."

"The thing is..."

He lifted his eyes to hers, unashamed of his emotions.

"When Margie told me I was being sent away, I didn't want to go. I wanted to stay just to be with you. You were the only person I felt safe with. You didn't judge me, and you didn't push me for anything. You just...loved me." She laid her head on his shoulder, and he rocked her in his arms.

Dex felt like his bones had shattered and the shards lodged beneath his skin. He should have figured it out. He should have asked, pushed, done something. The guilt laced his nerves, and this time when he took Ellie's face in his hands and looked into her eyes, he understood the shadows he'd always seen floating about like ghosts.

"I'll never let anyone hurt you again. Including me." He pressed a loving kiss to her lips.

"Don't. I know you blame yourself for not helping me, and, Dex, you couldn't have known. No one did."

Dex brushed her hair from her shoulder. "Were there other times, with other families?"

She shook her head. "Not that I can remember."

"Thank God."

Dex stared at the house, thinking of all the things he was going to come back and do to that old man as soon as he had Ellie somewhere safe.

"He's gone," she said, as if she'd read his mind.

"Gone?"

"Yeah. The police came and they found his body. He overdosed."

Dex would have preferred the guy suffered for a long time for what he'd done, but at least he was out of Ellie's life and couldn't hurt anyone else.

"I'm sorry I'm so broken. I don't want to be

difficult, but I only know how to be who I am, and I know I'm strong and I can handle a lot."

"Oh, baby, you're not broken. You're hurt. There's a big difference, and you're the strongest woman I know."

He watched her gather her courage like a cloak, pull her shoulders back, and set her chin. "I'm proud of what I've accomplished and excited about what I will accomplish, but things like the text from...Those things throw me right back to here. I'm terrified of being labeled a home wrecker and a victim—"

"Ellie—"

"Not by you, Dex. Anyone else. I just hate that I was involved at all. Some poor woman is hurting because I was naive. And now he's telling me it's not over, so here I ran away from him just to land in his backyard. And when I thought about telling you, I thought it was just going to mess up your life." She sucked in another hitched breath. "That you'd realize that I really am chaos." She buried her face in his neck and wrapped her arms around him. "I'm scared, Dexy. So scared. I've always been scared on some level, but the idea of losing you, that's my worst fear. I've never told anyone any of this, but I'm telling you. That has to mean something."

"Look at me." He drew her chin toward him so she had to look into his eyes. "You'll never lose me." He waited a beat while the words soaked in. "We'll deal with that together, but, El, baby, you're not chaos. And even if you were, I'd love you through it. If we can work on honesty, then we can make it through anything. Come on. You're shivering."

He helped her to her feet, and they walked down Carlisle to Marlboro and made their way to Dex's parents' house. The lights were off, and he hated to wake them this late. He led her around to the back of the house, intending to get the key his parents kept hidden beneath the pot on the back porch, but when they came around to his childhood bedroom window, he had another idea. He jimmied the window open; then he helped Ellie up and into the bedroom and hoisted himself onto the brick ledge and climbed in behind her.

He helped her take off her boots, then removed his own shoes and laid their jackets on the desk. They climbed into his bed, and Ellie snuggled in to him, bringing back all sorts of memories. She laid her hand on her stomach and let out a long sigh.

"Dexy?"

"Yeah?"

"Thank you," Ellie whispered.

"For what?" He kissed the top of her head.

"For not giving up on me."

"You never gave up on me," he said.

"You never asked me for anything."

"I did. I just didn't ask out loud. I asked that you would return. And I asked a lot of you tonight. Thank you for trusting me enough to tell me the truth." He felt the tension fall away from her muscles and melt into him.

"I'm sure of you, Dex. I hope one day you'll be sure of me."

"I'm sure of you, Ellie. More than sure." He covered her with the comforter. Dex laid his head back against the headboard, but he couldn't sleep. He was plagued by the image of Ellie lying in that house pretending to sleep—frightened and disgusted.

Chapter Twenty-Seven

BEING BACK IN his childhood bedroom with Ellie at his side had been exactly the right thing to do. Or at least that's what Dex hoped. He couldn't shake the image of Ellie walking down the street alone at night after what she'd gone through, and the feeling of helplessness was so strong that it made his skin prickle. If only he'd known. If only someone had known. He kissed the top of Ellie's head, silently thanking God that she'd come back to him. She needed him as much as he needed her. He'd always needed her.

Dex was nodding off when his mother appeared in the doorway in her fluffy blue robe and slippers. She came to the edge of the bed and sat down beside him. He smiled up at her sleepily, and she brushed his hair from his forehead.

"I knew I heard that window," she said. Her hair was loose down her back. Her eyes moved from Dex to Ellie, then back again. "Always the window." A breathy, quiet laugh slipped from her lips. "Is she okay?"

Dex nodded.

"What are you doing here?" she asked.

"We went to slay some demons."

His mother nodded, as if she completely understood, which Dex was sure she did. His mother had the uncanny ability to know what was going on in her children's lives, as she'd proven when they'd had lunch.

"And did you slay them?" she asked.

Dex slid out from beneath Ellie and settled her head on the pillow. She sighed contentedly and within seconds was once again fast asleep. Dex pointed to the hall, and his mother followed him out of the room.

"I don't know if we slayed them or not," he whispered. *I hope we did.* He glanced at Ellie. "It was a start. Mom, did you know about everything that went on when she was a kid?"

She touched his cheek, and her eyes filled with sadness. "Not all of it. We had our suspicions and found out the truth too late. Poor girl. She's been through so much. I'm glad she's here now. She always should have been here."

"How come you never told me?" Dex whispered, gazing longingly at Ellie and wanting to hold her again.

"Oh, Dex. You were so lost when she left. The last thing you needed was to know the truth of it all. Your father took care of it." She tightened the belt on her robe and patted his hand.

"Dad? What did Dad do? He was mad at me for missing her. I remember. He was kind of a pri—mean about it." His father's stern face and piercing eyes came back to him. *You're a man. Suck it up and move on.*

"Yes, that's your father's way." Joanie Remington was a realist. She didn't make up excuses for his father any more than she'd have made up excuses for him or his siblings. "But he did good, Dex. You should be very proud of him. He had wondered about what went on there, and he did a bit of snooping. He followed you the night you went there."

"Dad knew I went and didn't ride me for it? I can't believe that. He'd have given me hell if he knew." Dex's eyes locked on Ellie. As they spoke of his father, his gut clenched. Just like it always had. When they were kids, on the evenings his father had said particularly harsh things to him, he used to run his hands through Ellie's silky hair, and he remembered how it soothed his prickly nerves. *I always needed you, too.*

"He's not a bad man, Dexter. He loves you. He just doesn't know how to move with a tender touch. He was upset with you that night for sneaking out, but he was livid when things came to light much later. Now, it appeared that that man handed out his own judgment, although we'll never know if it was an accidental overdose or purposeful, but he must have been mentally sick to have done what was suspected. Your father found out that there were others before Ellie. So in a sense, he probably saved many more children by taking his own life."

Dex's eyes settled on Ellie. *She wanted to stay. Just to be with me.*

"Why was he so hard on me?" Dex asked. "If he knew what happened to Ellie, and he knew how I felt about her, why would he push me to let her go?"

"For the same reasons Ellie kept secrets. It's all

they know."

She said it so matter-of-factly that it threw him off balance for a minute. *It's all they know?*

"But..." He shook his head.

"Oh, sweetheart. Sometimes with your fancy apartment and your huge career, I forget you're still only twenty-six. You haven't experienced enough of life to see it for yourself yet, but we're all just doing the best we can. Your father learned from his father. He raised you doing the best he knew how. And as for Ellie, growing up in the foster system is difficult. The social workers do the best they can to decipher when kids are telling the truth and when they're vying for a new placement or for attention. And I'd imagine that Ellie spent years keeping quiet for fear of not being believed." She looked thoughtfully into Dex's eyes. "And as for me, well, I just do the best I can, too. I love each of you with all my heart, but without your father's stern love, you'd have grown up to be wishy-washy wimps." She smiled, and it lit up her eyes.

Her eyes lingered on Dex for a few breaths, and in those moments he realized that there was far more to his parents' actions than he'd ever realized. How much restraint had it taken for his father not to say something to Dex about Ellie being in his room at night? James Remington, control freak, six-foot-four retired four-star general. Stern father, harsh motivator, and when Dex was growing up...the man to be obeyed. To know his father had taken steps to protect Ellie cushioned Dex's mixed emotions toward him.

Joanie shifted her gaze to Ellie, and her smile faded. Dex's heart ached. "I worry about her. She's a sweet thing, and if she's anything like she was as a teenager, she's strong willed and very, very private. You can see that she feels safe beside you." She sighed. "She looks as precious as you used to treat her. Be careful with her, Dexter. As much as you think you can't take being hurt again, I'm not sure she could take it either."

"I love her, Mom. I've never been surer of anything in my life. But we have to trust each other. We're working on it, and I think tonight helped a lot, but it's kind of up to her." He shrugged.

"That's where you're wrong, honey. It's up to both of you. To trust is also to be trustworthy. She has to be able to tell you things when she's ready, even if it's way past the time that you're ready to hear them. And as much as that stings, you have to trust her enough to allow her to do so."

"That makes no sense. If you love someone, you share everything. You've always taught us that honesty was everything. I remember you saying, *As long as you're honest, you'll never be punished. No matter what you did.* Was that all a load of crap?"

She smiled. "No, honey. I don't dole out crap. Honesty and trust combined, they're everything, but forcing someone to tell you anything before they're ready is controlling. Trust in her and honesty will follow."

"But how? How can I trust when I know she's keeping things from me?"

"Do you trust me?" his mother asked.

"Of course."

"I kept what we thought had happened to Ellie

from you. Do you feel differently about me now that you know that?"

"Well, no, but..."

"Dex, until she can trust that you aren't going to hurt her like everyone else in her life has, she's not going to trust you." She narrowed her eyes in a way that said she knew exactly how they ended up back on Marlboro Street that night. "And that includes forcing her to come forward with things she'd long ago buried deep inside herself. Just as you can't trust her until she's sharing her deepest thoughts with you. It's a double-edged sword that needs to be danced around carefully. You'll figure it out, Dexy." She looked at the clock on his bedside table. "Goodness, we'd better get some sleep. When you mentioned she was back, I knew you would eventually end up back here. We'll have breakfast in the morning."

Dex settled in beside Ellie and closed his eyes, hoping his heart wouldn't get slashed too deeply. As he pulled her closer, he knew that even if he ended up hurt again, Ellie was worth the risk.

Chapter Twenty-Eight

ELLIE SAT ON the edge of Dex's bed, trying to ward off the memories that being back in his room brought careening back. The fear of lying in the bed at her foster home, listening to the grunts and noises of that awful man pleasuring himself, irritated her skin like dozens of spiders crawling over her limbs. She fought against every muscle to remain motionless when her mind screamed, *Get out!* She'd seen her foster father in every shadow all those years ago—heard his voice in the wind.

The only thing that had pulled her through and carried her young legs down the dark and eerie roads so long ago had been Dex. Dex had always been there for her, silently supporting her, loving her when no one else would—or could. She rubbed her hand over his pillow. She'd been so mad at him when she'd realized where he was taking her, and it had been a goddamn struggle to make it up that hill and face the nightmare that she'd tried so hard to forget. But Dex hadn't forced her to do it. She'd felt his steely resolve, and his anger, fall away. He was trying to make *them* possible. And Ellie wanted *them* more than she wanted her next breath. She covered her ears and repeated the mantra that had pulled her through many dark moments. *I'm okay. Just get through it. He can't hurt me anymore.* He couldn't hurt her anymore. She chewed on that thought for a while. Yes, he could. Every time she backed away from Dex, every time she wanted to run, she was letting what he'd done hurt her. *Well, fuck.*

DEX'S VOICE TRAVELED down the stairs to the lower level, where Ellie was debating how to handle seeing his parents again. When they were younger, Dex had complained about his father's pushing things on him, demanding good grades, manly actions, and respect. What Dex couldn't have known was how much Ellie had craved a parent who would care enough to demand those things from her. Of course, not manly actions, but respect, good grades. Hell, she'd have tried her damnedest to meet those expectations as if she'd had a real father instead of a heroin addict she'd never known. She listened to their conversation as she ascended the stairs.

"I wish you would have told me, that's all," Dex said.

"And what good would that have done?"

Ellie stopped at the sound of his father's deep, intimidating voice. She held her breath as he continued.

"You were already out of your mind when she left, Dexter. I took care of it. I wasn't going to dump a load of hurt on a boy who was already down."

"I get that, but maybe I could have helped her in those months afterward. Maybe it would have helped us somehow four years ago." Dex paused, and Ellie held her breath. She could guess at what they were talking about. Obviously, his father must have had an idea about what had gone on with her foster father. Of course he did. Adults weren't blind, like teenagers.

She heard a chair scrape against the floor, then footsteps across the kitchen floor. "I did what I thought was right. You can question it, but it's not going to change the outcome. What's done is done, son. Now you have to deal with what happens next. And that is on your shoulders."

"Ellie?"

Ellie started at the sight of Joanie Remington beside her. "Um...hi."

"Sweetie, how lovely to see you again." She opened her arms and embraced Ellie.

Shoot me now. "Uh...Good to see you, too. I'm just...um..." *Eavesdropping.* "Sorry we showed up so late last night."

"Oh, don't be silly. Come. Let's get some breakfast."

Ellie followed her into the kitchen feeling like an intruder. Dex reached his hand out to her, and she breathed a little easier. Sort of. Still stupefied by the discomfort of being a couple in front of his parents, her eyes darted from his mother to his father.

"Hey, you're awake," he said in a groggy, sexy voice, void of the earlier angst from his discussion with his father.

"Sorry I slept so late." She stood up straighter as her eyes shifted to his father. He stood with his shoulders square, tall and rigid. His gray hair was shorn close in short military fashion. "Good morning, Mr. Remington."

"Good morning, Ellie. Would you like some coffee?" His navy blue eyes softened as he pulled out a chair beside Dex. "Sit, please."

She let out a shaky breath as she lowered herself to the chair, feeling as though at any moment the elephant in the room might trample her. She reached for Dex's hand. Her leg began its let-me-out-of-here bounce beneath the table, and Dex settled their hands on her thigh and inched his chair closer to her.

Words pressed at her lungs. *Get it out in the open. Talk about it.* She accepted the warm coffee from his mother. "Thank you."

"Dex tells us that you've got a job at Maple Elementary. I taught a few art classes there back in the day." Joanie sat down across from Ellie. "Even back then their teaching methods were very individualized."

Thankful for something else to concentrate on, Ellie wrapped her hands around the warm cup to steady them. "I'm really excited about it. Did Dex tell you our idea to apply for an educational grant and try to develop an educational software program for kids?"

"Your idea," Dex corrected as he brushed her hair from her shoulder.

She felt her cheeks flush at the intimate touch, worried about how his parents might react to their relationship.

Joanie glanced at the two of them and smiled. "He did. It sounds like a great idea, and who better to help bring it forward than the two of you?"

His father lowered himself into his chair at the head of the table with a fresh cup of coffee and set his eyes on Dex. Even without looking, she felt the tension radiating from Dex. James shifted his gaze to Ellie, and Dex put his arm protectively across the back of her chair and grazed the tightly strung knot at the base of her neck, which she'd been trying to ignore.

"Are you here to stay, then?" he asked.

Ellie couldn't pull her eyes from his. "Yes. Assuming my job goes well."

He nodded. "And you're living in the city?"

"Well, for now—"

"She's staying with me, Dad," Dex said.

His father nodded. "I see."

"I was supposed to stay with a girlfriend, but she...It didn't work out," Ellie explained, feeling like she was taking advantage of his little boy, which was ridiculous given that Dex was twenty-six, and they were both adults.

He took a slow sip of coffee, looking at Joanie over the rim of his cup. When he set it back on the table, he locked eyes with Dex. "I think it's a good idea that Ellie stays with you. The city can be a rough place, and this way we know she's safe." His thin lips arced into a smile. His eyes softened as he turned to Ellie. "That is, of course, assuming Ellie wants to stay there."

The walls felt like they were closing in on her. Dex wanted her to be honest so badly, and her gut told her to claim him as he'd claimed her at his office, but what if she did and then his father nixed the whole thing? What if he thought she was bad news for his son? *What if...? What if...? The hell with it.*

241

"Mr. Remington, I know I've had a messed-up life, but I'm on a good track now." Damn it. Why were her eyes damp? Dex wrapped his hand around her shoulder and squeezed. *Thank you. Thank God you always know what I need.*

"Ellie, honey, you've always been on a good track," his mother said.

His father's stare iced over. His jaw clenched just as Dex's had the evening before.

Shit. I've ruined everything. She gripped the sides of the chair in anticipation of the trampling.

When his father pinned his gaze on her, she whipped her head to the side and looked at Dex, afraid of what she'd unleashed.

"What that man did in that house had nothing to do with you." His father's eyes narrowed.

Ellie froze at his fervent tone.

"He was a pig," he said. "A beast. And just because you lived in that house and bore the brunt of his sickness does not mean that you were on a bad track."

He reached out and took her shaking hand in his as a tear streaked her cheek. She couldn't wipe it away. She could barely breathe. Never in her life would she have imagined him reaching out in such a tender way, and for a moment, it scared the shit out of her.

"You have strength like no other, Ellie," his father continued. "Whatever happened in that house. Whatever he did or said. Remember, you are who you are because of your inner strength. Don't let that bastard make you feel otherwise."

Ellie breathed in hindered gasps for air. Her shoulders rose and fell as she tried to gain control of the tears she fought against.

"Ellie?"

Dex? She heard his voice, but couldn't focus. The hurt—*no*, the relief—was too great. They saw inside her. He recognized the girl she'd been protecting all these years. *Fuck. And now I'm blubbering like an idiot.* Her hand hung limply by her side as tears streamed silently down her cheeks. Dex's arms came around her. Joanie's comforting voice whispered in her ear.

"It's okay, honey. Let it out."

His father's enormous hand grasped hers.

She melted against Dex's chest, her eyes locked on his father's hands. Tears streaked her cheeks as her body trembled, overwhelmed by their support. She sucked in a breath. "I...I'm sorry. I just..." She wiped her eyes, feeling like a fool. She felt her cheeks flush. "I've spent my whole life proving who I was." She patted her chest. "Inside. Trying to separate myself from all the crap I grew up with."

"We've always known who you were." His father shook his head. A deep V formed between his thick brows.

Joanie touched his shoulder and looked at him disapprovingly. "Of course you have, Ellie, and you probably always will. And that's okay. But now you know. We have never seen you as anything less than the strong, beautiful person that you've always been."

How could his mother know just what she needed to hear?

"I'm sorry. I'm so embarrassed." She rounded her shoulders and shrugged away from Dex. He pulled her back. Of course he did.

"Embarrassed?" James said with a shake of his head. "Embarrassed to be with a twenty-six-year-old guy who plays games for a living maybe, but embarrassed by who you are? No. That's just unacceptable."

She smiled at his rare moment of levity. Dex rolled his eyes, but she saw relief in his sweet, compassionate smile.

"I like that he does something he's passionate about," she said to lighten the mood.

"Then he's a lucky bastard." He winked at Dex.

Dex gazed into her eyes, and there was no mistaking the love that welled there. That had always been there for her.

"That I am," he said.

But Ellie knew the truth. She had been the lucky one all along. She just hadn't been able to see it through the cloud of awfulness that she'd grown up in.

Chapter Twenty-Nine

DEX AND ELLIE spent the day with his parents. Throughout the afternoon, Dex had stolen glances at his father, trying to reconcile the softer side of him that had come through after he'd so vehemently damned Ellie's foster father. Dex had seen glimpses of that softer side when he was growing up, but his father's stern presence had made a stronger impression on him. Dex had been ready to go head-to-head with his father when he'd asked Ellie where she was staying, and when he saw Ellie floundering to answer, he hadn't hesitated. His heart led and his words followed. He didn't know what he'd expected from his father, but the kindness he'd exhibited was far from whatever Dex might have conjured up.

Now it was eight at night and his parents had just dropped him and Ellie off in the city. He'd had a dozen texts from Regina and Mitch about the review copies being sent out tomorrow, and they'd kept him up to date with reviews and prerelease events. With all that had happened, he realized that while the release was vital to his career—and the careers of his employees—Ellie was vital to his happiness. He drank her in now, the darkness of the past a thinner shadow than it had been just twenty-four hours earlier. He felt her heart open to him last night in a way it never had in the past, and he'd taken his mother's advice seriously. From now on, he'd tread a little more carefully. He had to believe that eventually, together, they'd slay all of her demons. Just as they'd begun to slay his.

"The last twenty-four hours have felt like a lifetime. Wanna get a drink?" Ellie asked.

Dex pulled her against him. "I thought you couldn't be trusted with alcohol." He slipped his hands beneath the back of her top and felt her silky, warm skin.

"Mmm. Maybe I don't want to be trusted. I can take only so much seriousness before I feel like I'm gonna explode." She pressed her hips into his. "Besides, I start work tomorrow. Then I'll be getting up early every morning while you're staying up all night, and we'll be completely thrown off balance."

"I think we'll figure it out." Since that morning, she'd moved easier, stepped lighter. He'd felt the shift in himself, too. Clearing the air and getting it all out in the open had breathed new life into them. And now, with her breasts pressed against his chest and her sweet, tender lips slightly parted, he desperately wanted to take her upstairs and rip her clothes off. He wanted to see what that lighter feel did to their lovemaking. Just thinking about it made him hard.

She hooked her finger in his jeans. "Seems like you have other things in mind." She licked her lips as she met his eyes.

"Can you blame me? I had to sleep next to you fully clothed last night. What do you think I thought about all night? Besides, you mentioned a drink and that made me think of NightCaps and you dancing like you wanted to have sex on the dance floor."

She blushed, and it made him want her even more.

"Fuck the drink. Come on." Inside the empty lobby of the Dakota, Dex wrapped his arms around Ellie from behind and kissed the back of her neck as they waited for the elevator to descend to the lobby. She arched her head back, giving him full access. The noise of the street was barely audible. He slid his hands beneath her sweater and cupped her breasts. She moaned, wiggling her ass against him. He was already rock hard. He slid a hand down the front of her pants and over her soft curls. She gasped a breath when his finger slid into her.

"Dex," she whispered.

"Shh." He sucked on her neck while he stroked her until she was wet and ready. The elevator reached the first floor and he withdrew his hand. She whimpered and turned to him with the hazy look of lust in her eyes.

The elevator doors opened.

"Hey, Dex." Josh Braden and his fiancée, Riley, walked out of the elevators. Josh wore a bright smile, and his dark eyes dropped from Dex to Ellie. "And, Ellie, great to see you." Josh wore dark dress pants and a white button-down shirt, and with Riley wearing a short black dress and sky-high heels, they looked like they were ready for a romantic night.

Ellie turned to face them, her cheeks burning red. Dex held her in front of his raging hard-on. Josh's eyes raked over the two of them.

"Josh, Riley." Dex's voice was heated, rushed. He knew he should take the time to talk with them. Josh was Savannah's brother, after all, but he had more pressing things on his mind. Or in his pants.

"Hey," Riley said. Her smile faded as her eyes passed between the two of them. Then her eyes widened and her smile returned as she grabbed Josh's hand and hurried along. "Um, we better..."

Josh looked from her to them with a furrowed brow, then blinked quickly, as if startled by the understanding of why Dex and Ellie looked so flustered. "Oh. Right." Josh and Riley headed for the entrance, and Dex hurried Ellie into the elevator with a soft laugh.

"It's not funny," Ellie whispered.

Inside the elevator, Dex hit the button for the top floor and pinned Ellie against the back wall. "It's kinda funny." His voice carried heated desire, the humor of the brief run-in with Josh and Riley forgotten.

"Hurry," she said, pulling at the buttons of his jeans.

He stilled her hands. "Not enough time." He lifted her shirt, taking her bra along with it, and brought his mouth to her luscious breast. She gasped, and he shoved his hand down her pants, adeptly finding the spot that sent her up on her toes. She breathed heavily, fisting her hands in his hair. When they reached the top floor, he hit the close door button repeatedly, which caused the elevator to stop for two full minutes, a glitch he'd uncovered by accident one afternoon when he'd been in a hurry. He dropped his pants and tore hers down, then lifted her up and pinned her back against the wall as he thrust into her hard and fast. Penetrating her to the hilt.

"Oh God, Dex."

With his hands gripping her ass, he thrust hard and fast. She clawed at his arms; her thighs tightened around him as her head dropped back and they rode the crest of their love up and over the edge, both gasping for breath. Two minutes later, the elevator rumbled to life and began its slow decent.

"Shit," Ellie whispered. "Can't...breathe."

"You're so fucking hot." Dex panted as he lowered her shaky legs to the ground and helped her pull up her jeans before righting his own clothing just in time for the elevator doors to slide open on his floor. He took her hand, already fumbling with the keys. Ellie's cheeks had an after-sex rosy glow. She nibbled on her lower lip, looking sexier than hell. Dex clutched the keys in his fist, unable to wait. He took her in his arms and kissed her again, stealing the breath from her lungs and feeling her heart pumping against his. She pressed into him again, and when he pulled back and looked into her eyes, his body reacted to her hungry gaze. He unlocked the door and pulled her inside.

"Shit. Ellie. I can't wait another second. I need to be close to you again. Now." Dropping his keys to the ground, he shrugged out of his jacket and tore at her clothes, tossing her jacket, sweater, and bra to the floor. He stepped from his jeans and drew his shirt over his head. That first stroke of skin-to-skin contact stole his breath again. He took her in a rough kiss before lifting her up again and staring into her eyes as he lowered her onto his hard length again, burying himself deep. They fit together perfectly. Ellie's eyes reflected pure, uninhibited desire, untethered by the links of the past that had previously held her captive. As they clung together, riding out their simultaneous release, it felt like a new beginning.

Chapter Thirty

LATER THAT EVENING, they lay in bed listening to the street noises filter in from the slightly open window.

"Tell me about the guy," Dex said.

Ellie closed her eyes. She didn't want to talk about him. She wanted to lie there soaking up Dex's warmth, listen to him breathe, and think about her first day of work. But she'd made a promise and she intended to keep it.

"His name is Bruce."

"Bruce. I kinda like *asshole* better." Dex pulled her closer.

Ellie rested her head on his chest as she spoke. "I already told you how I found out about his wife, but, Dex, there's more." She felt his body stiffen. "That night when I found out about his wife, he was pretty mad." She closed her eyes, felt his hand settle on her back. She fisted her hands beneath the covers, hoping Dex wouldn't go flying from the bed in anger. "He...he grabbed my arm."

His hand pressed down on her back.

"And...and he slammed me against a wall." She clenched her eyes shut, listening to Dex's heart beat faster against her cheek. He didn't say a word. He didn't move. And the silence scared the shit out of her. She turned to face him, and his eyes were closed, his jaw clenched tight. "I'm sorry I didn't tell you when you first asked, but I couldn't. I hate being a victim, or seeming like one, and I thought he'd go away and I'd never have to think about him again, but I made you a promise last night, and I'm keeping that promise."

He opened his eyes and pulled her up so they were eye to eye. "Now can I kill him?" His voice was dead serious. He stroked her hair and cupped the back of her head, drawing her cheek to his. "I'm so sorry, baby." He kissed her cheek and held her there.

"Are you mad at me for not telling you?" She didn't want to hear the answer, but she needed to ask.

"I'm mad at him for doing it. I wish you would have told me sooner, but I'm not mad at you for not telling me. We're past that." He kissed her cheek again. "I'm trusting that you'll tell me things when you're ready. That's all I can really do."

"Thank you."

"I think we should go to the police. He knows you're here. He saw you when you were in the Village. Ellie, that's stalker behavior."

"Can't we just see if it stops? Please? When he saw me in the Village, he didn't follow me. He travels all the time, or at least that's what he told me, so maybe he's not following me."

"Ellie."

She recognized the you're-doing-the-wrong-thing-but-I-won't-fight-with-you tone. "I'm starting a new job tomorrow. You're releasing your game next week. Can't we just have a little time without any craziness? Please? If he shows up anywhere, we'll go to the police."

"I'm really not comfortable with this, Ellie. How do you know he won't try to hurt you again? He's a scorned man who probably has a pissed-off wife."

"I was in Maryland for almost three weeks before moving here. If he wanted to take revenge, don't you think he would have done it then?" He'd called and texted relentlessly when she was in Maryland, but he'd never pursued seeing her. She had to believe that his being in New York was a coincidence. *Otherwise, wouldn't he have approached me when he saw me at the thrift shop?*

"Damn it, Ellie. I'm not going to argue with you, but I don't like it one bit. Promise me that if he contacts you again, text, in person, anything, that we'll file a report."

"Fine."

He leaned over her. "You mean it?"

"Yes. Fine." She popped her head off the mattress and kissed him. "Promise, and you have to admit, I'm getting better at this whole honesty thing. Like telling you that you are incredibly handsome and I'd like to make love to you again."

He leaned his forehead against hers. "You're the most frustrating woman I've ever known." He lowered his lips to hers.

Chapter Thirty-One

ELLIE LEANED OVER her desk as her students worked on a writing assignment. It was Friday afternoon, and although it was only her first week of teaching at Maple Elementary, she felt as if she were meant to work there. The staff was completely in tune with the students and their needs, they were excited about the potential software proposal, and since the first morning when they'd gathered in the teachers' lounge for coffee, she'd felt as though she fit in perfectly. Her colleagues were, in fact, her peers. She wasn't the only teacher who had something other than a middle-class childhood.

During her first few days of teaching, Ellie observed and listened. She met with each of the students and got to know them. She knew, for example, that Selma liked reading about horses and anything that had to do with animals, and that she once had a cat that her neighbor ran over with his car. Michael enjoyed only comic books and thought any other literature was boring. His mother, however, could not read at all. Kenny had a hard time with math but could read on a third-grade level, and he often prepared the grocery list for his family. Tabby could barely make her way through a sentence. During that initial get-to-know-you conversation, she'd also learned that Joseph lived with his aunt and her five children, and they had moved three times since first grade. The classroom was ripe with need, and Ellie was chomping at the bit to take them under her wing.

She watched the kids, some intent on the task at hand, others staring out the window, unable to stay focused for more than a few minutes at a time. And then there was Joseph. Joseph was a wanderer. Smart as a whip, socially awkward, and undiagnosed as anything other than a problem child, Joseph worked best when his legs were moving. She understood the need to not feel confined, and that was part of what drove her to ease up on typical "in your seat" guidelines and allow Joseph the freedom to move.

"Okay, girls and boys, it's time to put our work away for the afternoon." She walked down the rows of the high-ceilinged classroom as they put their work away. Sunlight filtered through the windows. Plywood blocked the holes where windows had been broken and not yet repaired, and as she glanced at them, she wondered what had caused them to break. Did it happen during school hours, or were they broken by rowdy teenagers over a weekend? The desks were standard student fare, small, metal, scuffed, and some covered with graffiti. Overall, the classroom was functional, and with a few colorful decorations, it would soon come to life.

"Joseph, good job getting your homework done last night," she said as the little dark-haired boy put his work into his backpack.

"Thank you, Miss Parker."

Blythe appeared in the doorway and waved her over.

"Three minutes until the bell rings. Be sure to take your jackets home with you. Check your cubbies for anything else you might need." She held up one finger to Blythe and continued speaking to the students. "I enjoyed our first week together, and I think we're going to have a great year."

"Me too." Missing her two front teeth, Selma flashed a toothless grin.

"Thank you, Miss Parker," Joseph yelled.

"It was a fun week except the reading," Michael said.

She met Blythe in the doorway.

"Great news. The grant program doesn't close until December twelfth, so we can still apply." Blythe's eyes widened as she smiled. "I'm so excited about this, and talk about fate! With Dex and his friends' help on the technical side of things, and our educational staff, I think we really have a shot at this."

"That's fantastic news. I can't wait to tell Dex. We've already begun the outline of the proposal. Why don't I bring it in next week and we can flesh it all out and get some opinions on anything that's missing?"

After the kids had left for the afternoon, Ellie gathered her papers and texted Dex.

We got the okay to apply for the grant! Wanna have

a drink 2 celebrate?

A minute later, her cell phone vibrated with Dex's answer.

NightCaps? 45 minutes? I'll wait out front.

K. See u soon. Xox.

Over the past week, Ellie had found a new side to herself. She no longer weighed her answers with Dex. She gave herself over to trust, and when he asked about Bruce, she answered fully and honestly. Luckily, she hadn't heard from Bruce all week. When Dex told her he loved her, she couldn't say she loved him fast enough. As much as she had lived in hopes of her mantra, *Everything will be okay*, she had never fully believed it. She was starting to believe that maybe everything really would be okay.

"WE'RE READY TO rock and roll," Mitch said as he came into Dex's office. He plopped his rumpled self into a chair with a wide grin on his lips. "Reviews are awesome; people are begging for the game. You know how many kids are going to miss school Monday because they downloaded the game Saturday at midnight and they've gotten so far it would kill them to have to stop?"

Regina was right behind him. "Way to ruin Dex's high, Mitch. He hates that kids skip school to play. Jesus, don't you ever learn?"

Dex shook his head. "What matters is that we're going out on time and we've got a great product. I don't want to talk about the kids skipping school. I wanna pretend they all have a father like mine." He lowered his voice and pinched his eyebrows together. *"Over my dead body will you stay home to play games. You're a man. Men don't play; they work. They provide."*

"That's actually pretty sexy," Regina teased. She carried a handful of Twizzlers and offered one to Mitch and one to Dex. Both of whom declined. "Suit yourself." She sat in the chair opposite Mitch and hiked her jeans-clad legs over the arm of the chair. She wore her black hoodie unzipped with a black ribbed tank top beneath.

"My dad is anything but sexy." Dex rose to his feet and came around to the opposite side of the desk. He leaned against it and crossed his legs. "I hate to jinx us, but I think we've got this release nailed."

"Yeah, no shit, Sherlock," Mitch said, then scratched his stomach.

Dex's phone vibrated with a text from Sage. *I've got a free night. Wanna grab a brew?* He knew Ellie wouldn't mind if Sage joined them, and he was excited to share their relationship with him. He texted back. *NightCaps half hr. Meet us?*

"Hey, how's Ellie's new job? I kinda got used to seeing her." Regina stuck a Twizzler in her mouth.

"She loves it. The work, the kids." He shrugged. "It's a good match. I'm on my way to meet her. Wanna come?" His phone vibrated, and he read a text from Sage. *Sure. C U there. Looking forward 2 getting 2 no Ellie better.* Then he texted Ellie, so she wouldn't be taken by surprise. *Mind if Sage joins us?*

"I don't know. The last time we crashed your date, you guys fought," Regina pointed out.

Dex's phone vibrated, and he read the text from Ellie. *Sounds good!*

"Sage is gonna meet us, too, so it's not like you're

imposing. Besides, we didn't fight." Dex could hardly believe it had been only a week since they'd gone to his parents' house. He and Ellie had come together in every way, and he felt like they'd been living together forever. Maybe in his mind, they had. Thoughts of her had always lingered in his mind. Was she okay? Was she happy? Was she thinking of him as much as he thought of her? She still loved to lie beside him while he read, or lie on the couch while he worked his way through a game. He used to cherish his privacy, but what he realized was that he just hadn't tried sharing his time with the right person.

"Right. What are we calling it now? A lovers' quarrel?" Mitch asked.

"Oh, like you'd know anything about dating." Regina swatted a Twizzler in his direction.

"Hey, I could date if I wanted to."

"Aren't you the guy who swears women don't want gamers?" Regina arched a brow.

"Hey, focus here or I'll be late. You in or out?" Dex headed for the door. Regina and Mitch were right behind him.

They arrived at NightCaps fifteen minutes late, and Ellie was nowhere in sight. They went inside to look for her. The bar was packed, but Dex didn't see Ellie.

"I'll check the ladies' room," Regina offered.

Mitch elbowed Dex. "You think Reg would go out with me?"

No way. How could Siena have seen that and he have missed it? "Dude, don't stick the pen in the company ink. It never ends well." Dex pulled out his phone and texted Ellie.

"I'm serious. We have the same interests, the same schedules." Mitch shrugged.

Dex only half listened, sidetracked by trying to reach Ellie.

"She's not in there," Regina said.

"Shit." Dex tried calling her cell phone. It rang three times, then went to voicemail. "I'm gonna walk down by the subway and see if I can find her. You guys can grab a table."

"I'll go with you." Regina fell into step beside him.

"I'm good. You guys wait here. I'll go alone." He turned so Regina couldn't see his face and winked at Mitch. Mitch pulled his shoulders back, which only made his gut stick out farther.

Regina shrugged. "Okay. Text if you need us to send out search and rescue."

Friday nights brought out the masses in the city. They came out early and stayed out late. Tonight Dex was looking at a sea of bodies moving fast and constant. He tried calling Ellie again before heading toward the subway. He held the phone to his ear, listening to it ring. He heard the ringtone Ellie had set up to identify his calls coming from the alley beside the bar. He lowered his phone, listening intently, then followed the ringing into the darkness.

"Ellie?" he called. He could barely see five feet in front of him as he entered the alley. He raced toward the ringing sound and found her phone lying on the ground, the faceplate cracked. *Fuck.*

"Dex!" Her voice was high-pitched, frightened. "Leave me alone, Bruce!"

"Like hell I will," a deep male voice seethed.

Dex ran into the darkness, his heart slamming against his ribs. Blood rushed through his ears as he came upon Ellie, her back against the brick wall, the man blocking her with a wide-legged stance. She took a step toward Dex, and Bruce pushed her back against the wall. Ellie sucked in a breath.

Moving on pure adrenaline and gut instinct, Dex grabbed Bruce and dragged him away from Ellie. Tears streamed from her terrified eyes.

"Dex!"

"Get outta here, Ellie," Dex growled just before slamming Bruce against the wall. His head met the brick with a loud *thud*. Ellie ran toward the street as Bruce's fist connected with Dex's jaw.

Ellie yelled, "Dex!"

The metallic taste of blood hung in Dex's mouth as he launched himself at the guy, blocking another punch and knocking Bruce off balance. Blind fury sent Dex's arm into motion, landing punch after powerful punch on Bruce's jaw. As his head fell back, Dex's fist connected with a blow to his gut. Bruce keeled forward, and Dex hammered an uppercut to his already bloody jaw, then threw him to the ground, landing on top of him with another *thud*. The anger and frustration of the last few weeks tangled into one massive surge of force. The sound of bone cracking and flesh pummeling flesh filled the darkness. Somewhere in the distance he heard Ellie calling out to him, but Dex was powerless to stop. He was pure adrenaline, rage personified. All of the men who had ever hurt Ellie blurred into the man beneath him. His fists flew hard and fast as the man went limp. A strong hand gripped his arm and he twisted out of its grip, landing another punch to the already bloody face beneath him. Then his arms were trapped, held firmly back as he was yanked from the limp body and dragged backward. He flailed and fought against them, burning to avenge Ellie's pain.

"Dex. Stop. Stop. You'll kill him."

Sage.

Dex's chest expanded with each angry breath. His fisted hands ached and burned. His knuckles dripped with blood. Some his, some the other guy's. Fury seeped from every pore. He struggled to break free, but stood no chance with Mitch and Sage holding him back.

"Ellie!" he growled. He heard her crying. He elbowed and twisted until he was facing the road, where Ellie shook and shivered within Regina's caring arms. "Lemme go!" He broke free of their grasp and sprinted to Ellie, barely aware of the crowd that now circled the man he'd beaten. Ellie's eyes and nose were red and puffy, her terrified eyes locked on his.

"Ellie." He pulled her against him, his own body shaking against hers. "Babe. I'm right here. It's okay. I'm right here." She clung to him, digging into him with her nails. He barely felt the moon-shaped cuts he knew he'd find later. She drew a shaky hand to his jaw.

"You're...bleeding," she sobbed.

He didn't care about the blood. Adrenaline and fear numbed the physical pain. Ellie was safe. She was in his arms, and he was never going to let her go. Ever.

AT THE HOSPITAL, Dex sat on the bed with a bandage secured to his hand. He'd needed eleven stitches to close a gash along his knuckles. Ellie stood between his legs, her hands on his hips. Regina leaned against Mitch, looking almost as scared as Ellie.

"I'm fine, you guys. You don't have to hang around." He was glad they were there, but the painkillers had kicked in and he felt fuzzy around the edges. He wanted to go home, lie down beside Ellie, and not move until his life would fall apart if he didn't.

"You sure?" Regina asked.

"Reg, I've got Ellie and Sage. I'll be fine." He watched her and Mitch exchange a glance, and he wondered if the closeness he noticed was caused by his drug-induced foggy state or something more.

"Okay. What about the release?" Regina asked.

"You know, I think I'll just hang with Ellie. Between the drugs and the stitches, I'm not sure I'll be up for it." He stroked Ellie's arm.

"Yeah, okay." Regina put an arm around Ellie. "I'm glad you're okay. It would have sucked if that guy hurt my new friend."

Ellie leaned her head against Regina. "For me, too," she said, but she was looking at Dex, and he knew she meant the both of them.

"All right, dude. Listen, you need me, I'm there. I'll text you updates." Mitch patted Dex's back. "Man, you'll do just about anything to get the girl, won't you?"

"Just about." *Anything. Anything at all.* "Thanks, you guys. I'm not blowing you off. I'm just really loopy."

"No worries. You're in good hands." Regina grabbed the front of Mitch's shirt. "Let's go. I need a veggie burger."

Mitch raised his eyebrows. "That's code for you know what."

Regina smacked him, and as they walked out of the curtained-off area of the emergency room, she looked over her shoulder and said, "In his dreams."

Ellie turned a soft gaze back to him, her pupils dilated as she ran her eyes along his face. "Dexy. Look at you. I'm so sorry."

"Don't be. It wasn't your fault."

"Do you believe me now? I'm chaos, Dexy. Bad news." Her voice was soft, riddled with worry.

Sage came through the curtain. "How're you doing, Dex?"

Dex arched a brow. "'Bout as good as can be expected."

"Good. The police just left. This guy, Bruce, he has a history of complaints against him from other women." Sage put an arm around Ellie. "You okay?"

"Yeah, thanks, but this is all my fault. I'm sorry to have gotten you involved with this." She touched Dex's cheek. "I'm so sorry."

"You couldn't have known. This guy's MO is to turn on the GPS on women's phones, so he always knows where they are." Sage let out a breath. "He wasn't married, Ellie. The woman who called you was some other woman he'd been seeing, who also thought she was his only girlfriend."

Ellie shook her head. "See? Pure chaos."

Dex lowered his forehead to hers. "I like chaos, so don't even think about walking away, Ellie Parker. You're not going anywhere. You have to nurse me back to health."

"I should have listened to you and gone to the police," she said.

"Maybe, but we can't change the past, remember? We can only learn from it and move forward. All I ask is that you not date any more maniacs." He felt the right side of his mouth lift into a teasing smile.

"I'm pretty sure I've found a guy that's only a little maniacal, and he usually plays out that side of himself in the virtual world."

He lowered his lips to hers and kissed her softly. "I thought I'd lost you," he whispered.

She cupped his cheek. "You'll never lose me again."

Chapter Thirty-Two

SUNDAY AFTERNOON, DEX and Ellie went to NightCaps to meet Mitch and Regina and celebrate the release of *World of Thieves II*. In the last twenty-four hours, *World of Thieves II* had broken new-release sales records. With that level of success, Dex had no concerns about KI or any other competitor.

"You sure you're okay with just Tylenol? It's been only two days," Ellie asked when they reached the entrance.

She'd hovered over him since they'd left the hospital, and her fierce protectiveness rivaled that of his mother, who had called him four times to make sure he was *really* okay.

"Ellie, it's just a few stitches. Bet you didn't know your boyfriend was so tough," he teased.

"I always knew how tough you were." She stood on her tiptoes, and he took her hand and led her up the first step, so they were nearly eye to eye; then he drew her close and kissed her.

A cab pulled up to the curb, and Dex reluctantly parted from the kiss, still holding Ellie's hand with his unharmed one. He turned just in time to see Siena spin around and snap a picture on her phone.

"Ha!" she teased.

"What are you doing here?" Dex asked.

"You don't think Regina would have a party without your family, do you?" Siena snapped another picture.

The door to NightCaps opened, and Regina and Mitch came outside. "Surprise!" they said in unison.

"Hey!" Dex hugged Regina and Mitch. "You guys could have told me you called everyone."

Siena took another picture. "Then I wouldn't have gotten that surprised look on film!"

"Wait," Ellie said, surprising Dex. She stepped in front of him, then grabbed his arms and wrapped them around her waist. "Okay, Siena. Can you please take another picture?"

Dex knew how much courage it took for Ellie to not only be in the picture, but to ask for it to be taken. With the others milling around him, he didn't want to call any more attention to her and make her uncomfortable, though his heart swelled with gratitude and love for her. He leaned down and whispered, "Thank you."

She squeezed his hands and lifted her chin so she could see him. "Thank *you*, Dexy."

"Oh, that is just the cutest picture I've ever seen!" Siena hurried over and showed it to them.

"I want a copy of that," he said.

Savannah and Jack came down the sidewalk hand

in hand. Jack looked happier than Dex had seen him in years. His thick dark hair brushed his collar, and as always, he wore leather hiking boots, making his six-four stature more like six-five. "Hey, baby brother," Jack called. He opened his arms and embraced Dex. "Heard you beat the snot out of that guy."

"To save his girl," Savannah said with a sigh. She brushed her auburn hair to the side and hugged Dex and Siena; then she wrapped her arms around Ellie. "I've heard a lot about you. I'm so glad we've finally met."

Ellie drew her brows together. "You have?"

Savannah touched Jack's arm. "Jack has a couple great stories about coming home to visit late at night and finding you two snoozing together in Dex's room."

"You do? Why don't I know this?" Dex asked.

Jack shrugged. "You were sleeping with your arms around her. I'm pretty sure you knew."

"No, jackass. Why didn't I know you knew?" Dex laughed.

"Wait, why didn't *I* know?" Siena complained as they made their way into NightCaps.

"Sisters are always the last to know," Savannah whispered to her.

As soon as they were through the doors, Mitch threw his arms up in the air and yelled, "Thrive!" There were only a handful of people in the bar, each of whom either laughed or looked at Mitch like he was crazy.

Dex high-fived him, then waited as the others filed past and greeted his parents and brothers. He pulled Ellie close. "I saw you cringe when Jack mentioned that he'd seen us sleeping together as kids."

"Jack knew," she whispered. "He must think I was a slut."

"No way. If he did, he would have said something to me. Besides, maybe you can pretend you were so I don't look like such a loser for not having sex with you back then."

She punched his arm.

"Hey, don't hit the wounded."

"Don't you dare let them think we did that." She narrowed her eyes, and he held his hands up.

"I never would."

"There you are," his mother said as she approached. She wore wide-legged slacks and a white turtleneck adorned with various chunky necklaces in a multitude of colors.

"You look really pretty, Mrs. Remington." Ellie let go of Dex's hand to hug her.

"Joanie, please. I might have gray hair, but calling me missus just makes me feel older." She embraced Ellie, then hugged Dex. She pulled back and brushed his hair from in front of his eyes. "You are a hero, but a scraggly one. Maybe you and Jack should go to the barbershop together."

Dex rolled his eyes. "My hair is shorter than Sage's."

"Maybe, but that's not saying much," Rush said as he and Kurt came to greet them. Rush had always kept his hair on the shorter side. He said it was easier when he was on the slopes, and as a competitive skier, he spent half his life on the slopes.

"Rush, Kurt, jeez. I haven't seen you guys in forever." Dex hugged them both.

Kurt was the quietest of the Remington crew. As a writer, he tended to observe the banter rather than spark new conversations. Dex watched him now with his thick dark hair and serious eyes and realized that he was very much like Ellie.

"You guys remember Ellie." He kept one hand on Ellie's back as they each pulled her into a hug. Dex hadn't ever thought about how his family had openly embraced one another, but watching them bring Ellie into their family fold brought that to the forefront. Remarkably, Ellie didn't shy away from the intimate gestures. And when she flashed her eyes in his direction, he saw relief. He made a silent note in his mind of another freight-train-like impact Ellie had on his heart at that very moment. Her relief spoke volumes of her love for him and how far she'd come.

"I think Ellie brings you good luck, son." His father wore a starched blue button-down shirt and dress slacks—always dress slacks. He patted Dex on the back with a proud smile. "She was there all those years ago while you developed that first indie game you released right after high school, and here she is again, the morning after another groundbreaking release."

Before embracing Dex, his father reached out to Ellie, and the gesture squeezed Dex's heart.

"Come on, little bro." Sage put his arm around Dex and walked him to the bar, away from the others. "You okay?"

"Yeah." Dex peered around him and was glad to see Ellie beside Siena and Savannah, looking at pictures on Savannah's phone.

"I'm proud of you, with the game and all."

"Thanks."

"Listen, Mom told me that you know I spilled the beans to her about Ellie four years ago. I'm sorry. I was worried and thought she might have some words of wisdom." Sage met Dex's gaze with an apologetic look.

Dex couldn't stay mad at Sage. "Whatever. No worries. What'd she say to you? Back then, I mean, because she never said a word to me."

Sage ran his hand through his thick, wavy hair. "She said, *Sometimes love hurts*, and told me not to try to talk you out of your feelings for Ellie."

Dex nodded. "You know, maybe Mom really is the smartest woman on earth."

"Don't let Ellie hear you say that."

They joined the others and sat at the tables that had been pushed together in the rear of the bar, where a buffet-style lunch had been set up. Dex leaned around Ellie and tapped Regina on the shoulder. "Reg, I can't believe you arranged all this. Thank you."

She held her finger above Mitch's head and pointed down at him. "He helped."

"Yeah, well, someone had to do the heavy lifting," Mitch said.

Regina rolled her eyes. "He means pushing the tables together." She laughed and shoved Mitch. "I could have done it myself."

"Well, thanks. I'm glad you got everyone together." Dex squeezed Regina's hand. "We have a lot to celebrate."

As they filled their plates, Jack rose to his feet. "I want to propose a toast."

Their mother gasped a breath. "You're getting

married!"

Jack laughed. "Maybe you can let me finish?"

His mother gasped. "Oh, Jack. Really?"

Savannah reached across the table. "No. He's pulling your leg." She swatted Jack.

"You'll be the first to know, Mom. I promise." Jack lifted his glass of orange juice. "To our little brother for his overnight success."

The game had released at midnight, and Dex and Ellie had stayed up watching the number of sales climb higher than Dex had ever imagined; then they'd celebrated by making love, eventually falling asleep in each other's arms.

Everyone clinked glasses, and Jack continued. "And to Ellie, for getting the approval to write the grant proposal. We're proud of you, Ellie."

Ellie blushed. "How did you know?"

Sage leaned forward from the other end of the table. "You'll learn that the Remington grapevine moves swiftly, Ellie. If you want to keep something a secret, then you can't tell any of us. We suck at secrets."

She shot a look at Dex. "That's okay. I think I'm done with secrets anyway."

"God, I love you," he whispered.

Kurt surprised them all when he stood and raised his glass. "And to our little brother for finally...*finally* coming together with the one woman we all knew he'd end up with."

Dex looked down the table at his siblings all nodding and smiling, raising their glasses. Except Siena, whose lip stuck out in a serious pout.

"Really? Everyone knew except me?" Siena shook

her head. "I'm your twin, Dex. How could I not know?"

"Maybe Dex's twin powers blocked you from knowing," Kurt mused.

"Save it for your novels," Siena snapped.

"Siena, I didn't know anyone knew about how I felt about Ellie. Hell, I didn't know how real it was myself. How could you all know?" Ellie's cheeks flushed, and Dex drew her close.

"Oh, please." Rush laughed. "You two used to look at each other and not speak. It was like you had this secret silent language. If only we could harness it and I could read the minds of my competitors."

Ellie bit her lip and looked down at their interlaced fingers.

Dex leaned in close. "You okay? Is this too much?"

She shook her head. "It's true. You're all I've always wanted."

The End

Please enjoy a preview of the next
Love in Bloom novel

Stroke of
LOVE

The Remingtons, Book Two

Love in Bloom Series

Melissa Foster

NEW YORK TIMES BESTSELLING AUTHOR

MELISSA FOSTER

stroke of

LOVE

the remingtons

Love in Bloom: Contemporary Romance

Chapter One

THICK BRANCHES SCRAPED the sides of the all-wheel-drive passenger van as it ambled along the narrow dirt road that divided the dense, unforgiving jungle. Sage Remington started as a mass of giant leaves slapped against the grit-covered window. Plumes of dust billowed in their wake, swallowing the road, and Sage wondered if they were really heading toward civilization or away from it. The van keeled to the left, sending Sage and the other passengers flying across their seats as the bus rocked back to center and found its balance. Sage had never experienced anything like the trek to the remote village of Punta Palacia, and as he listened to the other passengers bitch and moan, he turned a deaf ear—and focused his artist's eyes on the verdant jungle which boasted some of the most vibrant and interesting hues he'd ever seen. He'd been living in the concrete jungle of New York City for the past five years and rarely had a chance to venture beyond the streets, offices, and subways. When he'd heard about

Artists for International Aid (AIA), a nonprofit organization that brought educational, medical, and environmental programs to newly developing nations, he'd immediately volunteered to be a part of one of their two-week projects.

"This is such bullshit. Belize, my agent said to me." Actress Penelope Price gathered her long blond hair in her hand and pulled it over her shoulder, fanning her face with an exhaustive sigh. "Think beautiful beaches and sunshine, she said." After some fancy twisting and poking of a long, gold needlelike thing, she looked as if she were ready for the red carpet—or at least her hair was. The rest of her body—and her legs, which were long enough to wrap around any man's waist twice—glistened with sweat. "My Chanel is ruined!"

Sage shook his head at her Oscar-worthy performance. AIA worked with artists and celebrity volunteers, and as he listened to Penelope bitch, he wondered why she'd even volunteered for the project. He pulled a bandana from the pocket of his cargo shorts and wiped his forehead, which had long ago stopped beading with sweat and succumbed to the drenching wetness caused by the heat and humidity of southern Belize. Despite the sweat-soaked tank top clinging to his body like a second skin and the bitchy prima donnas he was traveling with, he didn't regret his decision.

"Stop your bitching," Clayton Ray snapped. Clayton was a country music star and—from what Sage had witnessed at the airport and during the long flight over—an asshole extraordinaire. "You'll have air-conditioning when we get there."

Sage hid his laugh behind a cough. *AC, my ass.* At least he knew what he was getting into. Apparently, the others hadn't been clued in to the realities of Punta Palacia. Sage was looking forward to the simplistic lifestyle, braving the heat and humidity of the jungle, and maybe, just maybe, figuring out why the hell a man who had enough money to buy half of New York, and a career doing what he loved most, felt so damn empty inside.

"All I can say is that if there's no air-conditioning, I'm heading back to Belize City. Pronto." Cassidy Bay, a B-list actress, dabbed at her streaked eyeliner. "I can't sleep in this weather, and without sleep, my eyes will be puffy."

Penelope whipped her head around to commiserate. "We can do that? Then why didn't we just stay there?"

Sage had been distracted and rushed when they boarded the van at the landing strip, and he had caught only a glimpse of Kate Paletto, the program director for AIA. He was six four and guessed she was about five foot two and weighed a buck ten soaking wet. He hadn't gotten a good look at her face, but as she led them through to the van, he couldn't help but notice her slim hips and sleek, feminine arms. Although from his seat in the second row, he could make out only her long, silky dark hair, he had a clear shot of her hand as it gripped the armrest so tightly her knuckles turned white. He wondered if it was from the banter or the bumpy ride.

"No, Penelope. We talked about this, remember?" Luce Palmer, Penelope's public relations specialist, sat in the back of the van. She was known in entertainment circles for being a hard-nosed negotiator, and most notably, for being able to turn around any celebrity's bad reputation. "You're here to rectify the damage you caused to your image. This is two weeks of...hardship to show you care about people other than yourself."

Hardship? Hell, Sage would relish being away from the stress and distraction of New York City. He worked late into most nights on his artwork and rarely even heard the phone when it rang. Maybe being away would help him to pay attention to other, more important things, too, and help him to not get so lost in his work. Spending two weeks in Punta Palacia seemed like the opposite of a hardship to him.

Kate turned in her seat, flashing vibrant blue eyes, dark lashes, and the softest-looking skin he'd ever seen. *The face of an angel. Jesus, where did that cliché come from?*

"I still don't see why I couldn't have gone on a vacation someplace else and gotten the same publicity," Penelope said to Luce.

"Because you're here for humanitarian purposes, not a vacation." Kate spoke with the confidence of a seasoned drill sergeant. Her harsh tone contrasted sharply with her soft features, giving her a good-girl, bad-girl vibe that she appeared to be completely oblivious to—and that Sage could not ignore.

Sage had come to Belize with a plan. His artwork commanded six figures, earning him a fine living and drowning him in feelings of unease. He'd always felt a desire to give back to the community, but no matter how much money he gave to charities, or how many hours he volunteered in New York City, he still felt hollow, as if, in the grand scheme of life, nothing he did made a difference. He hoped that experiencing a different type of giving back, in a country that wasn't so gluttonous, might spark a deeper level of fulfillment. And now that he'd smelled the humid jungle air and drank in the passing beauty of the jungle, an idea was coming to him—and a woman wasn't part of the plan. Not even a woman as beautiful and intriguing as Kate.

A whisper of a thought floated to the forefront of his mind while the others bitched and plotted about their *predicament*. Instead of just donating money, he could paint the local landscape and the people and send those paintings back to New York to be sold. The profits could come back to Punta Palacia. Surely they could use the money, and he couldn't imagine anything being more fulfilling than doing what he loved for a bigger purpose. A few pieces each year could bring significant funds for areas that needed it much more than he did. His pulse kicked up as the idea took hold.

"Well, this is *not* what I signed up for, so we'll just see about this," Penelope snapped.

Cassidy made a *tsk* sound and turned away.

The vehicle was taller and wider than a typical passenger van, with a narrow aisle dividing two rows of seats. Kate rose to her feet, clutching a clipboard against her small but perfect breasts. "This is exactly what you signed up for," she said to Penelope.

Clayton's leg stretched across the aisle like he owned it, and he made no attempt to mask his leering. His eyes took a slow, hungry stroll down Kate's body. Sage's muscles twitched. The guy was the epitome of the status-driven celebrities Sage sorely disliked. Entitled. Motivated by money and fame, he used people like pawns and stepped on anyone who got in his way with no regard for their feelings.

Kate narrowed her eyes in his direction. "Problem, Mr. Ray?"

Sage was drawn to her confidence, the way she wasn't afraid to challenge Clayton, and he was powerless to turn away. And her sexy little cutoffs weren't helping him any. With his artist's eye, he did a quick sweep of her features, hiding his glance behind his hand as he wiped his brow again. Her deep-set, slightly upturned, smoky blue eyes stopped him cold.

"You too, Mr. Remington?" Kate arched a brow.

Shit. Now he looked as bad as Clayton. *Am I?* He opened his mouth to explain—*I was just checking you out from an artistic standpoint. One quick glance. Jesus, you have the sexiest eyes I've ever seen. Fuck. Never mind.* Luckily, before he could put his foot in his mouth, she spoke.

"Let's get one thing straight. I'm sure this is very different from the harem-filled exotic resorts you're used to, but here at Punta Palencia, we have one goal. To help the community. And that does not include any sort of sexual action from me or any other AIA volunteer." She eyed Penelope, whose gaze was burning a path directly to Sage, and Cassidy, who was sizing up Clayton. "What you do among yourselves is your business, but we expect you to carry out your humanitarian efforts with respect for our staff and the community. Got it?"

The silence was deafening. Kate's lips held tight in

a *Don't mess with me* line.

"Got it." The words were out of Sage's mouth before he had time to think.

She gave a curt nod.

"Alrighty, then. We'll see where we end up," Clayton said with a heavy Southern drawl.

Kate exchanged a half smile with Luce, as if they were sharing an inside joke. "When we get to the compound, you'll be assigned a cabin. Once situated, we'll meet at the community rec area. The path behind the cabins will lead you to the rec area. Please try to be there within thirty minutes so we can get everyone up to speed as quickly as possible." Kate turned her back and lowered herself into her seat as the bus took a bumpy turn to the right and came to an abrupt stop.

Despite himself, Sage wondered what Kate would be like if she weren't wrangling self-centered celebrities. As he stole a peek at her profile, he realized that she'd lumped him in with Clayton, and he cringed. They hadn't even arrived yet and already he was on some celebrity shit list in her mind. Or on that damn clipboard.

KATE WAITED IMPATIENTLY while the prima donnas made their way down the dusty steps of the van. She'd been with AIA for almost five years, and this was her second assignment out of the country. Each assignment lasted for two years, with an additional three months of training. In a few short weeks, it would be over and she'd be flying back home to see her parents. She had misgivings about this assignment coming to an end. Punta Palacia had been her home for just over two years. She'd become close with the children at the school and the community, and she'd been lobbying for the installation of a well in the village. Just thinking about leaving everyone, especially before the decision on the well was made, caused her chest to constrict. Kate was good at a lot of things, but saying goodbye was not one of them.

She held Clayton's stare as he exited the bus. She'd learned early on with entitled celebrities that holding her ground was the only way to keep them in line. They were all the same: cocky, surly when she turned down their sexual advances, and goddamn needy. It would take less than five minutes after they checked out their small cabins for them to stomp back with a demand to leave. Kate had never given too much thought to what it must be like going from a world of having everything at their fingertips to a developing nation such as Belize. She'd grown up traveling with her parents on Peace Corps missions and had been surrounded by families who worked with the Peace Corps for her whole life. Once she'd graduated college, she couldn't wait to leave the United States and get on with helping people who really needed it. Lately, though, she'd also longed for something more, although she hadn't been able to put her finger on just what that *more* might be.

"Where to, darlin'?" Clayton flashed his perfectly capped teeth with a wide smile.

"You're in cabin one. The first cabin you come to." She pointed to the cabin, and when his smile widened, she knew she was in for trouble.

Sweat dripped from beneath Clayton's Stetson. He swiped at it with his forearm. "You don't need to worry about us. We're harmless." He took a step closer.

Kate was hyperaware of Sage standing behind him, his dark eyes narrowed, his jaw clenching.

"Unless, of course, you'd like to try ridin' a stallion." Clayton's smile morphed into a smirk, the left side of his mouth tilted up.

Kate had been propositioned by celebrities before, but that didn't stop her hand from fisting around her pen as she pulled her clipboard to her chest like a shield, but as she opened her mouth to tell him what he could do with his offer, Sage stepped from the bus in his sweaty tank top and cargo shorts and cleared his throat loudly.

"Cabin one, Ray." It was clearly a command.

His tattooed arms were solid muscle and so well defined that she had the urge to let her fingers travel the hard ridges. He was built for power, a protector, or...*No.* She wasn't going there. She'd seen too many temporary romances during these assignments to allow herself to be drawn in only to be forgotten after the guy went back home.

Clayton walked away with a swagger, turning back once and tilting his hat at Kate.

She groaned.

"Listen, I'm really sorry for the way I looked at you on the bus."

The command in Sage's voice was gone, replaced with sweet richness, as smooth as melted butter. Kate felt her cheeks flush. *Damn it. What is wrong with me?* She lowered her eyes, steeling herself against the warmth that had found her belly and was slowly traveling lower. She dared a glance at his handsome face. He had a strong chin, and his eyes hovered somewhere between gunmetal blue and indigo. *Shit. Really?* At least he wasn't perfectly manicured like the others. His eyebrows were a little bushy, a peppering of whiskers covered his cheeks, and his clothes looked like they came right off the rack at anyplace *but* a high-end store. Unfortunately, that only made him more appealing.

Focus.

Kate drew in a deep breath and ran her finger down her clipboard. Now she was stuck trying to figure out if he was just playing her—standing up to Clayton and apologizing like he was her savior—or if he was really a nice guy. She decided to ignore the conundrum altogether and focus on her job instead. Focusing on her job didn't require evaluating the motives of celebrities. Her job was safe.

"Remington, let's see. You're in cabin three." She pointed to a small cabin at the end of the complex.

He nodded silently and walked away with a dejected look on his way-too-handsome face.

Luce stood on the steps of the bus with her arms crossed. "Well, look at you, staring after him like he's a piece of meat. Maybe I'll start calling you Clayton." She stepped from the bus. This was Luce's third trip to Belize. Kate couldn't keep track of all of the celebs she handled PR for, but she was always glad to see her friend.

Kate realized she was not only staring at Sage as he walked away, but more specifically, staring at his perfect ass. She spun around. "What? Just making sure he figured out which cabin was his. They all look the same." *No. They sure as hell don't all look the same.* And she wasn't thinking about the cabins.

"Uh-huh. You stickin' with that story?" Luce's blond hair was clipped at the base of her neck in a low ponytail, and she reeked of bug spray. Luce was always prepared. It was one of the things Kate admired most about her.

Kate smacked Luce's arm with the clipboard. "Why didn't you warn me about those women? You said they were a little highbrow. That's different from—"

"No. No, no, no." Penelope traipsed across the yard, waving her arms and lifting her legs high to avoid the thick grass and flourish of dust that clung to her legs. "Luce, there is no way I'm staying in that bug-infested sauna." She crossed her lanky arms, rolled her eyes, and huffed a sigh.

Luce glanced at Kate and lifted her palms to the sky. "Sorry, Pen. This is what we've got. It's only two weeks, and—"

"Did you see the screened-in sleeping area?" Kate used as peppy of a voice as she could muster when what she really wanted to say was, *The cabins are fine. There are people who have real needs and you're here to help them. Suck it up and let's get going.* "The screen will allow the air in and it'll keep you cooler at night," Kate suggested. "There's a nice shower and bathroom that's all yours. I know it's not what you're used to, but remember, this was once a mahogany logging camp, so think of it like you're reliving a time in history."

"And that's supposed to make me feel better? The bathroom is awful." Penny let out a loud breath.

Luce put her arm around Penelope and guided her

back to the cabin, saying something Kate couldn't hear. Kate checked her watch. In another twenty minutes she'd hold orientation and then hand out the assignments. She'd been looking forward to working with Sage the most. She loved his artwork and she knew how much the children loved art as well, but whatever the hell was going on in her lady parts when he was around had her on high alert. She'd have to build a little higher fence than she was used to.

Who was she kidding? She needed ten feet of barbed wire—to keep herself in.

(End of Sneak Peek)
To continue reading, be sure to pick up the next
LOVE IN BLOOM release:

STROKE OF LOVE, *The Remingtons*, Book Two
Love in Bloom series, Book Eleven

"Contemporary romance at its hottest.
Each Braden sibling left me craving the next.
Sensual, sexy, and satisfying."
— *Bestselling author Keri Nola, LMHC (on The Bradens)*

LOVE IN BLOOM is a contemporary romance series featuring several close-knit families
Check online retailers for availability

SNOW SISTERS

Sisters in Love
Sisters in Bloom
Sisters in White

THE BRADENS

Lovers at Heart
Destined for Love
Friendship on Fire
Sea of Love
Bursting with Love
Hearts at Play

COMING SOON

THE REMINGTONS

Game of Love
Stroke of Love
Hearts on Fire
Slope of Love
Read, Write, Love

Acknowledgments

I would like to thank all of the readers who have emailed and sent messages on social media asking, pleading, and insisting on my next Love in Bloom novel. You inspire me to craft my characters with care and to create stories that are new and different. Thank you for taking the time to read my novels. I enjoy hearing from you, and I hope you will continue to reach out.

Thank you to the members of Team Pay-It-Forward, the blogging community, my friends, and the amazing volunteers—my sisters at heart—of the World Literary Café. I could not have made it through many days without having each of you to turn to. Thank you.

My editorial team continues to amaze me on a daily basis with their patience, persistence, and meticulous attention to detail. Tremendous gratitude goes to Kristen Weber, Penina Lopez, Jenna Bagnini, Juliette Hill, and Marlene Engel.

Kathie Shoop, you've pulled me up from under the waves too many times to count. Thanks for always being there. I appreciate your time, your brilliance, and your friendship.

My son Jake provided me with in-depth knowledge of the gaming world. I took many creative liberties, and any errors are mine and mine alone. Thank you, Jake, for sharing your time and knowledge with me. You're too cool for words. To my own hunky hero, Les, and to all of my children, you are my treasures, and I appreciate you.

Melissa Foster is a *New York Times* and *USA Today* bestselling and award-winning author. Her books have been recommended by *USA Today's* book blog, *Hagerstown* magazine, *The Patriot*, and several other print venues. She is the founder of the Women's Nest, a social and support community for women, and the World Literary Café. When she's not writing, Melissa helps authors navigate the publishing industry through her author training programs on Fostering Success. Melissa also hosts Aspiring Authors contests for children, and has painted and donated several murals to the Hospital for Sick Children in Washington, DC.

Visit Melissa on her website or chat with her on The Women's Nest or social media. Melissa enjoys discussing her books with book clubs and reader groups and welcomes an invitation to your event.

Melissa's books are available on Amazon, Barnes & Noble, and through most online retailers.

www.MelissaFoster.com

CPSIA information can be obtained
at www.ICGtesting.com
Printed in the USA
LVOW11s0920250617
539309LV00001B/200/P